*Christopher Priest is the autho[...]
several collections of short stor[...]
Best Young British Novelists i[...]
translated in many languages all over the world. His
most recent novel,* The Glamour, *won the Kurd Lasswitz
1988 Best Foreign Novel award. He lives in Wiltshire
with his wife and fellow writer, Leigh Kennedy.*

'Priest's chilling genius – he makes Stephen King look
unsubtle and John Carpenter's films contrived – is to
convey a series of minimal happenings that gently add up
to sheer horror on your doorstep . . . a tense master of the
not quite explicable'

Mail on Sunday

'The manoeuvring of material is expertly accomplished'
Listener

'*The Quiet Woman* and *The Glamour* stand as two of the
best novels published in recent years by any British novelist'
Oxford Times

'Priest writes with charm, grace and wistful individuality'
Guardian

'Engrossing . . . Christopher Priest writes fluidly and
subtly . . . a fine sense of the precariousness of truth, past
and present, are strongly realized'

Standard

THE QUIET WOMAN

CHRISTOPHER PRIEST

An *Abacus* Book

First published in Great Britain by Bloomsbury Publishing Ltd 1990
Copyright © Christopher Priest 1990
Published in Abacus by Sphere Books Ltd 1991

Typeset by 𝔸 Tek Art Ltd, Addiscombe, Croydon, Surrey
Printed and bound in Great Britain by Cox & Wyman Ltd, Reading

ISBN 0 349 10195 7

A Division of
Macdonald & Co (Publishers) Ltd
Orbit House
1 New Fetter Lane
London EC4A 1AR

A member of Maxwell Macmillan Pergamon Publishing Corporation

Memories of past lives are distracting Alice Stockton as she tries to make sense of her own recent past. Living alone after the break-up of her marriage, she is working hard to make a precarious living as a biographer, yet she finds herself powerfully and inexplicably influenced by other people's lives. Firstly, there are the six women described in her latest book, one of whose experiences now mysteriously threatens to jeopardize Alice's own personal freedom. Then there is her neighbour Eleanor Hamilton, brutally murdered without apparent reason, whose life Alice envied at first, before realizing that Eleanor might already have helped shape and influence her ideas. Finally, there is Gordon Sinclair, Eleanor's son, who enters Alice's life when he appears for the funeral. Why had Eleanor never mentioned her son? And why do Gordon's memories dwell on a confusing past life of loneliness and solitary imaginings, of which Alice herself seems already to be a part?

In his new novel Christopher Priest explores that tense edge that divides night from day, the real from the unreal and the everyday from the apocalyptic. His vision and assurance have never been so chillingly realized as in *The Quiet Woman*. It will haunt your days and nights.

TO THE MUDCAT

1

ALICE STOCKTON HURRIED in from the rain, trying to reach the telephone before it stopped ringing. The heavy plastic carrier bags collided with the door-post as she pushed through, and one of the flimsy handles broke in half, causing the lettuce on the top to fall to the floor. She got everything inside, scooping the lettuce in with her foot, then slammed the door behind her. She urgently needed to get upstairs to the toilet, but the phone call was likely to be from Granville. After a moment's hesitation, trying to decide her priorities, she let her leather bag slip from her shoulder to the floor and rushed through to her study. The phone stopped as she put out her hand to pick it up.

Her cat was there on the desk, lying flat across her papers and rousing to greet her, his legs straining at ninety degrees to his body, like those of the white horse engraved out of the side of the chalk Downs. He turned his face to her, yawning. The phone hadn't woken him, even though it was on the desk a few inches from his ear, but the noise of a supermarket bag, or of her own footsteps, could bring him out of the deepest sleep.

She stared at the phone, willing it not to ring again for a few minutes at least, while the cat stood up, arched his back, then nuzzled his head against her hand.

'Do you want some dinner, Jimmy?' she said. He turned an

ear in her direction. 'All right, in a moment.'

She left him on the desk and went quickly upstairs. A few minutes later, feeling queasy and depressed, she returned to her main living room, which doubled as kitchen and dining-room. Her leather bag was on the floor where it had fallen and she irritably pushed it aside with her foot, remembering too late that her only pair of spectacles was inside. Plastic lenses don't break, they only get scratched, she thought, wondering if it were true. The carrier bag with the broken handle had tipped to one side on the table, and two apples had fallen on the floor.

She picked up all the bags and took them across to the kitchen part of the room. The cat appeared as she opened the fridge door. He rubbed against her, 'loving' her legs, as Mrs Watson in the house next door described it. She pulled out that morning's can of food, talking to the cat as she did so. He always reacted to her voice, although there were only two or three words she knew he recognized, all of them to do with food.

The phone started ringing again. With a big dollop of unmashed cat-food on the plate, she dumped it on the floor and left the cat to work it out. She hurried into the study.

'Alice? This is Granville.'

'Oh, Granville. I hoped it would be you. Is there any news?'

'Well . . . not really, not until this afternoon.'

She imagined Granville in his office, the desk placed so that his back was to the window, the room obsessively tidy and clean, the houseplants, the carefully chosen furniture, and the neat rows of books by his clients on the shelf beside him.

'I thought we agreed this would be settled this morning.'

'Yes. I tried to call earlier. I wanted you to know.'

2

'I had to go to the shop. What's the excuse this time?'

'Some kind of meeting. I called Stackpole as I promised,but his secretary took the call. She said that the matter was in his diary for this morning, that a decision was expected, but that he'd been called away.'

Alice made an impatient noise, and waited for more.

'I've made an appointment to see him this afternoon. It would be helpful if you could be there too.'

'No, that's impossible. The car's broken down, and there's no train. I told you yesterday. Look, Granville, they've no right to do this!'

Granville said nothing, his way of telling her she was being difficult. Alice was standing beside her desk, the telephone cord stretched taut. She half-turned, looked in the mirror on the far wall. Her hair was still wet from being outside, and she knew she really ought to wash it as soon as she had a moment. Granville was speaking again, trying to placate her. The Home Office had every right to act as they did, he was doing what he could, the problem would be resolved by this evening, and so on.

'What am I going to do if they keep it? she said.

'They're not going to do that.'

'That's what you said two weeks ago! They've still got it.'

'It's not going to come to that. When I spoke to the secretary she made it sound as if everything had been settled.'

'Then why do you have to go in to meet him?

'I'm not sure. It could be to pick it up.'

'Well, I hope so.' Alice moved around and sat on her office chair. She leaned forward and rested her elbows on the desk, pressing the receiver to her ear, feeling bulky because she still had on the thick pullover she had been wearing under her coat. 'Have you found out anything else about Stackpole?

3

Like what his position is?

'Only that he's a department head.'

'Department of literary suppression.'

'He's quite high up,' Granville said.

'That makes it worse. Why the hell is the Home Office interfering with me?'

'I intend to find out this afternoon. Will you be in?'

'Yes.'

'I'll call you as soon as I get back to my office. I have to go now. There's another client waiting to see me.'

'All right.'

Granville always had someone in reception waiting to see him. An uninterrupted conversation with him was unusual. When she telephoned he often spoke to her while one of his other writers waited patiently on the far side of his desk. Or someone would arrive, or the other line would ring, or there was a client waiting. Most of Granville's other clients were more important, because they weren't just writers. Granville specialized in television personalities, sportsmen and politicians, whose opportunistic and often ghost-written books made him more money than books by real writers. That was Granville; she was used to that now.

She went back to the kitchen to finish unpacking her shopping. Jimmy had departed through the cat-door leaving most of his food untouched. In the middle of the day food was a social occasion for him, not a filling of the stomach. He would probably have cleaned the plate if she had stayed with him.

She glanced out of the window but there was no sign of him. He perversely liked rainy days. She noticed that three more dead birds were on the floor of the concrete yard. It always depressed her to see them. She went out immediately, scooped them up with a shovel and dropped them in the dustbin in case the cat grew interested in them.

She had washed her hair and was towelling it dry when the telephone rang again. This time it was the garage in the village. The distributor cap had cracked and they were having to get a new one in from Swindon. It should be ready to be picked up by the evening.

She made herself a cup of instant coffee and took it to her desk.

Her life was in suspense until the problem with the book was sorted out. There were letters to answer and people to call, but for the last three weeks she had been lying low, waiting for Granville to come up with some kind of answer. All the natural momentum of her life had halted until this was sorted out. There seemed no point to anything. Maybe she should take some direct action herself? But Granville's advice had been to lie low, not get involved, let him straighten it out. That was why she paid him. And so on.

Anyway, what could she possibly do on her own? She had no idea where to begin, and in practical terms was more or less powerless to do anything. She had barely enough money to leave the village, let alone to make repeated visits to London. The car was unreliable, and expensive to maintain. There were only a few trains a day: two in the early morning, for the long-distance commuters, two back again in the evening for the same people, and just one calling each way during the day. Granville was right, as always; it was best left to him.

She wrote two short letters, then made sandwiches for lunch. Jimmy reappeared and sat helpfully on her lap, watching her eat. She shared tiny pieces of cheese with him.

Two phonecalls came in quick succession after lunch. She

rushed back to the study to take the first, feeling slightly foolish at how dependent on the phone she had become. She had hardly ever used it when she lived in London.

The first call was from Bill, still living in their old flat in West Hampstead. She sat down at ther desk to talk to him, sensing a long conversation, dreading the emotional upheavals that might result. It was still too recent for any detachment. Bill did not have to say very much to upset her. But he was in a hurry, just about to go out somewhere for the rest of the day. He had posted a small cheque to her, part of the settlement that had been agreed, and he wanted her to know. He made it sound like a favour, and didn't say where the money was from. It was probably some of the furniture he had promised to sell for her last year, but it didn't matter.

He asked how things were 'going'; she answered in the same general way, with conventional vagueness. Bill couldn't care less how things were 'going' for her. He was only trying to be pleasant so she wouldn't ask about the rest of the money. He enquired after her book, a departure from his norm. She said it was all OK, wanting to end the conversation. Bill was the last person she would tell about the Home Office.

The second call came a few seconds after she had hung up. This was from Mrs Lodge, who worked part-time in the post office in Ramsford. Alice knew her through the Natural History Society in Ramsford, which she had joined during the summer.

'I thought you should know straight away,' Mrs Lodge said. 'Has anyone else told you about Mrs Hamilton?'

'Eleanor?' Alice said, sensing bad news. 'No . . . what's happened?'

'I'm afraid she's dead. They found her body this morning.'

'Oh, no!' Alice stared at the littered papers on her desk,

looking blankly at the muddy prints where Jimmy must have jumped up earlier. 'But how could that be?' she said, feeling inadequate. 'I saw her only two days ago.'

'Yes, and she was in the post office yesterday, just like normal.'

'Was she ill? Was it a heart attack?'

'That's the mystery, you see,' said Mrs Lodge. 'There are police cars outside her house, and apparently she was found away from the house. Out in the woods, somewhere near the river.'

'Um, are you *sure*?'

'Yes.'

'I meant . . . is there anything I can do?'

'I wouldn't like to say, dear. You were friendly with her, weren't you?'

'Just a little.' Alice felt an irrational surge of selfish worry, and quickly suppressed it. Why were the police there? The business with the Home Office and her book had made her paranoid. 'This is terrible,' she said. 'Does anyone know how she died?'

'That's not for me to say, dear. But there are others who do say she was murdered.'

'Oh, that's ridiculous! No one would kill a harmless old lady like Eleanor.'

'That's exactly what I said. I heard the doctor had been called, so I reckon she must have had a seizure.'

'Yes,' Alice said, then repeated the word to make herself sound more sure. 'Look, do you think I should go over to her house? Maybe I could help in some way.'

'I'd say that was up to you.'

'Doesn't somebody have to identify a body? She was all alone. I could do that, I suppose.'

'I don't think there's any need. They say her son is coming to the village. He'll take care of that.'

'I didn't know she had a son! She never said anything about him.'

'So it seems. He lives in the north, up Manchester way, and is driving down tonight.'

Alice was thinking, trying to remember whether Eleanor had ever mentioned children. She knew that her husband had died about ten years ago, that before she moved to Wiltshire she had been living somewhere on the south coast near Portsmouth . . . but a son?

'Well, thank you for telling me. What terrible news!'

'That's all right, dear. Goodbye.'

Alice went upstairs and sat on the end of her bed, looking down at the garden. It had stopped raining but the soil looked sodden, and the overgrown grass of her lawn and the late flowers seemed laden with water. She could see the sun shining weakly on Salisbury Plain, a mile or two to the south. She sat quietly, thinking about Eleanor and her sudden death, still disbelieving the news, trying to come to terms with it. And all mixed up with it, her book and Granville and Bill with his small cheque in the mail. All troubles, mounting up, yet none of them as shocking as the news about Eleanor.

Jimmy came in and sat on the bed beside her. She stroked him while she cried, listening to him purr. He tried to clamber on her lap, but she pushed him gently away, went on stroking him. Soon he settled down beside her, curling up in a contented ball of tabby fur.

She thought bleakly how her life revolved around the cat these days, or seemed to. She lived in daily dread of him developing more symptoms, or perhaps, just as likely, being killed by a passing car. The countryside was dangerous for cats. The roads were quiet, but when traffic passed it was travelling quickly. She had several times seen Jimmy sitting in the lane outside the house, calmly waiting for a speeding motorbike to flatten him.

What would she do without the cat? He was her only company. More so now than ever, if Eleanor really was dead. Writing the book had seemed at the time like an answer to the loneliness and the sense of failure. The single-mindedness of hard work was a distraction from everything else. It had helped her through the physical and emotional upheavals of leaving London, and her constant shortage of cash had been less of a worry while the book was in progress. It was easier to lie to the bank manager so long as she believed the book would earn some more money when it was finished.

Now it was, but it had become in its turn a part of the problem. Minor worries were all around her. She lived alone, a single woman in a house where the only neighbours were elderly, and along a narrow unlighted country lane. The house had lost at least half its value since she bought it, while her mortgage repayments had increased sharply. The place still needed repairing. The building society had placed a retention on the original loan until various structural improvements had been carried out, but apart from some patching up done by a local builder soon after she moved in most of the work remained undone. She was in a part of England she barely knew, and where she had no roots, no family, no real friends. The only close friend she had made locally was suddenly dead. Her car had broken down. Bill was a bastard. She was worried about her health. And someone in the Home Office had seized her latest book, and served a restriction notice on her, her literary agent and her publisher. All because of something she had written.

9

The only thing left to her was the cat, purring beside her. She stroked him affectionately, and wept.

2

ALICE WAITED AROUND all afternoon for Granville to call her. At the last minute, just before his office closed for the day, she could contain her worries no more and telephoned him. The receptionist answered, to tell her that he had gone out without saying when he would be back. Alice left a message for him to call her urgently, but she knew she wouldn't hear from him until the next day. The news was not going to be good.

It was a cool but pleasant evening, with an hour or so remaining before darkness. The sky was clear after the rainfall. Alice put on her coat, still damp from her trip to the shop in the morning, and went for a walk.

Her cottage was one of three small terraces that had originally been labourers' cottages for one of the local farms. Now only two were occupied: hers, and the one belonging to Mr and Mrs Watson next door. Alice had loved the house when she first saw it, seeing it as a consolation prize for the mess she had made of her life, a symbol of starting again. It had been neglected for years. The previous owner lived in another part of the country and had rented it to soldiers living out of the Army camps on Salisbury Plain. The house had not been repaired or decorated for ten or more years, and the surveyor's report had been intimidating and depressing, with its litany of rising damp, antiquated wiring, rotten timbers and leaking roof. For some weeks it had been difficult to raise a loan, but she was desperate to move and more or less by sheer willpower had finally managed to get the money. After the essential repair-work the place had become liveable, and as soon as she had settled down to writing her book she had grown to ignore the vague background smell of damp, the uneven walls, the unpredictable plumbing, and the house had simply become home, a symbol of neither past nor future.

It was about a quarter of a mile away from the main part of Milton Colebourne, if a village that consisted of a scattering of small houses, one general store and a pub could be said to have a main part. The only access to the house was along the lane where Jimmy liked to sit, and this led into the wider lane that ran between the rest of the houses. Two cars passed her as she walked along, turning off into her lane and accelerating towards the house, reminding her nervously that the cat was out. She wished she did not love him so much.

She could see Eleanor Hamilton's house as soon as she reached the main road to Ramsford. Nothing seemed out of the ordinary from this distance: it was a tall, white-rendered house with a thatched roof, standing back from the main road in a large garden. Until she met Eleanor, Alice had assumed the house was occupied by a family. It looked too large for just one person, but Eleanor had easily filled the house by herself, finding a use for each of the rooms, content amongst her possessions. She was an enthusiastic gardener, a collector of old furniture ('Not antiques,' Eleanor once said to her), a hoarder of books and records, photographs and silly mementoes. At the back of the house, overlooking the garden, was the large room Eleanor used as her study. Her typewriter and desk were here, but Eleanor had said she no longer wanted

12

to write, that her fingers were too stiff for typing. She was happy as she was.

Alice had sensed a kindred spirit in Eleanor. Initially it was because she was, or said she had been, a writer, but when they grew to know each other better this diminished in importance. Eleanor had a quiet, self-absorbed life, retired and contented after the business of living. Alice had admired this, thinking how she too wished to be contented now that a major and disruptive phase of her own life was behind her. They became friends easily. Alice had been glad to meet her and at first had tried to do several small favours for her. She had quickly learned that Eleanor's frail physical appearance was deceptive. She needed no looking after: she was an active and intelligent woman with a good mind; she was widely travelled, wise and alert to the events of the larger world. She was stimulating company for Alice, reading the manuscript of her book and showing a constructive interest in it. She had lent her books from her own collection that had saved Alice several trips to libraries.

When the manuscript was impounded Eleanor had been a sudden ally. It was to no avail, but it helped Alice through the first aftermath of the news. Until then Alice had felt paranoid and helpless, wounded by the thought that someone in authority saw her as a threat. Eleanor at least had made her feel she had done nothing wrong.

In spite of their closeness, Alice had never really learnt much about the other woman. Eleanor did not like talking about herself, and usually avoided personal questions. Alice knew that she and her late husband Martin had been teachers, that she had written a number of novels when younger, that she moved to this house after his death, and so on, but very little more.

The novels in particular intrigued Alice, because she sensed that to read some of them might afford insights, but Eleanor so consistently downplayed them that she soon stopped asking about them. (A search through library catalogues – with an unmistakably furtive feeling - revealed nothing. None of the titles was even listed, and the only authors with the name Hamilton were other people.)

Alice was now thinking about Eleanor in an awkward and disturbing combination of past and present tenses. Just as she had felt when her own parents died, it was impossible to believe that Eleanor was really dead. Yet she already accepted it, even to the point of realizing that she had been prepared for this kind of news. Eleanor had seemed in good health, but she said her joints were stiffening with age and the cold weather was a torment. She had always moved, and sometimes talked, like an old lady.

Alice reached the gated entrance to the house and glanced towards the door. Mrs Lodge had said there were police cars at the house, but if that was true they had already left. Alice hesitated, wondering if she should go to the house. It felt strange not to push the gate open and walk naturally to the door, as if it had become forbidden to her. But it was no longer the same. For one thing Eleanor's son might be there, and Alice was reluctant to interfere.

While she was still standing undecided, the door to the house opened and a uniformed police officer appeared. He closed the door behind him, then stood inside the porch with his hands clasped behind his back. He looked towards Alice.

Feeling that something had been decided for her, Alice went through the gate and walked up the drive. She recognized the policeman: she often saw him when she was in Ramsford, the larger village two miles down the road,

14

where he ran the one-man police station.

'Can I help you, miss?' he said.

'I wanted to know. Is it true about Mrs Hamilton?'

'Yes.'

'I was a friend of hers. I live along the lane over there. I was wondering – '

'Do you have information about Mrs Hamilton's death?'

'No. I only heard the news an hour or so ago. It was a terrible shock.' The officer regarded her steadily. He was not reacting except as a cop on duty reacts, no small-talk, no conversational offers. He was making her nervous, anxious to explain herself. 'I think there might be something of mine inside the house.'

'And what would that be, miss?'

Of course she instantly regretted having said anything. Until that moment she hadn't thought consciously about the tapes . . . but she knew they had been at the back of her mind ever since she heard the news. They were innocent enough, preparation for her next book, but Eleanor had after all been murdered and the police were presumably searching for clues, and –

The Home Office had made her feel that everything to do with her writing was in some way guilty or suspect.

'I'd lent her some books,' she said, feeling implausible. 'They're not important. I can pick them up some other time. I was passing, and . . . I'm sorry, I shouldn't be here. I was very upset about the news.'

'I can't let you into the house, miss. If you could tell us what the books are, I'll see they're returned to you.'

'Just a couple of recipe books. They don't matter.'

She could feel the lie making her blush. She hated herself for allowing the policeman to intimidate her. She started to move away.

The policeman said, 'I'd like your full name and address, please.'

'It's all right. I don't want the books back.

'We're conducting a murder investigation. We might want to ask you a few questions about Mrs Hamilton.'

'But there's nothing useful I can tell you.'

'A lot of people think that. It's just routine.' He had his notebook out and was flicking the pages over, like a stage policeman. 'I'd like you to meet the investigating officer. Would you call into the station, or would you prefer him to come to your house?'

'I'm going to be in Ramsford tomorrow. I'll call in.'

The policeman wrote down her name and address, using block capitals. He seemed as uncomfortable as she felt. He was young, but she had been used to that for several years, and not tall, which usually surprised her. He looked harmless enough: a country policeman standing outside a house. But these days that was a deception, a reassuring myth created by chief constables. Modern policemen were moved around: inner city slum to affluent suburb, drug squad to regional crime prevention, riot control to country village. Just as they were about to become corrupted or softened by a posting, orders moved them somewhere else. There was an official rationale behind it, something to do with the broadening of experience, but it meant the concept of community policing had gone for ever. She had learnt all this, ironically enough, from Eleanor herself. Eleanor's uncompromising and mistrustful attitude to the police was one of the first things about her that had intrigued Alice.

She felt irritated with herself and self-conscious as she walked away down the drive, imagining the policeman was

16

watching her, but when she glanced back from the gate he had turned away from her and was going into the house again. She wondered how he would get back to Ramsford without a car.

Alice walked along the road in the direction of her house, thinking melodramatic thoughts. If Eleanor had been killed by someone, perhaps she was now a suspect. Her visit to the house had been noted, her name would be on the Hamilton file. She imagined the constable telephoning his superiors at that moment: a woman from the village was at the house, said she knew the dead woman, something about property still in the house, I called her in for questioning tomorrow, etc.

It was crazy to think like this! But she knew why: it was the damned Home Office seizing her book.

She had fretted about this for three weeks, endlessly thinking through the book in her mind, wondering what it was about it that had concerned the authorities.

The book seemed harmless enough to her: it comprised the biographies of six women, examining their lives and careers through traumatic events that had occurred in childhood. There was nothing political, anti-establishment or radical about it. The women were not particularly famous, and none had been arrested for subversive activities, or been shot for spying, or had made pornographic movies, or *anything*.

Another possible explanation for the seizure was that it might have been thought of as a feminist tract. Alice had heard about several feminist writers who had been harassed in recent years. But her book was not overtly feminist, except by the implication of being about women's lives. Anyway, she took an independent line on feminism.

It seemed ridiculous that anyone could read something subversive into the book. Maybe it was her choice of subjects?

But the women themselves were politically 'safe', by whatever standards of 'unsafeness' the Home Office might be looking for. Two had lived in the nineteenth century, one had lived most of her life abroad, one had married a diplomat, and so on.

Even so, a government official had confiscated the manuscript, quoted Section I7 of the Copyright (Crown Property) Act – a law of which she had never even heard until she received the terse, unsigned note – and the book was impounded. But now she was thinking about the tapes, somewhere in Eleanor's house. They too seemed harmless enough to her, but what would police conducting a murder hunt think of them? She tried to remember what might be on them.

Just two conversations, rambling over the four sides of the cassettes. She hadn't even had a real purpose in mind, simply an unspoken awareness that Eleanor was old and possibly frail, that she had a lively mind and was full of unexpected ideas and opinions. Alice knew that she had been politically active when younger, that she monitored news reports and government statistics and scientific reports . . . and that there might be a book for her somewhere in all this.

Eleanor knew what she had been planning, and had been amused and flattered by her interest. She readily acceded to the idea of taping some conversations, and had even offered to write down some notes for her. But if it was going to be a biography, then so far it was only a biography in outline. As yet, Alice had no real idea of what she was seeking. Perhaps it would turn out there was nothing at all.

As she walked along the lane towards her house Jimmy appeared, trotting towards her with his tail raised in welcome. She stood still while he rubbed against her legs, then went into the house.

She realized then that she had completely forgotten to collect her car from the garage.

3

I WAS DRIVING through the night, tired for the usual reasons after a day at the office, irritated with myself for having agreed so promptly to co-operate with the police, and above all fighting back feelings of guilt.

The guilt was the worst. I had been expecting the news about my mother for years, and had always anticipated the consequences, yet when the moment arrived the guilt came at me as if it had been formulated especially for the occasion. Nothing prepared me for the impact it had on me. Her death was a relief; I was glad it had happened at last. While she lived she undermined everything that I was, as she had done from the start, and I had always expected that I would feel the same when she was dead. But now it had happened and I found myself the guilty party, her last act against me. The guilt began with the call from the policewoman, whose calm and factual message seemed underlaid with unspoken accusations. Why had I not been there when she died? How long was it since I had visited her? Why did I live so far away? Answers existed to all these, but they did not ease the feeling.

Driving alone at night encourages circular thinking, and I had been going over all this for some time. Otherwise, I was concentrating on driving. I had not touched alcohol all day. In spite of my general tiredness I was not feeling drowsy. All this is relevant to what happened next.

I was nearly at the end of the journey, driving across the Marlborough Downs, somewhere to the south of the town itself and in the thinly populated countryside that surrounds Devizes. The sky was cloudy, but through breaks in the cover I had been able to see the stars even with the car headlamps fanning across the empty road ahead. The way was straight and the ground on each side was level, with higher land some distance to the sides humping blackly against the sky.

In the loneliest part of the road, and without any warning, the car's engine died. The headlamps and dashboard lights went out, the radio fell silent. The car freewheeled for a few yards until I pulled it over to the side and brought it to a halt. It came to rest at a slight angle, the two nearside wheels on the sloping verge. I tried the starter, but I knew it was hopeless. There was no response. When I picked up the cellphone even that was dead.

I cursed my luck, and looked around to see if there were any house lights in the vicinity, or if other traffic was approaching. I reached over to the back seat and grabbed the torch, but when I tried it I found the batteries had gone flat: there was not even a dim glow from the bulb.

I felf under the dash to release the bonnet, then climbed outside to try and work out what was wrong. Once, years before, another car had refused to start when one of the battery leads worked loose. I imagined that something similar to this could be the only explanation.

The darkness outside was eerie because of the unrelieved black of the ground and the spectacular broken sky. There was a cold wind, uncannily quiet because of the lack of trees. All I could hear was the sound of grass, or crops, moving in the wind. I was alone.

21

Looking up, I could see some of the stars, a sickle moon, the clouds scudding by on the wind. I was frightened. I have always been scared of the dark, the childish fear that for me had persisted into adulthood. I was never calm when alone in the dark; reason died. I felt the fear rising, the first hint of panic, but I managed to suppress it. I groped under the loosened bonnet lid, trying to find the spring catch. Opening it was always awkward, even in daylight, the feeling that touching it would trigger the tautened spring with a finger-crushing recoil. I was trembling, and my hands felt weak and soft. At last I released it, but as I raised the lid it slipped from my grasp and slammed shut again.

Something was out there in the field beside the road. It was a huge object which had not been there before.

Disbelief occluded my vision. At first I seemed only able to glimpse it without focusing, like trying to keep the eyes open when first waking. My mind rejected what I saw, made me glance away, but because it was there and had to be seen, I forced myself to look. In persisting I made it more visible. Once I had located it, and once I knew it was real, my eyes fastened on it and I could see it clearly.

It was a tall black cylinder, standing on end.

I stared at it in amazement, listening to the wind in the grass, feeling it press coldly on my back and drum in my ears.

The cylinder loomed over me, seeming as tall as an office building, towering up against the sky.

Because of the darkness I could not properly see where the base of it joined the ground, but where it was profiled against the sky I could see sharp curvature. The dim moonlight was not reflecting from its matt sides. Nothing was clear. It was like an *absence* of light, a darker black against the night. It hurt to look at it, just as it hurts to stare at a bright light.

I was paralysed with fear. I stood with my hands resting on the metal bodywork of my car, and stared in fixed terror at the immense object. Rationality briefly took over, and I tried to estimate the size of the thing, but I recoiled from calculation: two hundred, three hundred feet high?

How close to me was it? A vast object two hundred yards from me? Or something smaller near by? Why could I not see it properly?

Why was it rotating?

Irregular, improbable fitments were attached to its sides, pressing close against the cylindrical wall. I could see them now as they came into view, briefly silhouetted against the sky. I fixed on these, trying to use them for scale, or as some judge of the speed at which the thing was going round. It was rotating from left to right, anti-clockwise if seen from above, but these angular attachments did not appear to stay on one part of the side. The main cylinder rotated, taking them behind and temporarily out of my view, but when the turning brought them back into sight they were no longer at the same level as before. Somehow, they were moving up and down on the wall, but never in my sight, *only when hidden from me.*

The wind was gusting, and in the quiet moments I could hear noise coming from the base of the object. It was not a mechanical sound, like that of an engine, but a product of the motion; where the great cylinder turned against the earth it made a crushing, scraping, grinding noise.

There was another cylinder beyond it.

This was smaller, but it too was made of the impenetrable dark substance, it too had inexplicable objects attached to its side, it too rotated inexorably.

I turned away, full of fright, to look behind me, dreading what might be there ... but there was nothing to see. The clouds in this direction were faintly orange, the sky-glow of a distant town. I could see the shape of the rounded hills, feel the dry wind on my face.

When I looked back there were five huge cylinders upright in the field, and all of them were rotating slowly.

Two of the ones that had just appeared were small compared with the others, but the last, furthest away of all, was the largest, the tallest, the bulkiest . . . the worst.

I closed my eyes, incapable of looking, because to look was to see and to see was to face the impossible.

Fear has limits, and soon I reached mine. I felt my mind swimming, nausea rose, I slumped forward across the car. I gave up. I could accept no more.

I pressed my face against the cold metal roof of the car, feeling the wind lifting the flap at the back of my jacket, chilling my spine.

Then came clarity, transcendent from the fear.

I stood up, looked again. A sixth cylinder had appeared, a relatively small one, less than fifty yards from where I stood. I could hear the crops tangling and tearing as it twisted them, and the stones and chalky soil crushing and shattering under the weight.

I thought:

This is real. What I can see is there. I know by seeing and hearing that these cylinders objectively exist. But I do not know what I am seeing, only that I can see but that this does not explain what I have to know. However, there must be an explanation, something that solves the mystery.

They are farm machinery. (Impossible). Something to do with the military. (Improbable, impossible . . . nothing like this.) Alien spaceships, UFOs, flying saucers. (Improbable, impossible . . . but for other reasons.) A natural phenomenon.

24

(Then what? What is natural that is cylindrical and black and huge, and turns of its own volition? What is all of these, and is six in number?)

A seventh had appeared.

I am mad. (Possible, but I was not mad a few minutes ago.) I am dead and this is the afterlife. (Possible, now that I have eliminated the rest.) I am neither mad nor dead, but hallucinating. (Possible, because anything has become possible.)

When I turned away I could see the road, pale silver in the light from the moon, stretching behind me the way I had come, stretching ahead the way I had intended to go. I could touch the car, feel the wind, hear the sounds, see everything else around me and explain it to myself. I was not hallucinating. Nor was I dead.

I did not feel mad.

I noticed, in my new transcendent clarity, that the angular things attached to the wall had disappeared from the cylinder I had first seen. Without them I could no longer tell if it was rotating.

It no longer mattered: it was lifting slowly into the air.

It went straight up in dead silence.

The others followed, irregularly, not in formation. The last to lift was the one closest to me.

I watched, looking for signs of light, of propulsion, of clues to human manufacture or (at least) the humanly explicable. The cylinders had not risen very far before they disappeared from sight.

I do not know where they went, or how they went. It was simply that I could no longer see them.

The headlamps of my car suddenly came on, spreading light across the verge and along the side of the road. The

25

inside of the car was illuminated. I could hear a woman's voice coming quietly from the radio, reading the news, or intoning the shipping forecast.

Still in shock, still tortured by clarity, I climbed inside the car and slammed the door. The torch was on, the beam slanting upwards from where I had dropped it on the floor.

I switched everything off, locked all the doors, then sat in the silent darkness, protected by the car's capsule of metal and glass. I felt secure at last. The fear had left me, the sharp intensity of the trans-fear rationalism died away. I was not mad, I had not hallucinated. It had all been real.

A car went past, dazzling me with its headlamps, I turned my head to watch it pass, trying to catch a glimpse of the driver. Why were you not here when I needed you?

I sat quietly for a few more minutes, not unafraid. I listened to the radio, switching through channels. I heard part of a pop song, an interview with a television celebrity, a phone-in coming from Bristol. I did not look out towards the place where the cylinders had been.

At last I started the car, switched on the lights and moved off the verge to the road. I looked carefully for any other cars that might be approaching, then reversed a few yards, backing into the middle of the road.

I swung the car around, moving directly up the verge until it was level and until the headlights played across the field. I saw crops of some kind blowing in the wind. Taking the torch with me I left the car and walked out into the field, staying within the arc of the headlamps. I soon found the place where the nearest cylinder had been.

An immense circular impression had been made in the ground, thirty or forty feet in diameter. The crops were tangled and flattened, crushed into a level spiral where the

26

cylinder had pressed and turned. At the periphery of the circle the plants grew normally. The circle was as precisely made and as clean-edged as one lifted with a circular cutter from pastry dough. I knelt down and felt the ground through the mat of broken vegetation. It was hard and smooth.

I was unwilling to venture further away from the car, because the immensity of the land and the sky above was bearing down on me. I felt the beginnings of the fear again. I quickly flashed my torch around. I glimpsed other circular marks where the cylinders had pressed against the ground.

I returned to the car, reversed back to the road, then continued with my journey. Soon I felt again the weight of guilt turning in me, grinding me down, reminding me of the chore that lay ahead. I still had to face the final explanation from the woman I had loved the least.

4

ALICE HAD EXPECTED Granville to telephone her first thing in the morning, and so she was out of bed before eight o'clock, sitting in the kitchen drinking coffee, reading her mail and the newspaper, distracted by the silent telephone. By eleven she had worked herself into what she felt was an entirely rational state of impatience, and called him.

He came on the line without the customary delay, and immediately disarmed her with a friendly greeting.

Then he said, 'I've been trying to reach you, Alice. The girl on the switchboard said there was no answer. Have you been out?'

'No, I was here. What happened yesterday?'

'Well . . . I met Stackpole.' His tone had changed. 'There isn't much good news for you, I'm afraid. They're not going to let the manuscript go for a while.'

'I thought you said – Never mind.' Alice felt a familiar dread growing in her; familiar, that is, for the last three weeks. 'Did you find out what's going on?'

'Let me tell you exactly what was said. Stackpole explained the Home Office regulations under which your book was seized. They amount for the time being to a complete banning order. Officially, the book no longer exists until they decide to release it. The restriction order means rather more than I thought –'

'Granville, I don't understand!' She was feeling dizzy, losing track of what he was saying. 'What do you mean, the book no longer exists? Have they destroyed it?'

'I'm trying to explain. They haven't physically destroyed it. But the effect of the restriction order is that the book has no existence until they decide otherwise.' Granville paused. 'It means rather more than that, unfortunately. I admit that until yesterday I thought it simply meant they could stop you having it published. It's more serious. So long as the order is in effect we can't tell anyone that it exists, or that they've taken it in. You mustn't talk about it, Alice.'

'I haven't . . . that's what the note said.'

She thought guiltily about Eleanor, and the letters they had been planning to write.

'Yes, but they're concerned about other copies. How many copies did you make?'

'Just the two. The one they've got, and the one we sent to Harriet.'

Granville said, 'They have that copy as well.'

Alice groaned. She was sitting at her desk, her head bent low. Her free hand was clasped tensely against the side of her neck.

'Stackpole asked me if you had made any other copies, for your own use.'

'No, just the two.'

'No carbons? or photocopies?'

'No.'

'Are you sure?'

'I used my word processor. I can't make carbon copies.' She closed her eyes, suddenly realizing. 'I still have it on disk.'

'Then you'll have to send the disk to them. Or wipe it.'

'I can't do that! It's my only copy! Granville, I can't stand this!'

'They can search your house, Alice. And they don't need a warrant. They were here at my office yesterday, while I was with Stackpole. They were looking for extra copies of your book. I don't think you realize how serious this is.'

'I can't believe it's happening. Not to me! What I have I done? What's in the book they're scared of? I'm convinced they've made a mistake. Did you ask him that? Did you ask if they're sure they got the right book?

'The disk, Alice . . . will you wipe it?'

She looked despairingly at her plastic disk box, standing neatly beside the computer. The disks were somewhere in there with the others, in no particular order. She had never really thought about them since she had finished with the book.

'I'll do it as soon as we hang up,' she said. 'Should I smash the computer while I'm at it? In case I'm ever tempted to write another book?'

'I'm sorry, Alice, I know how you must feel.'

Actually, she thought grimly, no you bloody don't. Granville had never written a word in his life. You had to get a book written to know how it felt. She was wondering if Harriet might have made a photocopy before it was seized. Publishers did that sort of thing: they usually had a manuscript read by other people, and held the original back for safe keeping. Maybe a spare copy had already been sent to an outside reader, and she could get hold of that one somehow.

But what good would it do if they could search her house?

'There's a little good news in all this. Stackpole seemed to imply that they might release the book before too long.'

'Then what's all this about? Did he give a date?'

'You know how civil servants can be. Nothing was said directly. I was given to understand . . . that's the sort of phrase he was using. I was given to understand that if you do what they tell you they might let you have it back eventually.'

'Granville, what am I going to do about money? I was counting on this.'

'I might have an answer to that.' She heard a familiar manner. Granville was good at money. 'I'll be speaking to Harriet later today. I think I can get her to release the rest of the advance. If she doesn't, or if she can't, then I'll see what we can do here.'

'No. No loans, Granville, if that's what you mean. But thanks. I just want my book back.'

A few minutes later, when they had hung up, Alice remained at her desk, glaring at the wall. She still blamed Granville, irrationally. It wasn't really his fault, of course, but ever since she heard the manuscript had been impounded he had sounded like a mouthpiece for *them*. She kept wanting him to dream up one of his marvellous schemes, the sort that she sometimes read about in the *Bookseller* after he had done a clever deal for one of his other clients. She knew and accepted her lowly place in Granville's scheme of things – in every hierarchy someone has to be near the bottom – but now would be a good time to feel he was working for her.

She found the two computer disks on which she had written her book, and slipped them into her pocket. There was no power on earth that would make her destroy them.

But she knew Granville was right: her house might be searched. There was simply no point in hiding them somewhere.

She thought for a moment, then switched on her computer. She hunted around in her box and found a couple of old disks, painstakingly peeled off the old sticky labels, and put new ones in their place. She scribbed '*Six Women*, first draft' on one of them, and '*Six Women*, final draft' on the other.

Feeling that she was at last doing something constructive in her own cause, she used the computer to wipe everything off the disks. When she had finished she used a different pen to write 'deleted' on both labels, and added the date.

She made herself another cup of coffee, then played with the cat for a while, feeling she had out-manoeuvred them in some small way.

A few minutes later another thought occurred to her, a rather more sinister one. She remembered reading some-where, probably in one of the computer magazines, that when a disk was wiped it didn't become completely blank. There were programs that could read disks that only seemed empty. For a moment she felt a renewed helplessness, but the sense that she was now in a battle to save her book was making her devious.

She quickly copied the real disks to the fake ones, made sure the text had arrived safely, then wiped them a second time. Now if someone broke into her house, and if they took away the disks, and *if* they had that program . . . then all right.

She put the fakes back in the box, closed the lid and switched off the computer.

With the genuine disks safely in an envelope in her pocket, she put down some food for Jimmy then walked to the village to see if her car was ready to be collected.

She had no conscience about what she had just done, no sense that it was illegal . . . although it almost certainly was. Instead, she had an inner certainty that it was *right*: she could no more have destroyed her book than a mother could destroy her child. What this therefore meant was that the law must be wrong, and the thought gave her a heady sense of recklessness. She had never flouted the law before, at least not seriously. Smoking dope at college with everyone else, breaking the speed limit, fiddling her tax expenses, etc., did not count. She knew that if she were caught she could be imprisoned; the note had said so. But some things were bigger than the law, and anyway they would have to catch her first.

The disks were safe for the time being, so long as she carried them about with her, but if they had powers of search without a warrant there was nowhere around her she could keep them for ever. Fantasizing morbidly, she thought of a gang of Home Office thugs kicking down her door, a butch female stripping her of her clothes, pulling the disks triumphantly out of her bra, or wherever.

The whole situation was unreal to her. As she passed the houses in the centre of the village she said hello to a couple emerging from their cottage, and she thought: I'm carrying illegal substances and isn't it a lovely day?

Her car was waiting. She paid the bill with a cheque, wondering if the bank would cover it, then drove into Ramsford. The disks were ever-present in her mind. She imagined being stopped by a police car for some trivial traffic offence, and having to watch as they pulled the car apart in search for her contraband. Until she could think of a better place, she put the disks in the glove compartment, behind all the rubbish that was there.

Although she lived a couple of miles away, Ramsford always felt as if it was the place to which she really belonged. She had tried to find a house here when she was first looking, but had been driven out to Milton Colebourne by the prices. Ramsford was a village that had grown into the local market town, and had branches of the main clearing banks, a post office, a railway station, doctors, dentists, shops, and everything else. The centre was still more or less unmodernized, and it was possible to imagine what Ramsford might have been like a century or so before. In his book on Wiltshire, Nikolaus Pevsner called the architecture of Ramsford 'non-committal', a comment which always puzzled Alice when she was actually there, and other historical references were few and far between. William Cobbett had stayed overnight in 1821, and in 1687 Celia Fiennes had made a long detour around the place on her way to Bath, for fear of rutted roads and lurking vagabonds. Alice liked Ramsford for its undiscovered and underrated quality, and was content for it to stay that way. Although she had lived in Wiltshire for less than a year, she already thought of it as home.

She went first to the post office to buy some stamps. Mrs Lodge was working behind the counter, very anxious to gossip with her about Eleanor, but it was pensions day and there was a long queue waiting. Alice was glad to get away without having to say more than a few words.

The police station was across the road from the post office, but Alice went to the fruit shop first to buy a grapefruit. As she walked by she glanced at the police station and saw the constable she had spoken to standing by the window. Looking straight at her he beckoned unsmilingly. Alice nodded, and went on into the greengrocer's. A huge green-painted truck belonging to BBC Television News was parked outside.

Ramsford was too small for a proper police station. There was just the house where the policeman lived, with a modern extension serving as an office. One of the windows at the back had bars over it. This was the only indication from outside of the use the building had. Otherwise it was as noncommittal as the other houses in the centre of the village. When Alice went in the constable was still by the window, while an older man, in plain clothes, sat at a desk.

The interview lasted about ten minutes. Before she arrived Alice had not really known what to expect, although the conversation with Granville had left her in an unusual state of mind: what he had told her about her manuscript had heightened her paranoia, but her falsification of the disks had made her feel defiant. The two conflicting moods balanced out into a feeling of detachment.

The plain-clothes officer introduced himself as Superintendent Bowker from Salisbury Police, and his questions turned out to be as routine as the constable had said they would be. How long had she known the dead woman? How well did she know her? When had she last seen her? And so on.

At the end, though, the detective said, 'Have you seen anyone recently you didn't recognize? In Milton Colebourne, or in the vicinity of Mrs Hamilton's house?

'No, I don't think so.' She was trying to remember, conscientiously doing what she could to help. 'I've only lived around here since last winter. I don't know very many people.'

'All right. But you say you were friendly with Mrs Hamilton. Have *you* any idea why someone might want to kill her?'

'No, of course not.'

But the detective had emphasized the word 'you', as if other people might have thought differently. It cast everything into a subtly different light. She wondered who else they would have interviewed. Tradesmen, the son, other people in the village? Would any of them think differently? Did they know something about Eleanor that she did not? The odd thing was that when she befriended Eleanor she had felt she was being

35

taken into the older woman's confidence. She remembered their first conversation: village concerns, banal gossip, offers of neighbourly assistance, and so on. How that had changed later! Eleanor had frequently said, 'You don't know what it means to me to have someone I can talk to.' as if she was finding an outlet in Alice she had with no one else. Alice remembered her feelings of selfish guilt as she later spent long hours finishing her book, closeted away in her study with the word processor, not visiting Eleanor as often as she had. That was how the tapes had come to be made, a way of justifying the time away from the book, thinking that the next one might develop from them.

She recalled what they had discussed: Eleanor's membership of CND and Friends of the Earth and Greenpeace, her conviction that the British Government was embroiled in a conspiracy with the United States to increase defence spending still further to keep the economy on the boil, and so on. When she talked about these things she seemed fierce, radical, rather cranky. She saw enemies everywhere, talked of secrecy, censorship, high-level conspiracies, political repression. It was all fairly familar. In an odd way Eleanor had reminded Alice of her student days, when she too had been convinced about everything.

Was it then a political killing? Three weeks ago such a thought would never have crossed Alice's mind, but the business of her manuscript had opened her eyes to many things. Would someone have killed Eleanor for her beliefs?

'Are you sure?' the detective said, perhaps seeing Alice's uncertainty. 'No one Mrs Hamilton might have mentioned?'

'No, I'm certain.' Alice said, and tried to look ingenuous. 'She was just a harmless old lady. I've no idea what could have happened.'

36

5

MY DEAR ALICE,
I've already started this several times, without success, and so I have decided to write it to you as a letter. I send so many letters these days that I only feel 'at home' when I can address someone directly. You will of course be able to reply to this in person, but I want to say a few things first, in my own way, while I am sitting here alone.

I suppose the first thing I should deal with is your intention of writing a book about me. (I presume it is a book, or at least part of one? You haven't said so in as many words.) I could not of course stop you if you went ahead against my wishes, so I'd like you to know that you have my blessing. I've given this much thought, because your interest has created many contradictory feelings in me. I am flattered, of course, but also very much afraid that you would find little to write about. Many year ago, while my books were still in print, a pleasant but awesomely intelligent young man from America approached me with the same request. I had then much the same conflict of feelings, but on that occasion I decided to turn him down. (I feared he would write something anyway, but so far as I know he never did.) Afterwards, I gave a lot of thought to how I should react if someone else asked the same. I made the decision that I would neither encourage nor obstruct, and that decision still stands today.

I believe you are a good writer, Alice, and I enjoyed the manuscript you lent me. I think you are a sympathetic person, and that you make a genuine effort to understand the people you write about. In this sense I don't feel threatened by your interest in me, but I owe it to you to say very clearly that these notes will not tell you what I think you would like to know. Instead, they will make a few suggestions about places where you might start your own researches.

For instance, you have asked me several times about the books I have written, and the last time you asked I thought you did so rather deviously. Please don't be devious with me! If I had wanted to tell you about them I should have done so directly. I am not a secretive person, but my books were written during a very distinct and difficult period of my life, that period is now a long way behind me, and in a very real sense they no longer mean much to me.

However, the *Oxford Companion to Children's Literature* has a short entry on my work (as do several less weighty reference works on children's books), and a long essay was published in an American journal called the *Maryland Literary Quarterly*. This was hostile to the books, but, I thought, contained several perceptive remarks.

The books themselves are difficult to find, but not impossible. Most children's books, don't survive being owned by children, the few that do end up in jumble sales, and after that God alone knows what happens to them. But if you put your mind to it you should be able to find one or two of them. (The last time I was in the second-hand shop in Marlborough I saw they had a copy of one of them on sale. £75!!) They are most certainly no longer in print in any edition, the publishing house was taken over years ago, and I imagine the only places which still have complete sets would be the copyright libraries. But if you are determined to find them you should not, as I say, have too much trouble.

You have also asked several questions about my background, and here too I should prefer to give you a few trails to follow, rather than answer you directly.

I was born in 1915. I was christened Eleanor Seraphina, and throughout my childhood I was called 'Nell' or 'Nellie' by mother, and 'Seri' by my older brothers. I have always detested my middle name and never normally use it, although for a few years after I left home I called myself 'Seri' because of my brothers. I thought it was a name other young men might find attractive.

My mother's name was Lilian Mary, and her maiden name was Bartholomew. I never knew my father. He was killed in France two months before I was born. He was a Lieutenant in the Royal Welch Fusiliers, and his full name was David Michael Fulten. (We do not have Welsh connections. His commission to this regiment came about, I understand, through a professional contact.) He was an architect before he joined the Army, and an active member of the Liberal Party. He was 25 when he died. Most of what I know about my father is of course from what my mother told me when I was a child. I possess the only photograph of him still in existence. His death while still so young has affected my whole life. I have always hated war, and those who pursue it. This is not unusual in people of my generation, because we were born during one terrible war and spent our young adult lives in another.

My mother remarried many years after the war. Her second husband, a doctor, was several years older than her, but I believe they were happy together. My brothers had already left home by the time this happened, but I was still attending school. My stepfather died a year before the outbreak of World War II. My mother died in 1943.

I was working in Greece when Britain declared war on Germany. I had gone there in the summer of 1939 because war seemed inevitable, and because I had thought, naively, that I would be well out of it when it started. There was another reason, too: I was making a fool of myself over a young man called Hugh, and he had also gone to Greece. After that had sorted itself out I stayed on afterwards, doing what work I could. When war broke out I had a job with a shipping company in Athens, and was already wishing I was at home. (Hugh became infamous later. You will find several references to him in Rebecca West's *An Understanding of Treachery*, and I think there should be sufficient trails in this for you to discover what he had been doing in Greece, and why I had been such a fool. His case is well covered by other books, and I am mentioned in a few of them.)

I was finally evacuated to Britain in January 1940. By this time I had joined up with a young Englishman called Peter, who had been convalescing in Greece after a serious illness. He attached himself to me, and during the long sea voyage back to England we became lovers. It was doomed never to last. He had not entirely recovered from the illness, and was preoccupied with his own complicated life at home. Once we had landed safely, the unpleasant realities of war readiness, and all the inconvenience that went with it, drove us apart.

I eventually joined up with an old schoolfriend called Joyce, and we rented a small flat in London. Flats were easy to find in those days. Joyce had joined the WRNS and was working at the Admiralty, but I kept as far away from war service as I could. I got work as a clerk at Guy's Hospital, but during the blitz I found another job as a typist with the BBC.

I'm skipping a lot, perhaps missing out the part you would find more interesting. I've said nothing about being at school (I was something of a swot, and most of the others hated me), nor about the days when I went wild ... all those dancing parties and boyfriends and late nights! (In reality I was a bit shy, and a wild party in the thirties is, I imagine, rather tame when compared with what young people get up to these days. Even so, by the time I set off for Greece I was no longer innocent.) I've also said nothing of my brothers (my older brother Philip would make a much more interesting subject for a book than me.)

I realize as I write this down, Alice, that you might think I'm just playing games with you, tantalizing you with snippets while holding back the real information. I'm constantly tempted to tell you everything I can think of. I'm also tempted to tear this up before you see it. I have read enough biographies of still living subjects to know that it's almost impossible for such a biographer to write objectively. Perhaps you should wait until I'm gone ... whatever you decide, while I am still here and can have a say, I want to help you without influencing you.

It's difficult to judge accurately how to do this, though, and I am getting tired, so I will take a few more days to think about it. Maybe then I will add a few more details. I must tell you about Peter, who came back into my life, and you will want to know something more about the background to my books.

All this later, then.

6

AFTER SHE LEFT the police station Alice drove back towards her house, wondering what to do about her disks. Her book was still her priority, and the disks were her last remaining link with it. She had complex feelings about the book. The ones she talked to Granville about were all real: the need for money, the sense of puzzled outrage, the paranoia of being picked on. All these would be enough on their own. But there was something extra that no one else could understand. Not even Granville, perhaps especially not Granville. The book felt unfinished because no one else had read it.

Eleanor, of course, had read the manuscript, but she had made changes since and they were important. Maybe not to someone else,but they mattered to her. They altered the emphasis subtly, gave the book greater depth. Of the two copies she had given to Granville, one had gone straight in to Harriet, the other – the one that was seized – had been put in the mail to go to her American publisher. Granville, knowing how desperate she was for money, had done as he promised and sent the book straight out, saying he would read it later.

Alice needed feedback on anything she wrote, feeling that until then the work was somehow incomplete. It probably revealed insecurity, or vanity, or some other besetting sin peculiar to writers, but that was how she was. This was why she had forced the manuscript on Eleanor, knowing it was not quite finished; then, when Eleanor made her comments, why she had gone back to her desk and worked through the entire text, tinkering endlessly with it. All this gave her a feeling of suspense that had not changed from the day she delivered the manuscripts to Granville's office. The instruction to *destroy* her last copy was impossible to obey.

The problem remained of what to do. While driving to Ramsford she had thought of asking Bill to look after the disks for her, but that would introduce too many problems. He was not exactly unconnected with her, and if people were going to be searching for copies of the book they would obviously pay Bill a visit. This was the practical drawback, but there were other reasons, more personal and therefore more compelling. Bill had never been sympathetic to her writing, and he was unlikely to have changed. He would be naturally curious and she would have to tell him what had happened . . . or make up some unconvincing lie. She no longer trusted him. All that had gone when the marriage went wrong, and he would be sure to make capital of it somehow. Also, he had the same make of computer as hers, which he liked playing around with. She didn't want him near the book. No, not Bill.

A short distance outside Milton Colebourne the road widened slightly where there was a farm entrance. Alice stopped the car here, and took the disks from the glove compartment.

She had remembered that the carpet under the front passenger seat had been loosely attached ever since she bought the car, so she pulled up a corner and slipped the disks underneath. She pushed them as far under the seat as she could, where anyone in the car would be unlikely to put their feet, then straightened the carpet and pressed it down to make it look undisturbed.

Before driving off again she glanced around, wanting to be certain that no one, however innocent or unaware, had seen what she had done. Again, there was the weird feeling of unreality, the sense that she was acting like a criminal, and indeed literally was a criminal . . . but that it was her and the blameless book she had written, and that this was just England, the familiar lanes and trees and countryside, exactly as she had always known them. Why had it all changed?

A few hundred yards further on she passed Eleanor's house and noticed a dark-maroon car parked on the drive.

She slowed, intending to pull in, but suddenly changed her mind and let her car go on past. Then she changed her mind a second time. She stopped the car and reversed back to the gate. She parked on the drive, behind the maroon car.

A man came to the door a few moments after she had rung the bell. He looked tired, distracted.

'Hello,' Alice said. 'Are you Mr Hamilton?'

The question appeared to irritate him. He looked past her as if to find out if other people were with her, then he said, 'No, but I'm Mrs Hamilton's son.'

'I'm Alice Stockton. I live in one of the houses over there, and I was a friend of Eleanor's. I don't know if she ever mentioned me.' She waited for a cue, but none came. 'I was so sorry to hear the news. It must be dreadful for you. I was passing, and I saw your car, and I was wondering if there was anything – '

'I don't think so, thank you. Unless . . . you don't happen to know if there's a restaurant around here, do you?'

44

His voice had the faint trace of a northern accent; Lancashire or Yorkshire, modified in some way.

'Not in the village,' Alice said. 'There's a fish and chip shop in Ramsford, but if you want a real restaurant you'll have to drive into Marlborough or Salisbury. Is there any food in the house?'

'Nothing fresh, no. Look, would you care to come in for a moment?'

'Would I be interrupting anything?'

'I'm just trying to sort out her things. I'd be glad of a break.'

She followed him through the house to Eleanor's sitting-room, which looked much as she remembered it. The place had always been a homely mess, but a number of cardboard boxes were there, on the top of the table and piled on the floor.

Alice repeated her conventional condolences, but he listened to them without response, then asked if she would care for some coffee. 'It's instant coffee, with powdered milk. Would that be all right?'

She sat at the table while he put on the kettle and searched awkwardly for a second cup. Alice remembered the occasions she had sat in the same room with Eleanor, nibbling at cakes or home-made biscuits and drinking numerous cups of tea. Once, on the day they talked about her manuscript, they had shared a bottle of wine. The house smelt as it always had done: that vague but distinctive smell of other people's homes. Knowing nothing about the actual circumstances of Eleanor's death Alice had half-expected to find signs of a struggle, or macabre stains, but instead there was just this pleasant old house, full of mild but happy memories.

She wished she had not called in, though. Eleanor's son seemed put out by her presence, in spite of what he said. He looked as if he was a little older than she was, tall, his hair

45

starting to thin on top. He was dressed casually, but looked as if he was someone who only did so when he had to. He had a disconcerting mannerism when she spoke to him: he would stare straight into her eyes, without apparent expression, then hold the gaze for a moment or two longer before replying. As he moved about the room while the kettle boiled he was avoiding her eyes, but at last he sat down across the table from her, and stared at her once more.

'I've just been to see the police,' she said, as if explaining something, but realizing as she spoke what a non sequitur it must sound.

'Are you a suspect?' he said, surprising her.

'I shouldn't think so.' The thought hadn't occurred to her until that moment. 'They asked me if I'd seen anyone around the house, or if I knew anyone who'd done it.'

'What did you say?'

'Nothing much. I never see anything.'

'That's what everyone thinks. People see more than they admit.'

She shrugged, thinking that this was a bit blunt. The kettle started to boil, and he went over and filled the cups. Alice wondered if he had used water from the tap.

'I actually didn't see anything at all.' she said, 'I've been busy for the last few days, I've hardly left the house.'

'Do you smoke?' he said, taking a cigarette for himself.

'No.' She had quit when she moved to Wiltshire. It was all part of her new life, a conscious throwing off of the old. 'Do they know how your mother died?'

'I understand she was strangled. They're not completely sure yet. Her heart had given out . . . she might have died of that while the man was attacking her. There were bruises on her throat, but no other signs.'

'Oh,' Alice said, wishing she hadn't asked. The cold description had suddenly made Eleanor's death feel very direct and personal. She could imagine her fighting back, but ineffectually, because she was so old. 'Did it happen here, in the house?'

'That's something else they don't know. Her body was found by the river. How far's that from here? About half a mile? She could have been dragged there, or taken in a car. A lane runs a few yards from where they found her. Nothing was stolen from the house, so far as they know.'

'Was this during the day?'

'At night. They can measure the time of death.'

'I'm sorry . . . I shouldn't ask so many questions. You must be very upset.'

'Yes.' He stirred his pale-brown coffee idly, staring at her. 'Actually no I'm not, to be candid. I'm surprised and I'm shocked. But I don't feel upset. Maybe that will come later.'

'Yes, these things are delayed,' Alice muttered conventionally.

'They've been delayed for about thirty years so far.'

'I don't understand.'

He made a gesture with his hand, indicating the house, the generality of the room. 'I hardly knew my mother. We were never close.'

Alice felt uncomfortable, still distressed by the image of Eleanor's violent death. She knew she was intruding. She needed to hear none of this. All it explained was the minor mystery of why Eleanor had never mentioned her son. Now she was finding out, and she wished she did not have to.

She drank her coffee too quickly, scalding her tongue.

'Thank you. I must let you get on. I'm sorry about your mother, I really am. She was my only friend around here. I

47

still haven't got used to the idea she's dead. I shouldn't have come.' She stood up, knowing she was about to cry. 'Thanks for the coffee.'

He followed her to the door.

'Did you say your name was Alice Stockman?' he said.

'Stockton. If you need me for anything my telephone number's in the book. I'm sorry I troubled you.'

She hurried to her car, aware that he was watching her. She started the engine and drove away quickly. She was trembling, and her eyes were full of tears. When she arrived home she went to her bedroom and lay down, feeling wretched.

Her mood was broken abruptly when the cat came in. He prowled around the room, hunching and looking from side to side. Alice watched him attentively, suddenly alarmed. He did not respond when she spoke to him, but crouched down in the middle of the carpet, made a pathetic grunting noise, then vomited.

Alice moved towards him quickly, trying not to alarm him. The cat sniffed the little wet pile, then backed away, cowering and looking up at her. There were traces of green in the vomit.

'Have you been eating grass, Jimmy?' she said. The cat scuttled away from her.

She rushed to the bathroom and grabbed the pills the vet had given her. She kept the lawn uncut, because that was the first advice she had heard, and simply hoped he wouldn't try to chew on it. She grew cocksfoot grass in a tray in the kitchen, but he never seemed to use it.

Alice caught the cat, held him tight, and forced one of the pills down his throat. She held him until she was sure he had swallowed it, then released him. He got away from her,

48

dashed downstairs and clattered through the cat-flap. She watched him from the window.

He walked as far as the centre of the lawn, and began retching again. She watched, full of compassion, as the pill purged his stomach.

Later, when he would let her near him again, she held him in her arms, stroking him and speaking to him gently. 'Don't eat the grass outside, Jimmy, don't eat the grass outside . . . '

The cat purred. He never understood what she said.

At the end of the day, when she was worn out from worry, and worn out from feeling miserable, and was thinking of listening to Radio 4 all evening before having an early night, someone knocked at her door.

It was Eleanor's son.

He said, 'I'm just about to drive into Marlborough for a meal. I was wondering . . . would you care to join me?'

7

THE DAY WAS grey, with low clouds moving in on the wind from the North Sea. It was far too chilly to sit on the beach, so we all walked up through the town, passed across the low headland that separated the beaches and went on the pier on the other side. I was six years old. My brother Frank was nine.

We weren't often on this side of town because the guest house where we stayed faced the other beach, which had been specially cleaned up for visitors. Most of the other beaches along this stretch of the Suffolk coast were still polluted with oil spillage from wartime sinkings. 'Our' side of the town had been repaired and rebuilt, but in the main part there were many vacant sites and piles of rubble where shops and houses had been bombed. During the war, German aircraft had routinely released any unused bombs as they headed home across the English coast, and this town had been repeatedly hit.

The pier, though, was open and was a special treat. It was normally a place to which our parents would never take us, it being full of dangers for small children, but on this windy day it was a distraction for us all. The imagined dangers were of course what we loved about the pier. The noise and lights from the penny arcades, the exotic smells of onions and sausages from the snack bars, the whirling lights and deafening music from the rides. Further out towards the end there were the lonely men with their fishing rods, the views of the distant seashore, the cracks in the elderly planks through which the sea could be glimpsed below.

We walked to the end, watched a speedboat bouncing and dashing through the choppy waves, leaned perilously over the rail, found loose planks that wobbled when you jumped up and down on them, pestered our parents for goes on the rides, and begged them for silly hats and sticks of seaside rock.

In the end Frank and I were allowed free rein in the amusement arcade, each clutching six pennies for the machines. My own favourite was the machine with the movable hands, made of shiny metal, which hovered temptingly over a slow-moving turntable filled with toys. When the penny went in you could make the hand slide out across the turntable, then propel it down to make a grab at the toys. When this happened, the fingers, each tipped with a spiked thimble made of red rubber, clenched magically . . . and sometimes, but only sometimes, grasped a toy and deposited it neatly in the prize chute. I loved to watch these hands at work, even when they failed to grab me a toy. They seemed possessed with magical life, worked by a hidden brain which made arbitrary decisions about when to take, and when not to.

After the penny arcade we went to the rides. Here we ran into our parents' wall of opposition to everything we wanted to do. Frank and I wanted to go on the Giant Slide, the Ghost Train, the Dodgem Cars, the Waltzo; they would permit only the roundabout and the miniature railway.

Unexpectedly, my father announced that he would like to ride on the Ferris Wheel. Frank was selected to accompany him, while I had to wait below with my mother. We watched as they clambered into the rocking cradle, and the man in charge lowered the safety bar across their waists. My father had a camera with him, and as they waited for the machine to start he took a photograph of us.

The wheel went around once, then came to a halt to let on more people. Frank and my father were halfway up, rocking to and fro in an exciting way, waving to us. The wheel started and stopped as more people got on and off. Standing below, looking up, my envy of my older brother made this wheel seem as if it was the most thrilling ride on the pier . . . but at the same time, with that perverse ability of children to hold two conflicting ideas at once, it looked dull and predictable. What was the point in just sitting there, while the thing went round and round? This did not stop me pleading with my mother to be allowed on anyway. I was told to be quiet, and to wait.

Soon after the ride had properly begun, and the wheel was turning rapidly, something went wrong.

The drive machinery at the bottom made a loud bang, a plume of dark smoke gusted around the platform, and the wheel came to an abrupt halt. My mother clutched me, and dragged me backwards. I was staring up at the wheel. The cradles were all rocking violently, and some of the passengers were shouting and screaming. As the smoke cleared, my mother snatched me up into her arms and rushed forward.

There followed a period of great excitement. People came from all over the pier to see what had happened, and as the crowd built up some of the men who operated the other rides tried to make everyone move back out of the way.

I noticed two men in dark-green uniforms, carrying rifles, standing at the back of the crowd. I asked my mother who they were, but she wasn't listening to me.

Frank and my father were in the cradle at the very top of the giant wheel. Now that the cradles had steadied they were waving down to us reassuringly, and we waved back. My mother shouted something up at them, but in all the noise it was impossible to make herself heard.

The passengers whose cradles were at the bottom of the wheel were taken off, and a stepladder was found for those a little higher. Most of the cradles were too high to be reached, and the passengers sat helplessly, rocking in the sea-wind.

The men in charge were trying to repair the machinery. Meanwhile, two men from the St John's Ambulance Brigade arrived, and they took over control of the crowd. Most of us were reluctant to move back, and there was much pushing and jostling.

The two men in green uniforms stepped forward to help, and at the sight of their rifles the crowd at last began to disperse. As one of the men came towards us I explained that it was my daddy who was on the wheel and that we wanted to stay. My mother did not hear this, but let herself be moved to a position that was out of the way of the rescue attempts. She was staring at the sky.

A long period dragged by without any progress. A large group of firemen arrived, adding to the excitement. They had brought longer ladders, and a few more people were rescued. The top six cradles remained beyond reach.

My father kept waving down to us. We waved back. I was jealous of Frank, because it was he who was having the adventure, not I. I wanted him to come down and describe it all to me, and at the same time stop having all the fun without me.

The rescue entered a more complicated phase. This

involved the firemen building a high wooden platform around the base of the wheel, then trying to raise their ladders from this. The novelty began to fade, and I felt bored. I wanted to go back to the penny arcade, and wait for the other two in there. It was cold standing in the wind, not doing anything except look at the cradle so high and far away. At last I tugged on my mother's hand and told her I wanted to go to the toilet. The nearest public lavatory was on the sea front, and my mother scolded me and told me I had to wait. We were not going to leave until Daddy and Frank came down from the wheel.

I won the argument by starting to cry.

I was hustled away, off the pier, my mother glancing back towards the wheel as she tugged me along.

A few minutes later, my bladder relieved, we hurried back along the promenade towards the entrance to the pier. A bigger crowd had gathered here, drawn by the sight of the two red fire engines. There were more men in the green uniforms, holding everyone back.

Distantly, borne on the wind, there came the sound of a scream.

My mother snatched me up and started to run along the promenade. Lifted high, I could see past her head towards the wheel. She too was staring out at the pier as she rushed towards it.

We saw flames and sparks shooting around the main axle of the wheel, and firemen on ladders were directing what looked like intense white clouds of dust around the fire.

The wheel started to rotate, then halted, making the cradles rock violently. The wheel jerked again. I saw someone falling from one of the highest cradles, landing out of sight amongst the crowd at the base. The people there scattered, and we heard more screaming.

My mother came to a halt, and we stood by the sea-rail of the promenade close to the entrance to the pier. We could see everything.

There was another loud explosion, followed an instant later by a second one, much more powerful. I saw one of the firemen hurled backwards from the ladder on which he had been standing.

The wheel collapsed, crashing down vertically on the surface of the pier, balancing for a moment, then tipping slowly to one side. As it fell against the raised balustrade of the pier it flipped like an immense coin, and crashed in large broken pieces into the sea. White spume shot up from a dozen scattered places.

It was then that I believe my mother went mad.

She had been holding me tight against her shoulder, but now she pulled me away and held me at arm's length in front of her. Her hair was tangled from the wind, and her eyes were crazed. With her jaw sagging she fixed me with a blazing look. She had turned me away from the view. I could not see what was happening, could only hear the surging of the sea, the wind gusting around us, and the shouting and screaming from the crowd. She held me like this, silent in all the tumult of noise and confusion, fixing me with her wild expression. I was terrified of her, but only when I yelled with fear did she release me. She held me against her chest, cradling my head in her hand, and I bellowed with terror and shock.

Everyone who was still on the wheel when it fell into the sea, including Frank and my father, died. One of the firemen and three of the people in the crowd were also killed. Several more were seriously injured.

Many years later, while going through old boxes in the junk

55

room, I came across my father's camera, which had been recovered intact from the sea. I discovered that it still had film inside it, and, not realizing straight away what it might contain, I sent it away to be processed. When the prints came back – slightly faded and speckled, but perfectly viewable – I realized that these were the pictures my father had taken from the cradle at the top of the Ferris Wheel.

One of them showed my mother and myself, seen from aboard the cradle, waving and smiling inanely from a few feet away. Others showed long views of the pier-head, receding in exaggerated perspective out to sea. Most of the pictures were views of the sea, lacking detail, grey areas with a few flecks of foam, poorly defined distant objects, slanting horizons.

The last was a downward view of a ball of flame: a technically brilliant photograph, sharply defined, full of contrast, showing horrified faces and upraised arms beyond the explosion, the limbs of a fireman spreading wildly as he fell, the jagged splinters of a broken spar.

This must have been my father's last conscious act: to release the camera shutter in the last two or three seconds of his life.

It is also the moment in which my mother lost her mind, fifty or a hundred yards away, clutching me in her arms. Although I had never seen the picture before, or anything like it, the picture brought back to me the moment my mother moved me away from her, held me at arm's length and turned on me with her mad stare. My mind was full of that terrible image of the wheel crashing into the sea, but what I was seeing was my mother's face. I felt her horror as if it were my own, transmitted to me from her.

And afterwards, when she was silent and calm and in morbid grief, and all through the weeks when she was confined to hospital and I was cared for by strangers, and again afterwards, when she was home and her memory had gone, and yet again, all through my childhood and teenage years when we were together and her traumatic amnesia put the block in her mind, and on again, into adult life . . . all this time I retained her horror because she continued in some terrible way to transmit it to me.

She never recovered her memory of that day.

There seemed to be a time in her life when my father and brother had existed, and she could talk about them as naturally as if they were still alive. And there was another time when they were not there, and never had been there, and this was the longer time, the fullness of the rest of her life. There was no link for her between the two. They had been removed from her life without explanation. With them went a part of her mind.

It was the single crucial moment of her life, depicted indirectly in that accidental photograph.

I remember little of my own life before the day of the accident, except that I have vague and happy memories no different from those of other small children. I have normal memories of all my life following, with sharp recollections of this and that, lapses and mistakes, dull and indistinct periods. But I remember that particular day in every detail.

Somehow my mother made sense of her life with the accident censored from her memory. Somehow she pieced together the two parts, made them internally consistent. She never seemed puzzled, or aware of the real inconsistencies I noticed every time she talked about herself. Her life became whole, fully explicable, but never to me.

I took it all into myself. I carried the load of the memory. Her life was marked in that moment of the accidental photograph, but so too was mine. My mother became mad, but I became sane and whole.

8

HIS CAR SMELT of tobacco. The ashtray was stuffed with cigarette ends, the floor was littered with empty Dunhill packets and Eleanor's son lit the next cigarette only a minute or so after the last. Alice liked all this, though. She had made a private vow, on quitting, that she would never become an anti-smoker. The smell of someone else's tobacco was always pleasant to her.

He drove well without showing off. Some men could not resist driving too fast when they had a woman in the car, or would display meaningless expertise in something to do with the gears, but Eleanor's son drove as if he was used to spending a lot of time behind the wheel.

She wondered what he did for a living and whether it involved driving. She knew so little about him, not even his correct name. She felt embarrassed about this detail, because a time naturally arises when you can enquire about a stranger's name, and that time had now passed. All she knew for sure was that he was not called Hamilton. Because she had told him her own name she felt obscurely at a disadvantage.

But she was glad of the invitation to dinner. She spent so much of her time alone. Her infrequent visits to London were the only chances to see her old friends, but very often the trip was a hurried one to see Granville or Harriet, and if she went by train she was subject to the tyranny of Western Rail's minimalist service. Because she never had much spare cash she usually headed straight for home afterwards without contacting anyone. There was always Jimmy to think of. She didn't like leaving him alone for too long. In the past friends had sometimes visited her at weekends, but after her first few weeks in Wiltshire, when they had been curious about where she was living, visitors became increasingly rare. Her departure from London had left only a small hole in the social lives of her friends, one which apparently filled up quickly. Anyway, most of them were still in touch with Bill, and that created a subject of conversation no one wanted to bring up. After the accident at Cap la Hague, the excuses weren't even offered.

She had not yet sorted out her feelings on all this. She missed her old friends but was sustained day to day by the thin consolations of a new way of life. The countryside was pretty, she told herself when she felt lonely.

Eleanor's son made small-talk during the drive to Marlborough. He told her about the car. It was a German import, a BMW, and although it had been converted to right-hand drive for the British market, it remained ergonomically (he used the word, oddly) a left-hand drive car. He pointed out that it was almost impossible for the driver to reach the ashtray without reaching awkwardly around the gear lever.

He showed her the radiophone, and how it linked in with a computer console. This enabled him to keep in touch with his work while he was away from the office. (Alice passed no comment on these, remembering the numerous times she had been overtaken on the M4 by a powerful car hurtling along, driven by a man – it was always a man – chatting on his phone or fiddling with equipment below the dashboard.)

They parked in Marlborough High Street, and after briefly looking around for places that were open he suggested one of the hotels. Had he asked her Alice would have opted for the Chinese restaurant tucked away behind the town Hall (when the cash started running out her weekly Chinese dinner was the first luxury to go), but since it was his treat she said nothing, happy to let him make the choice.

He wanted a drink before they ate, and led her to the bar. She scanned the menu while sipping at a gin and bitter lemon, feeling hungry. She wished he had given her a chance to put on clean clothes or wash her hair. She felt dowdy in her daytime clothes. Better still, she would have felt more at home in a less expensive restaurant.

She was not warming to him. He was wrapped up in himself, her present role appearing to be that of convenient but essentially uninteresting female company. Turned away from her, he chatted to the barman. Meanwhile, she read through the menu for the third time, noticing the prices more than the selections on offer. When the head waiter came to take their order, Eleanor's son asked for a steak; Alice ordered the grilled trout, on the principle that it was the least expensive item. The waiter led them to their table in the dining-room, and the usual rigmaroles began: taking places, having napkins placed on their laps, ordering wine, and so on.

'You still haven't told me your name,' she said, thinking that she would take the conversational initiative, even if he would not.

'Is that so?'

He was fiddling with his cigarettes again. There was no ashtray on the table, and he turned away from her to ask the waitress for one.

61

'Well?' Alice said. 'Or is it a secret?'

'It's Gordon. Gordon Sinclair.'

'Thank you. I'm sorry about the mistake I made, thinking you were a Hamilton.'

She waited for more, but the gambit had apparently died on the air. She was irritated by him, and was already wishing she had not agreed to this. She had known when she said yes that he would be merely using her for company, but he now seemed so bored with her that she wondered why he had even bothered. She was an appendage, a way of not having to eat alone.

Then she felt ungracious and mean. His mother had just died, he was in a strange part of the country, he knew her no better than she knew him. He had rightly sensed that she was lonely, knew she had been a friend of Eleanor's, and the invitation to dinner had been polite rather than friendly. What had she been hoping for? A romantic interlude?

'How do you find living around here?' he said. 'After Cap la Hague, I mean.'

She felt the muscles in her abdomen tighten, a reminder of the old fears.

'I suppose it's all right,' she said.

'Aren't you worried?'

'I was at first. But it seems fairly normal now.'

'I'd heard the radiation was below danger-level again. I suppose this explains why there are so many people still around here.'

'A few people did leave, but I think they were the ones with weekend cottages.'

'Weren't a lot of people evacuated?'

'Only from towns along the south coast. Southampton and Portsmouth mostly . . . but I believe they're all back now. The

Channel Islands are still empty.'

'What about you?' he said. 'Weren't you tempted to leave when it happened?'

'It was never really an option. I've nowhere else to go.'

She was relieved they were actually talking about something at last, but given a choice of subjects she would have put the nuclear accident low on the list. She toyed with the cutlery on the table in front of her, feeling herself tremble. She moved her hands away, and clasped them together in her lap.

'Were you here on the day?'

'Yes.

'Did you know it was happening?'

'Of course.' It struck her as an odd question. 'I woke up and heard it on the BBC news. I had the radio on all day, like everyone else, and as soon as I realized how dangerous it was I stayed inside. My real worry was my cat.'

Jimmy had been out in the rain, and he wouldn't come when she called. She had gone into the garden with an umbrella to find him, but he'd thought it was a game and dodged her. For an hour she had been in an agony of worry, torn between fears for her own safety and for his. She had caught him on her third foray outside: he was fooling around under a rose bush while the deadly rain dripped all over him. As soon as she had him inside she hosed him down in the bath with her shampoo spray, using water from the head-tank in the roof, knowing it was as yet uncontaminated. Jimmy had scratched and bitten her for her trouble, and fretted inside the house for days afterwards, resenting the fact that she wouldn't let him out. She had been forgiven in the end, but even now, when it was probably safe again, she hated him being outside.

'Things must have changed,' Gordon said.

'In some ways . . . But life goes on. It has to.'

'The worst is over now, though?'

'I suppose so. It's impossible finding anything out. All you hear is fragments, and you can't get an idea of the whole picture. "Don't do this," they say, or, "That's OK now," . . . but what you really want to know is – '

She left the sentence unfinished, because she didn't want to say it. *Am I dying because of the fall-out?* She couldn't face up to that. She had no choice but to stay where she was.

'I thought the official advice sounded rather sensible.'

'Maybe because you didn't have to act on it,' Alice said. He didn't respond. 'They were full of advice at first . . . you heard nothing but spokesmen on the radio saying scary things. But they don't do that any more. None of it seemed to apply, anyway.'

'What do you mean?'

'All right . . . two days after it I happened I had to wash some clothes. Without thinking, I hung them out on the line to dry. It was a sunny day, there was a good breeze, and it was just something I did without thinking about it. About half an hour later it started raining. I was in my office trying to work, and I didn't notice. By the time I got outside the clothes were wet through, and I realized what that probably meant. My first thought was to take them inside and wash them again. But they were saying on the radio that the water in the taps was contaminated, and not to use it. So whatever I did, my clothes were going to be radioactive. I couldn't just throw them away.'

'What did you do?'

'I washed them again. It seemed the natural thing to do. I used a lot of soap powder. That made it feel safer.'

64

She realized how daft that sounded. He apparently thought so too because he grinned, the first trace of amusement she had seen.

'Are there other problems?' he said.

'Water's the main one. It's supposed to be safe for washing, but we get drinking water in plastic flagons, and it costs a fortune. I'm not supposed to mow the lawn, pick flowers or fall in a river. I read about that in the local paper. The farmers can't move or slaughter livestock. I haven't heard that anywhere, but it's what all the locals say. Milk comes in cartons. From France, as it happens, which a lot of people feel resentful about. There are no local vegetables . . . no official reason, but everyone knows why. Bread comes from somewhere up north, and it's always stale. Fruit is expensive. A lot of small differences like those. But there's a good side to it too.' The meal had arrived while she was talking, but she ignored it. 'They were building a lot of new houses. Estates full of semis, retirement homes, that sort of thing. Parts of Ramsford were beginning to look like a London suburb. That's all over now. No one in their right mind would buy a house around here. And that's the other side of it again. I couldn't sell my own house even if I could afford to advertise it. Would you want to move to this area?'

Gordon had started eating while she spoke, and did not look up when she asked her question. Had he been listening? She waited for a response.

'Well . . . would you?'

He glanced at her plate as if to tell her to begin, then put more food in his mouth.

Alice picked up her knife and fork. The brief conversation was apparently at an end. They ate in silence.

She was fuming inwardly. She could not tell whether

Gordon was being deliberately rude, or she had been boring him by talking too much, or she was simply incapable of relating to him on even the most prosaic level, or –

Her last few words kept running through her mind, as if there was something in them that had caused the antagonism. She remembered a time Bill had hung up the phone on her in mid-sentence. The result was the same: she felt angry, humiliated and wretched all at once, not because of the rudeness but because what she had been saying was made to seem worthless. Even if this was not the real reason, the very fact that she reacted meant she was over-sensitive, and that was bad too.

She ate quickly without savouring the food, determined to get the meal over as soon as possible. All she wanted was to be taken home. She could hardly bring herself even to look at him across the table, but when she did he was concentrating on his meal, bending his head forward to take up the food. She noticed the small patch on the top where his hair had started to thin, and she felt like asking him about it, deliberately to hurt him.

She had lost her appetite, and after a few hurried bites left most of the food uneaten. She waited for him to finish, and when he had she sat up straight, trying to convey the message that she was restless and wanted to leave.

'Coffee?' he said, lighting a cigarette. 'Or would you like a dessert?'

'Just coffee, I suppose. Thank you.'

She waited in silence, staring at the tablecloth. When the waitress removed the plates Gordon ordered coffee.

'What do you do for a living, Alice?' he said.

Half a dozen sarcastic retorts crossed her mind, but she said lamely, 'I'm a writer.'

'Oh . . . that explains it. What do you write?'

That explains *what*? Alice thought. 'Books, a few reviews.'

'What sort of books? Novels?'

'No. They're non-fiction. Partly historical, partly biographical – '

'Have you had any of them published?'

'I'm a *professional* writer,' she said. 'Of course I get them published!'

His eyes widened. 'I'm sorry.'

Alice thought: My God will this evening never end? Next he'll tell me about the book he wants to write. He'll give me the idea, I'll be expected to write the damned thing . . .

He actually looked a little crestfallen at her vehement response, and against her own will Alice felt herself softening again. She'd heard that question many times. Most people knew very little about what it was to work as a writer. They thought you could somehow 'be' a writer just by calling yourself one, and that publication was a dream beyond the reach of mere mortals. She had never snapped at the question before, and now she felt in the wrong again.

She waited, deliberately calming herself, then said, 'What did you mean, that being a writer explained something?'

'You were friendly with my mother. You must have known she used to write books.'

'Oh yes.' But she had befriended Eleanor long before she found out about her books. That wasn't why. It explained nothing. 'I don't know much about your mother's books. What sort did she write?'

He shrugged, losing interest.

'I don't know much about them,' he said. 'It was a long time ago, before she retired.'

He drank his coffee, and turned around to catch the

waitress's eye. The meal was over, just like the conversation.

'Can you remember any of the titles?' Alice said.

'I've forgotten them, if I ever knew them.'

'But were they under her own name?'

'She used a pen name. Don't ask me what it was, because I can't remember.'

I wasn't going to ask, I wasn't going to bloody ask! Alice fumed silently while he paid the bill, then walked back to the car with him. But she *had* been about to ask, which was even more irritating, and she did badly want to know about Eleanor's books. She forced herself to calm down, remain civil to him, but as he drove out of Marlborough he missed the road to Ramsford and she said nothing. She waited for him to notice, and have to ask her for directions, but he drove as if he knew where he was going. The car headed to the south-west, towards Devizes and across the lonely Downs.

She settled back in her seat, lulled by the car's quiet engine and the smooth ride, and breathing his cigarette smoke. This was a road she never normally used at night, partly because it was out of her way, but also because of its local reputation.

She said, 'I never normally use this road at night.' He said nothing in reply, but for an instant he glanced towards her as if showing interest, so she went on, 'You probably know what it's like around here. People say they see UFOs, and circles appear in crops.'

'You don't believe in that stuff, do you?'

'No,' she said, but realized at once that she had already admitted the opposite by saying she avoided this way. 'How about you?'

'I believe nothing until I've seen it for myself. Then I usually discard it.'

'What do you mean?'

68

But he said no more.

After he had taken another wrong turning she pointed it out, and he turned the car around. Within a couple of miles they saw signposts to Ramsford, and he again drove more quickly.

She said, 'I'd be very interested to try and find your mother's books. She must have copies in her house somewhere. And her files. Would you have any objection to my looking for them?'

'You may do whatever you like. The house has to be cleared soon, but it won't be for a week or two.'

'Eleanor gave me a spare key,' Alice said. 'I don't want to be a nuisance. Perhaps after the funeral I could let myself in and have a hunt around. Would that be all right?'

'I won't be there. Take everything – as much as you like. I don't want any of it. the more you can take away, the less I'll have to think about.'

She had to direct him again when they reached Ramsford. She was fully expecting him to drive straight to Eleanor's house, leaving her to walk home the rest of the way, but she had misjudged him. He drove her to the front of her house, and switched off the engine.

He said, 'I'm sorry about this evening, Alice. I know you haven't enjoyed it. That was my fault. I'm under a great deal of strain.'

'I am too, as it happens.'

'Yes, well – I suppose you'll be coming to my mother's funeral?'

'I was intending to, yes.'

'Good. I'll be returning home immediately afterwards. I can't afford any more time away from my job. I plan to come back here as soon as I can, and tie everything up. If you need to visit the house in the mean time, that's all right.'

A thought occurred to her.

'What about the police?' she said. 'Will you tell them I might be calling in?'

'I don't think there's any need, but I'll mention it to them.'

He reached across her to the door handle, but did not open it.

'Well, thank you for dinner,' Alice said.

'I'm sorry it wasn't a more pleasant evening for you. Things will be better next time.'

Because he was reaching across her to the door, his face was close to hers. Shrinking back from him, Alice said, 'Next time?'

'Would you have dinner with me again soon?'

'Um . . . yes, of course. Thank you.'

'I'll call you, and we can fix it up.'

He opened the door, and Alice wriggled out before he tried to kiss her.

She thanked him again, then slammed the car door. He restarted the engine and turned on his headlights, then waited with the engine idling until she was inside the house.

She closed the door behind her, and listened to him drive away.

She shut her eyes, opened them again, puffed up her cheeks and expelled breath noisily. She giggled. She hadn't had such a terrible date since her teens!

Jimmy had run through the house to greet her as soon as he heard the door, and now he was nudging and pushing around her legs, purring with his back arched. She picked him up, cuddled him for a few moments, then let him escape to his food.

She followed him into the kitchen and made herself a cup

of tea. The house felt cold. Soon it would be the time of year when being at home all day meant having to heat the house expensively. Either that or be cold herself. Unless money turned up from somewhere soon she wouldn't have much choice.

She took the tea to her armchair and sat comfortably, cradling the cup in her hands and sipping at it.

She was still thinking about Eleanor's dreadful son. It wasn't surprising Eleanor had never mentioned him! She wondered what had gone wrong between them. There must have been a family rift some time in the past. Gordon had obviously not visited her in years. His surname was different; had Eleanor married twice? Maybe that had something to do with it.

Alice mused about all this, plotting out what might have happened. The cat came to join her, pushing his way under her arms and establishing himself on her lap.

The evening had not been a complete waste of time. She had learnt something indirectly about Eleanor's background, and she had Gordon's permission to go and look for her books. Also, not to be dismissed lightly, the evening had temporarily taken her mind off her own troubles. That in itself was like a holiday. She realized how worn down she had become over the last few weeks, obsessed with the shortage of cash, the paranoia and outrage about her manuscript, all interfering with the even larger process of recovering from a broken marriage, which until then had been going well enough. It had made her inward-looking, bitter, a little selfish and self-pitying.

And in the middle of this Eleanor had been murdered. Wasn't that bigger, more shocking and appalling than all her troubles put together?

71

She knew that it was, of course. She wondered again about who could have killed Eleanor, and why. None of it made sense.

When she had drunk her tea she undressed, took a bath and went to bed. After a few minutes the cat came in and took up his usual position at the end of the bed. She read for a while, but sleep would not come. A disturbing thought was nagging at her, and to put it out of her mind she climbed out of bed and pulled on her dressing-gown. She went downstairs to her study.

The two fake disks had been removed from the box.

Back in the bedroom she knelt down beside the cat, pressed her face miserably against his warm furry back.

'Did someone come into the house, Jimmy?' she said, but the silly cat only blinked at her and nuzzled his face affectionately against hers.

9

I SUDDENLY DECIDED that I wanted a permanent record of the last moment of my mother's life, and that I should like a photograph to be taken as her coffin was placed in the ground. It was obviously going to be difficult for me to use a camera during the ceremony, so I asked one of my assistants, Larry Norris, to come to the funeral and take the picture for me. I explained what I wanted him to do, and he agreed to drive down to Wiltshire on the day, return to the office after the funeral and have the photograph ready for me when I returned.

My mother's will directed that she wished to be buried in Ramsford churchyard, and she had set aside some money for this. After her body had been formally released by the coroner I put the arrangements in hand with a firm of undertakers in Marlborough. I then returned home briefly. All this had happened at a busy time, and there was a backlog of work I had to deal with in the office.

I drove back to Wiltshire the day before the funeral to spend the night at her house. I could have driven down with Norris, but I planned to take Alice Stockton out for dinner again, as we had agreed. Unfortunately she was not at home when I called, and I spent a depressing evening alone in my mother's house. I disliked everything about the place. The whole house needed repainting, and it was inconveniently cluttered with furniture. My mother, apparently incapable of throwing anything away, had surrounded herself with junk.

Some of the furniture was all too familiar from my childhood, and I was surprised that she should have kept it for so many years. The place was full of reminders; a plump, dark-leather pouffe on which she had sometimes made me sit when she told me her stories, the lampshade made of yellow parchment that used to hang in our living-room, the dark-stained gate-legged table that had once crushed my hand. I was tempted to make a bonfire of it all in the back garden, but her will directed that it must be auctioned, so I had to put up with it. The house itself was also to be sold, although the solicitor in Salisbury confirmed what Alice had told me, that property in this area had almost no market value at present. None of this directly affected me, as I was not a beneficiary under her will. I had not expected to be.

When I turned up at the church I was annoyed to discover that the BBC had sent a news crew to record the funeral. I should have expected this, and had I been in my office all week I would certainly have known in advance. I found Norris, and consulted briefly with him. He had already spoken to the news editor in London, but lacked the authority to have them called off. I passed the crew on my way back to the car, and I could tell from their expressions that they knew what was about to happen. It took only a short call. Five minutes later, they had packed their gear and driven away.

I saw Alice Stockton had already taken a seat in the church. She looked poised and calm in her formal clothes, but she cried quietly throughout the brief service. Whenever I tried to catch her eye she did not acknowledge me.

Afterwards, I walked beside the coffin as it was carried to

the prepared grave. The weather was cool and bright, with a fresh breeze. Traffic went by noisily in the road beside the church. There were about twenty other mourners in all, mostly my mother's women friends from the village. There were one or two young men I did not recognize, so I assumed they were reporters from the local press. (I said nothing, but later that day I dealt with the problem.) Two uniformed police stood by the gate of the church, watching the proceedings; I could see their Panda car parked next to the hearse. Larry Norris was not in sight, but I knew he would be waiting unobtrusively somewhere with a clear view of the grave. I stood next to Alice Stockton beside the grave, and at last she greeted me with a quiet, formal nod. She looked very pale and distressed.

As the vicar intoned the words of the burial service I was distracted by the sound of a large jet aircraft moving slowly towards us at low altitude. I pretended to ignore it, but the engines had a distinctive note that of all the people present only I, and perhaps Larry Norris, would recognize.

The sound increased, and I turned my head. I saw the aircraft at once. It was about half a mile away, close to the rising scarp of Salisbury Plain, and banking to the left to veer away from us. The autumn sun glinted briefly from its delta-shaped wings.

I was astonished to see it.

The plane was one of the new series of highly secret low-level 'stealth' nuclear bombers. I knew that three prototypes had been sent to England from the USA, and that they were undergoing evaluation trials while being placed, in direct defiance of superpower accords, on active service. Anyway, the plane should not have been flying: I knew that for the past two weeks all three aircraft had been grounded. There were design and handling problems. On top of this, a team of Soviet military observers was due to arrive in Britain within the next day or two, on one of the INF Treaty inspection visits. I had personally seen orders that restricted all three aircraft to a base in Scotland for the time being.

If it had not been my mother's funeral I should have gone straight to the phone to find out what was happening. Trapped by the conventions of the moment, I continued to watch the aircraft while the familiar words of the burial service droned on. The plane seemed to be circling, probably intending to land at one of the former RAF airfields on Salisbury Plain; the undercarriage was down. Once more it headed towards us, gaining a little height, but moving slowly with its nose raised at an unusually high attitude. I knew then that something was seriously wrong: the aircraft had a high stall-speed, was known to be unstable at low speeds, and notoriously difficult to fly with the wheels lowered. The engine note changed perceptibly, whining more loudly.

The pilot seemed to recover control, and the flying attitude improved. Seconds later, the aircraft passed directly over-head, drowning the sound of the vicar's voice. The plane passed out of sight beyond the church tower, flying across the village. The engine noise reverberated around us.

Moments later the plane came back into view, having circled away from the village. Once again its nose was raised in the dangerous position of an incipient stall, and although the engines were at full thrust the aircraft was clearly out of control. It wallowed uneasily in a power stall, losing height and falling rapidly towards the ground.

I tensed in horror, knowing what was almost certainly on board the machine, and what was therefore about to happen. I could not breathe, could not wrench my gaze away from the terrible sight. In a matter of five seconds after it had reappeared the plane smashed into the ground, falling out of my sight into a dip in the ground beyond some trees.

A tremendous explosion followed: an orange fireball, black-streaked, a thick mushroom of oily smoke.

Two more explosions came in quick succession: smaller, intensely blue-white, lingering horribly. I had to flinch away, my eyes temporarily blinded by the flashes.

The deadly radiance was still glaring across the church-yard as the blast from the first impact hit us, a shattering roar, slashing through the trees around us, echoing flatly from the faces of the houses across the road from the church. A stained-glass window shattered, the church bell rang once.

They were lowering my mother's coffin into the grave. Beside me, Alice tried to control a sob. A sidesman tossed a handful of gravel down on the pale cedar lid of the casket. There was a long moment of silence, in which we all stood with our heads inclined. I wanted to take Alice's hand to comfort her, but she had moved a step or two away from me.

We dispersed in sombre mood, and several of the women from the village spoke sadly to me about how much they had liked and admired my mother. I thanked the vicar for the service, then returned to my car. Alice Stockton had already departed.

(Three days later, Norris gave me a print of the photograph he had taken at the moment of burial. He had been standing at the edge of the churchyard, concealed by trees. The picture had been taken with a telephoto lens and showed myself and Alice Stockton in close-up. Alice's head was lowered, and partly concealed from the camera by the brim of her hat. I was staring away to the side, my eyes stark with terror. This was the last moment of my mother's existence, one that I experienced in my own way, captured by the conscious release of a camera shutter some fifty or a hundred yards away.)

10

A FEW DAYS after Eleanor's funeral Alice left home early and drove into Ramsford, where she caught the morning train to London.

One of the many changes the accident at Cap la Hague had brought in its wake was a reduction in the number of trains calling at Ramsford. Within a month of the melt-down Western Rail had cut the service in half. The station had always seemed like a charming anomaly to her, because Ramsford was not an important village outside its own immediate area, and at this distance from London the commuter population was tiny, but it was on the main line between Paddington and the West Country. People in the village said that a year ago there was talk of improving the service, because so many people had moved down from London to live in the village, but all that had changed. Wiltshire was now an area of population decline, and Western Rail were hastening the process by making it that little bit more inconvenient in which to live.

Nevertheless, there was still a service of sorts, and because most of the trains started from Plymouth they usually had buffet and restaurant cars. Alice went straight to the buffet and treated herself to a toasted bacon sandwich and a cup of tea.

The mood of depression and paranoia that coincided with Eleanor's death had lifted, and she was feeling more like her old self. A trip to London often had that effect on her. It was after all her home town, and she had never really lost her love for the place. Sometimes, when the loneliness had been at its worst, she had cursed herself for leaving, but on days like this she could feel she had the best of both worlds.

She arrived in Paddington with three hours to spare before her appointment with Granville, so she dawdled for a while in the station bookstall, browsing through the magazines and noticing how few of them were normally sold by the newsagent in the village. There were several titles she hadn't seen before. She wished she had more cash, because she was missing the glossy trivia she had once taken for granted.

Alice called into a sandwich bar for a cup of coffee, then, still with time to spare, decided to make an unannounced visit to see Harriet. She hadn't seen her editor for several weeks, and their telephone conversations subsequently had all been short and, at least as far as Alice was concerned, guarded in tone.

She walked to Harriet's office, partly to use up a little more time but mainly because being back in London was a tonic to her. Much as she loved the countryside she knew she was basically metropolitan by nature. And she felt able to breathe freely at last; ironic, because people were supposed to move to the country for fresh air. Since the accident Alice had felt her breathing was constricted. When she was in the open air she could not let herself relax. Her breath was always half-held, like that of a child tiptoeing. It was pointless, of course. The danger had been greatest in the first few days, when no one knew how bad the accident had been. London had been lucky. Dirty old London, with its traffic fumes and grit and crowded streets, had been to the side of the fall-out plume. It was the same unhealthy place it had always been, but whatever the reality it smelt good to her.

Harriet's office was in a tall terraced house in one of the squares near the British Museum. As Alice went through the front door a motorcycle despatch rider, huge and anonymous in helmet and leather, pushed past her. No one in London ever seemed to use the post any more: the place was full of motorcycles weaving through the traffic, ridden by legitimized Hell's Angels with printed satchels and two-way radios. One had probably been sent from the Home Office to collect her manuscript from this very building. There was a security area beyond the main door, and here a uniformed guard checked the contents of her bag, and ran a metal detector around her. The machine appeared to give a reading, but the guard did not seem too worried by it. He gave her a lapel badge, and waited for her to pin it on before allowing her inside.

The reception area itself consisted of a desk built into the space beneath the wide staircase, piled with large packages addressed to printers or marked for collection.

'I wondered if Harriet Blair was free?' Alice said to the woman behind the desk.

'Do you have an appointment?'

'No . . . I was just passing.'

'I think she might be in a meeting.' The receptionist picked up the internal phone. 'Who shall I say it is?'

'Alice Stockton . . . no, say I'm Alice Hazledine.'

There was a pause, then the woman said into the phone, 'There's a Miss Hazledine in reception, to see Harriet. Thanks.' She looked up at Alice. 'They've gone to find out.'

Heavy footsteps sounded on the stairs above, and a young man Alice vaguely remembered meeting in the art department hurried past her. He was carrying a large piece of art card with the painting for a book cover; a glimpse of tantalizing colour. They glanced at each other with cautious recognition. He gave an ambiguous smile and went through the door at the side of the reception desk.

It had been too long since she had published her last book, and been involved with all this. She couldn't recall the young man's name, and she knew that he wasn't sure who she was. His recognition had been just in case.

'All right.' The receptionist put down the phone. She said to Alice, 'Harriet's with one of our authors at present. Would you like to leave a message?'

'Not really ... just tell her I dropped in to say hello. Nothing important.'

The woman dutifully scribbled on her message pad, made Alice repeat her name, then turned away to take an incoming phonecall.

Back in the street Alice felt irritated with herself, and with Harriet. More with herself, really. She knew you could never just drop in on a publisher, however far outside London you lived, or however infrequently you did it. They were always doing something else. 'One of our authors.' Alice wondered who it was. If the damned Home Office hadn't stolen her book, it might have been her. She and Harriet had always got along well personally, and when her last book had been going through the system she had been a frequent caller at the office.

That was the old days, though, when she lived only fifteen minutes from the centre of London. No security guards, then, and a lady in reception called Betty who knew her by sight. She had been away too long, and lived too far out. People who worked in London didn't realize what an event it was to spend your last few pounds on a trek up from the country for a day. She wondered if Harriet had been told who it was in reception.

It didn't matter, it didn't matter.

At least she had an appointment with Granville. She should have gone straight to see him.

To make some kind of meaningless point Alice deliberately arrived five minutes late, but even so Granville kept her waiting. His office was on the second floor of a nineteenth-century block in High Holborn. It looked small when you went in, but once you were past the reception area there was a warren of rooms and corridors cluttered with modern technology. Telex and fax machines, computers and photo-copiers; they all looked a bit out of place in the high-ceilinged and rather grand rooms. Granville was a great enthusiast for modern gadgets.

In contrast with the reality beyond, the reception area was self-consciously 'literary' in appearance. A glass-fronted display cabinet stood along one wall, its shelves lined with recent books by the firm's clients. Alice recognized most of the names and titles. She always felt the other clients were more famous and successful than she was. At least two of the books had been recent bestsellers, and the rest had all received wide review coverage. She had never seen one of her own books in the cabinet . . . though to be fair she had not actually visited Granville around the time her last book was out.

Another wall carried numerous photographs of authors. This was an open joke, even among the staff who worked at the agency. Only dead authors went on the wall. Everyone knew that was where the real money was: authors were never profitable until they died. The publishing industry would be altogether more prosperous and convenient if every author was dead from the start.

Sitting there quietly, Alice wondered if this was the week that Eleanor's photograph would go up on a wall in some other literary agent's office.

At last she was told to go through. Knowing the way, Alice went along the first corridor towards Granville's room, but he had come out to greet her, and he hugged her effusively. She wished he wouldn't. Granville was at least ten years younger than she was, and when he did this he made her feel like an aunt.

'I have news for you!' he said, and beamed at her. He led the way into his office, and closed the door.

'I hope it's good news,' Alice said.

'Sit down.' He waved his hand at the visitors' chair. 'Would you like a cup of coffee?'

'Maybe later. Tell me the news first.'

'I was speaking to Stackpole just a few minutes ago. He sounded quite hopeful – ' The telephone rang, and he broke off. 'Yes? All right, put him through.'

Alice subsided into the chair while Granville spoke to the caller. It was ever thus: she never seemed to get his undivided attention.

Granville must have seen her expression, because when he had finished the call he immediately picked up the internal phone.

'No more calls,' he said. 'I'll be engaged for a while.' With the phone back on the hook, he said, 'I think Stackpole's prepared to let you have the manuscript back.'

'That's wonderful!'

'Well, yes it is. But he intends to release only a part of it at first. You can have some of it straight away, but they want to keep the rest a bit longer.'

'How much longer?'

'He wouldn't say.'

'What about the restriction order?' Alice said.

'That stands for the time being.'

'So what's the point of getting a bit of it back? I can't do anything with it, even if there was something I *could* do with part of a book!

'That's how it seems.'

She exhaled noisily, glaring at Granville. He was fiddling with some of the papers on his desk. Since all this began a small but perceptible change had occurred in their relationship. She continued to blame Granville for the loss of her book, and he knew that she did. At the same time they both knew it wasn't *really* his fault, not even indirectly. The official letter she received had referred to her book as if it was something they had known about all along – even while she was writing it, the letter seemed to imply darkly – so the fact that Granville had mailed the package to America with the legendary label was only incidental. They didn't talk about the label any more. (CONTENTS : BOOK MANUSCRIPT. MAY BE OPENED FOR INSPECTION.) But it was constantly in the background and it always put him on the defensive, the guilt making him sound to her like a spokesman for the civil servants who were really responsible, and giving her more just cause for irritation. It gave her a certain amount of grim satisfaction to realize that this change had taken place.

The agency no longer used that mailing label.

'I have more news for you,' Granville said. 'You'll like this. I told Harriet about your predicament, and she managed to talk her accounts department into releasing the rest of the

85

advance. No strings attached. They obviously assume the manuscript will be released soon.'

'Oh, good!' Money, money! What a difference it made! 'I hoped she might, but I didn't like to press her about it.'

'It came in this morning, special delivery. They're drawing up your cheque in accounts. You can pick it up before you leave.'

'Thanks, Granville!'

'Thank Harriet. Frankly, I don't know how she pulled it off. They've been the most tight-fisted house in London since the takeover.'

'I'll ring her as soon as I get home.'

She couldn't help smiling. A problem solved, at least for a while. She had been putting off small but important expenses for weeks. One of her priorities was to get the cat to the vet for another check-up. She hadn't even been able to think of that until now. She wanted to go to the hairdresser. And unpaid bills could be paid at last. A trip to Marlborough to buy some food for the freezer. It was ridiculous to be so anxious about money.

'Stackpole asked me again about copies. You did destroy them all, didn't you?'

'Yes . . . of course. You told me this a long time ago.' She felt a stirring of anger. 'Anyway, Stackpole knows I destroyed them.'

'He does? What makes you think that?'

'Someone broke into my house and stole some computer disks. They were the ones I'd written the book on. After you phoned me, I wiped them blank. But someone took them anyway.'

'Was anything else stolen?'

'No, just those.'

Granville was looking serious. 'Alice, I'm terribly sorry. I hadn't realized . . . But are you sure it wasn't an ordinary break-in? Did you call the police?'

'No. I *knew* it wasn't just a burglar. Anyway, I can prove it. Three days later I found them again. Whoever took them put them back.' Granville had written something on his notepad. 'Do you have any real proof . . . did you see anyone?'

'No, I was out both times. Which makes it much worse, incidentally, because it means they must have been watching the house.'

She hadn't even dared to look and see if the real disks were still in her car. The knowledge that Stackpole's men were monitoring her movements could also mean they were watching everything she did. Anyway, the importance of the real disks was only symbolic. She couldn't do anything with them. So long as she only thought they were still hidden, then they were, in one sense at least, all right.

When some coffee was brought into the room, Granville asked if she had any ideas yet for a new book.

'I do, as it happens,' Alice said. 'Of course, some of the urgency has gone out of it, if I've been paid for the last one. I was going to ask you . . . well, if you could try and sell an outline now. But I think I can probably get by for a few months. Or maybe you still could – '

'I'm always willing to try. What sort of book would it be?'

'That's part of the problem. I'm not yet sure there's enough to make a book. Normally, I'd get most of the research done before sending in an outline, but I've been so desperate for money . . .'

Granville was smiling encouragingly at her. This was the old Granville, the one who always made her nervous by trying to put her at her ease.

'Go on,' he said.

'OK.' For some days Alice had been trying to think of a way of presenting this, to make it sound interesting. 'You see, a friend of mine was murdered two weeks ago. A woman I knew locally.'

'Not Eleanor Hampton?'

'Hamilton . . . yes! How do you know about her?'

'It was on the television news. I thought of you. She lived in your village, didn't she?'

'Just a couple of hundred yards away from my house. She was a terrific lady, very interesting to talk to, and after she died I started thinking. Well, I'd been thinking *before* it happened.' She wished Granville didn't look quite so attentive. 'She was a writer. I'm not sure what her books were about because she would never talk about them, but she had several published. I can find out about those – '

'There's someone I think you should talk to,' Granville said. 'One of my other authors is connected with CND, and he thinks she was murdered for political reasons. Apparently, she was very active in the anti-nuclear movement.'

'So she said. I thought it was because of the accident.'

'Yes, but didn't she go on demonstrations against the American bases?'

Alice fell silent, realizing how little she knew about Eleanor. Even Granville seemed better informed. And what about this other author? Was he going to write a book about her?

'I didn't see Eleanor that way,' she said, eventually. 'She was just a friend, someone I knew. She was good to me, and she intrigued me. She was always surprising me with what she knew. I don't know much about her politics . . . I was more interested in finding out about her books.'

'It sounds very promising to me. That would add another dimension.'

'Do you think my book should be political?'

'Whatever you think is right, of course,' Granville said tactfully, and Alice knew he didn't mean it. He wanted a book she hadn't even thought about. 'Obviously, the fact that she was murdered would make it very commercial. Would you like me to ring Harriet now?'

'Oh no! please don't. I'd like to think about it more, first. I've a lot of research to do. I want to find out what kind of books Eleanor wrote, for instance.'

'I thought you already knew.'

'No. She wouldn't talk about them, and I couldn't find them in any libraries.' Alice was looking into her lap, thinking how little preparation she had done, how born out of desperation the idea had been. 'I found Eleanor kind and motherly . . . but she hadn't let old age get at her. Before she died I'd started talking to her, with a tape recorder running. I didn't have anything in mind. I thought something might come of it, but there was nothing definite. We didn't really touch on politics, except in a general kind of way. She didn't seem political to me, in the sense you mean it. She was just very concerned about everything that was going on. I thought she was like me, living in a part of England that had been contaminated by the fall-out and worried about what was going to happen. Since then, I've met her son, and he's given me permission to go through her things . . . and I thought, once I've found the books she wrote, and read them, and had a chance to transcribe my tapes, I'd know more about her and more about the kind of book I could write.'

It sounded lame, and she was wishing she hadn't started. She should have known better than to tell Granville about it at this stage, but without Eleanor she had no one to confide in. She always talked about her books when she was planning them. This was probably the real if subconscious reason for trying to see Harriet this morning. Granville's job was to look after writers' business, but he had no idea what writers really needed when they were trying to work something out. His receptive smile was betrayed by his restless eyes and hands. Perhaps she was embarrassing him. He thought it sounded as lame as she did, or his other writer had already put in a proposal for a work of investigative journalism exposing conspiracy in high places.

She stumbled over the thought. An investigation . . . ?

'So you would see it as a biography?' Granville said.

'Yes. A literary biography, I think.'

But already she could feel the book changing in her mind. It had never occurred to her before to wonder if Eleanor's death was anything more than just a squalid but straightforward murder.

'Of course, that's what you're known for.'

'I might be if I ever get *Six Women* published.'

She was thinking: Why had Eleanor been killed?

Nothing had been stolen from the house, just as nothing had been taken when Stackpole's men broke into her own cottage. Eleanor had been a political activist, a writer. Her death had been important enough to be featured on the national news. Was Eleanor more famous than she had realized? How little she knew! Obsessed with her own trivial problems, thinking vaguely about a biography, she had overlooked the real story!

'This client of yours,' she said. 'The CND man. Did he say anything else about Eleanor?'

'I believe not.'

'He wasn't thinking of writing a book about her, by any chance?'

Granville was now looking at her steadily, and Alice noticed that his face had started to turn pink.

'Alice, I've been insensitive. I know what you're thinking. No, he's busy on something else. I shouldn't have said anything.'

'No, I'm glad you did. Do you think he could help me?'

'I'm sure he'd be delighted. I'll give you his phone number. His name is Thomas Davie.' Granville found a diary in his desk drawer, then scribbled the name and a number on a scrap of paper and passed it to her. 'It was just a casual comment he made. In fact I was telling him about you.'

'About me?'

'I thought he might have had some experience of Home Office restriction orders. He told me CND has had several served on them in the past, but he had never heard of an individual writer getting one before. I think he was impressed. From his point of view it's quite an honour.'

'Did you tell him I believe they've made some kind of mistake?'

'No . . . I was trying to find out what he knew.'

'It *was* a mistake, wasn't it?'

'Of course. I think we simply have to wait until they either realize it was, or until they're prepared to admit it.'

Later, Granville took her along to meet the lady who ran the agency's accounts, and she was given her cheque. Alice slipped it into her bag, trying to look gracious about it, but now it was hers she felt embarrassed about it. It was only money, after all, a temporary solution to a few practical problems. It was always the same when she received a cheque: everything depended on it before it arrived, but as

91

soon as she had it in her hand there was a sense of anticlimax, a feeling that all she was going to do was spend it.

She went to the nearest bank to pay it in. Her account was at a branch of the Midland Bank in Ramsford, and it would be credited more quickly if she were to pay it in tomorrow, but she felt superstitious about walking around with an unused cheque. While she was in the bank she withdrew some cash, using her cheque guarantee card. There was a long time to wait before the next train to Ramsford, so she went to the West End to look around the shops. The first place she went to was Collett's bookshop in Charing Cross Road, because she knew it carried a huge range of left-wing books. She spent an hour searching through the shelves: nothing by Eleanor Hamilton, and nothing either by Thomas Davie. (He had a book out in paperback, but according to the assistant it was no longer in stock.) Alice bought a selection of recent paperbacks about the peace movement, and the anti-nuclear lobby, then treated herself to a hardback of the new novel by Anne Tyler. Later, in Oxford Street, she bought herself a pair of jeans, a blouse, jacket and skirt, a pair of good shoes and at least six months' supply of tights. In Paddington Station, before she boarded the train, she spent several pounds on magazines: *Elle* and *The Tatler* and *Vogue* and *Private Eye*. She lugged everything home, feeling rich and deliciously spend-thrift.

11

OF COURSE WE must talk about what we can do to get your book back from the Government. Don't leave it to your agent. These things can only be sorted out by direct action. I know of several voluntary groups who will take your side in this, and the next time I see you I'll have their addresses ready for you.

I have just re-read the first part of this letter to refresh my memory. I'm still having serious doubts about it all, but it is done now and I don't want to write it out again. I'll keep the rest as brief as possible, and trust you will understand why.

I finished by telling you about the flat I had moved into with Joyce. Almost as soon as I was there I discovered I was pregnant. I suppose the signs had been there earlier, but I simply hadn't taken any notice. My first thought, when I finally woke up to reality, was to hope that the father was Hugh . . . but I did the arithmetic and realized it must have happened with Peter on the boat coming back from Greece.

This created a problem (perhaps less of one, with hindsight, than if the father really had been Hugh). I liked Peter a great deal, but in spite of what we'd done I hardly knew him. Anyway, I had no idea where he was, and I really didn't know whether I *ought* to tell him, even if I could find him. And there were practical problems, too. There was no welfare state in those days, and as a single woman I had to work for a living. The war was getting worse, with Hitler invading Norway, etc. I couldn't face burdening my mother with the problem. I suppose it was irresponsible, but for a month I tried to deal with everything by ignoring it. Then everything was solved when Peter turned up. He had traced me through a friend. His personal problems were sorted out, he said all the right things about having missed me, and seemed as if he wanted to stay around. I gave him a week to show some sign of changing his mind, then broke the news to him. He wasn't at all put out by it, and in fact said he was delighted. We were married on the day that Belgium surrendered, and immediately afterwards we moved into another flat together. My first baby, Frank, was born at the end of October. I went back to work a month or so later, and Peter and I took it in turns to look after him. Peter eventually found work as an interpreter with the Free French, but it wasn't very well paid. We survived. None of this is very interesting. Our biggest concerns were the baby, and the bombing. I had a second baby boy in 1943. Peter had a real job by then, and the bombing wasn't so much of a problem. By the time the war finished we had moved to Cheshire, because of Peter's job, and I went to a teacher training college. I'll leave this as another trail for you to follow, an easy one this time.

My first book came out while the war was still on, but paper rationing was in force and not many copies were printed. The publishers seemed to like it, though, so I wrote them another. That one did a little better, and from then on I wrote one or two books a year. By the middle of the fifties I had a regular readership, but I never made a lot of money from the books. I had so many expenses that as soon as any money came in it went straight out again. You probably know all about this side of a writer's life. I stopped writing at the end of the fifties and have never wanted to take it up again.

I expect there's nothing I can do to stop you finding and reading my books, so let me, just once, say what I have to about them.

Firstly, I think you'll find them rather old-fashioned and slow-moving. That was the style then, when I was writing. There's no point apologizing for this, or attempting to explain. You'll understand, I know. But the second thing is more important, because it relates to you.

What I admire about your writing, Alice, is that you attempt to tell the truth. You research everything in great detail, and try your honest best to interpret your subjects as you feel they would interpret themselves. I could never do this. Telling the truth in that way has never appealed to me. I am by nature a concealer and disguiser, a natural fiction-writer. I have always enjoyed misdirecting the truth.

It's the same with the books I like to read. A book should *seem* to reveal something about its author, and there should *seem* to be intimate details of the author's life coming out. But there should also be little facts that don't add up, that misdirect the truth, e.g., a book by a female author that feels authentic, and which seems to have been experienced, but which has a male protagonist.

You see, all writers write about themselves, or should do, but some of us are less straightforward about it than others. My life is in those books I wrote, because I wanted the children who read them (perhaps you were even one of them?) to believe in them by identifying with the stories. The best way to do that, I thought, was deliberately to put in everything I had known or experienced or thought about. But then I

95

changed it around, hiding it all again in fiction, a small boy as my protagonist, the vehicle for the metaphors.

There's nothing unique about this, because a lot of writers do it. I suppose this is a warning. When you find my books you will be right to make assumptions about me from them, but you will be wrong to make too many. There are more trails for you to follow, but they are disguised.

My real point, though, and the reason I have taken the time to write all this down, is that you too are a natural deceiver. I don't think you realize this. You seem to write about the lives of other women, you are genuinely *interested* in the lives of other women, but I believe that in reality you are disguising yourself in your subjects. We are friends, so I can presume to say this. In the manuscript you showed me, three of the women you described were writers of one sort or another, four of them had broken or unhappy marriages, and *all* of them had a drastic physical upheaval in early middle age, just as you have wrenched yourself out of London to live in Wiltshire.

Now you plan to write about me. Is this because you see yourself in me, or an element of yourself? I obviously can't answer this, but if it is true then I want you to accept the idea wholeheartedly. It will make a better book for you . . . and possibly offend me less when I eventually read it.

Now, briefly, a few more reliable trails for you to follow. I met Martin Hamilton in 1960, and we married at Southampton Register Office the following year. He was then teaching English at a grammar school in Fareham, and managed to find me a position at the same school. We stayed there until we retired at the end of the seventies. Martin eventually became headmaster. We lived together at various places, all in the immediate neighbourhood of the school. The house in which we were happiest was a converted guest house

96

in Gosport, overlooking the Solent. We had no children together, although Martin had a son by his first marriage. (His name is Theodore, and he moved to Canada many years ago.)

It was Martin who first involved me in the work against nuclear weapons. He had been a member of CND since the fifties and had taken part in the first two Aldermaston Marches. Like my father he was a member of the Liberal Party, although of course that meant something different in the sixties. Martin served in the Royal Air Force during the war, but he was in ground-crew and so he was not directly involved in any fighting. Martin was a kind, decent and gentle man, I loved him all the years we were together, and was devastated when he died. I moved to this house the following year. I carry on the work he did, partly because of my own convictions, but mostly, I confess, because of Martin.

So this is my paltry story, which to me seems unremarkable. Where I speak of 'trails', these are not clues to a secret or hidden life. If you follow them up you will probably find extra details, but no surprises. The only exciting or 'interesting' thing I ever did was to throw myself at Hugh, and of my whole life this is the only incident about which I still feel embarrassed. I was young, more or less inexperienced, and completely naive, so spare my blushes. I dare say many young women have made equal fools of themselves over some self-centred but handsome young man like him, but it was something that cast a shadow over me for a year or two, and I have never forgiven myself.

You will want to ask me questions when you've read this, and I suppose I shall probably answer them. But I sincerely believe that you should plan to write your book in your own way, without hindrance from me. This is the way to find me, and also to find yourself.

(I am writing this on Wednesday afternoon, and plan to give it to you on Thursday or Friday. Will you be at home over the weekend? If so, I will be here on Saturday evening and should be very happy if you would like to come over for supper.)

With love,
E.H.

12

'HOW ARE YOU planning to get back to Wiltshire?'
        'I came by car. It's parked just over there.'
    'Do you think you should drive?'
    'Am I drunk?'
    'I don't know. Are you?'
    'A little. What about you?'
    'I don't have to drive.'
They were standing in King's Road outside the wine bar
they had just left. It had been raining earlier in the evening,
and the traffic went by in a rush of tyres against wet road
surface. People pushed past them. It was cold and city-lit and
dauntingly busy, and Milton Colebourne seemed a long way
away.
    'We could have some coffee at the Chelsea Kitchen.'
    'All right.'
She knew she was postponing a decision. Inside the wine
bar, warm and candlelit and shaking with loud music, she
had been feeling sexy and restless, and when Tom Davie
suggested leaving she had walked with him to the door, ready
for anything. Outside on the draughty pavement, with her
head reeling slightly from the wine, she was thinking: I've only
just met him, this is ridiculous, I should know better than this,
I don't know anything about him, etc.

They sat for a long time over espresso coffee, making further postponements, but eventually they were once again outside in the same cold wind, and Alice was an hour further into the night and no closer to making up her mind.

Then he said, 'I don't think you should be driving home. Why don't you stay over at my place and go back in the morning?'

She saw by his expression that he meant what she thought he meant.

'I don't think I should.'

'My place isn't far away.'

'I don't think so. I've got some work to do in the morning. And I forgot to feed the cat before I came out.'

She meant none of this.

'All right,' Tom said, but he stood there without conceding defeat.

'I'll ring you,' Alice said. 'I'm really grateful for all the help you've given me.'

'You still have my number?'

'Yes.'

He moved closer to her. 'Come back with me.'

'No. Not this time.'

And that was the end of it. They kissed briefly and demurely, a peck on the cheeks, and Alice set off to find where she had left her car.

She drove home along the M4, feeling drunk and excited, and already kicking herself for saying no. Near Reading she passed a car that had been pulled over to the side by the police, and this worried her, so she turned off the motorway and took the slower route home, through Newbury and Hungerford.

The way the evening had developed was a complete

100

surprise. It started ominously: the wine bar where Tom Davie had suggested they should meet turned out to be one of the coffee-bar haunts she and Bill used to go to in the old days, with a different décor and new prices, menu and clientele. Simply going through the door had given her a chill of alienation. Everything looked simultaneously familiar and strange, and charged with deceptive memories.

But meeting Tom himself had soon put all this out of mind. She had been dreading what he might be like, because on the telephone he had sounded busy and distracted, and at first she had had to explain who she was. (Granville, apparently, had forgotten to tell Tom she was going to phone him. From this, and from what little Granville had told her about him, she had expected him to be a dour and intellectual Marxist, or some kind of trendy journalist. He had turned out to be an affable and talkative man of about her own age, easy to get on with, and only too willing to divulge the results of his own researches.

When they first started talking it all felt very promising and fruitful from this point of view. She noted down a few of the books he mentioned, listed the other people he recommended her to get in touch with, and wrote down the address of a library he said she should try . . . but soon after this they began to drift away from the subject.

He had spent much time travelling in the USA, Australia and Eastern Europe, and he talked interestingly about these places. He started with the social differences, as he saw them, but moved on quickly to more personal anecdotes. By the time they had started on the second bottle of wine all pretence of exchanging information about the state of the world had been abandoned, and they were asking personal questions about each other. Alice was charmed by him. Starved for too long of attractive male company she had opened up, talking about her life and hopes, about the books she had written and still planned to write, and even a little about Bill and the mess that they had made of their lives. He told her about himself, the most immediate and memorable fact being that there was someone else in his life. This was Pamela, his girlfriend of long standing, now declared rather unconvincingly to be on the way out.

Alice made it home safely, feeling guilty about having driven such a long way while over the legal limit, but anyway back in one piece.

The next day she glanced through the notes she had made at the beginning of the evening, but they sparked no ideas in her and only reminded her of what Tom had been like.

She still regretted saying no to him, although the sensible fraction of her knew she had done the right thing. She wasn't yet ready for another lover, and the inevitability of the proposition had put her off. Not because he had made it, but because she had been so ready to accept it. Then there was Pamela, although Pamela was not apparently a problem. (For him perhaps not, but there were always problems when there was someone else.) All this left her with a glowing feeling – part excitement, part anticipation, part guilty indecision – that seemed unlikely to cool away. She didn't care to think where it all might have led, and still might lead.

His telephone number was in her diary, and hers was in his, and she kept thinking she should call him. She also kept thinking she should not.

She had not found out much from him about Eleanor, which after all had been the whole reason for the meeting. She knew if she rang him she could ask some direct questions. She also knew that the very fact that she had called him would be interpreted as a pretext, and it would be harder to turn him down next time.

She stared at the phone, thinking about it anyway.

The only interesting thing that Tom had told her about Eleanor was that he thought she had once been prosecuted unsuccessfully under the Official Secrets Act. Other people were involved, civil servants, a serving member of the armed forces, and a journalist. If he was thinking about the right case, it had been seen at the time as a test of the independence of the press, the right of journalists to protect their sources, and the basic freedom to demonstrate against government policy. Much had been said in Parliament. Tom had promised to find Alice some newspaper clippings about the affair.

This created more indecision, stemming from her interest in Tom. She knew perfectly well how to research Hansard, court records and newspaper files, and she could easily find such material on her own. It would be quicker and more satisfactory to do all this on her own, but she wanted Tom to get in touch with her again.

She had an old book on her shelves about the government intelligence service. This had a section on the Official Secrets Act, but there was no mention of Eleanor in the index. The book had been published some seven years earlier.

That evening Tom telephoned her and they talked for an hour. Eleanor was not mentioned.

13

THE PROOF FOR me that my mother was irremediably mad was the way she told me her stories.

I was still a small child when I became aware of them and so I have no idea when or how they started, or what the first ones were about, but they were a feature of my life as far back as I can remember. I suppose the very first stories have become a part of my subconscious: remembered details, a few images and names, all confused now with real childhood memories, swirling around in the slow currents of growing up.

Because of their unpleasant associations I have never discussed them with anyone else, but I know that listening to stories is something most children traditionally enjoy. My mother's stories were different: they were not about fairies, animals, magic. Her stories were adult, both in their content and in the manner of their telling. They were about subjects that did not concern me, and dealt with matters I could not properly understand. They confused and bored me, and often, especially in later years, seriously embarrassed me.

It was always a penance to listen to her. When I was small it meant that I had to sit still when I would rather have been active. When I was a little older I had to leave my playthings or my friends. As a teenager I found her stories intrusive and humiliating.

I tried not to listen. I developed a passive state of mind, one which enabled me to fix an attentive expression on my face while letting my thoughts wander, but she always knew when I was not listening properly because she would break off unexpectedly from her narrative to ask me questions about it. I learnt to deal with this problem, although not until I was older. My method then was to ask questions back. This had two advantages: it deftly avoided the need to come up with answers, and it usually sent her back to her narrative, often diverting the story into a new direction. My ambiguous state – a passive expression, a rebellious mind – could then safely return, and all would be bearable again.

These storytelling sessions never happened without prior warning signals, which I learnt to recognize from very early on. She would seem fretful and irritable for days. I could do nothing right, and was held responsible for all manner of trivial accidents and spillages, and her own absent-mindedness. Dread grew in me, because I knew what was about to happen.

In later years, when I sensed one of her moods coming upon her, I would try to jolly her out of it, or distract her with suggestions for trips away from home, television programmes to watch or films to go out to, small gifts bought as conscious bribes against her endless and compulsive narratives. These only delayed her, because inevitably the story would start. I would be told to sit before her on the leather pouffe, and she would settle opposite me on her favourite chair, then, with those fearsome eyes gazing into mine, defying me to look away, she would begin.

What was it about her life that gave her so much to tell? How many different events could happen to one person, and stand retelling?

Not very many in my mother's life, or so it seemed to me. I heard her stories repeatedly over the years. They did not change much, so presumably they had at least some grounding in fact, but from my point of view the repetitions only made the listening worse. Perhaps she sensed this, because she would sometimes try to dress up the narrative in new words or motives. She had remembered something else . . . she had never told me why . . . she knew I had been wondering about . . .

Then a familiar tale would be told, and I, stuck betweeen boredom and the perverse interest of checking for variations, would be forced to listen again.

Most of the time I was not really listening, only pretending. The narratives drummed in my subconscious, distracting me from my own thoughts, forcing me out of my own present into her past life. So what I remember most are my own feelings, and her stories are secondary to these. They became like wallpaper in a familiar room, always present yet rarely noticed.

Once when I was in my late teens, driven to asserting the rage that was in me, I interrupted the flow to ask her, 'Why do you tell me all these stories?'

'Listen to what I'm saying.'

'Tell me why I must. Why should I listen? Why do you keep on? Why do you do this to me?'

She frequently used her madness to intimidate me. I was scared when the crazy look came into her, and she knew it. Her response this time was to widen her eyes, tilt her head back and turn it slightly to one side.

I said, 'I'm not going to listen, I *hate* this!

She held the affected pose for a few more seconds.

'I want you to understand,' she said. 'You know nothing.

You hate me because you do not know me.'

'I don't hate you,' I said, 'I hate your stories, I want to know why you talk so much.'

'These are explanations. Even if you don't understand them now, you will one day.'

I got up to leave, but she commanded me to stay. I complied. Her stability was restored and she returned to the story.

So what was this particular story I interrupted? I've no idea. It was one among so many.

Here is a typical example of one of her 'explanations'. It is one I heard so many times that it requires a conscious effort to recall it *as one of the stories*. Everything about it is so internally familiar, so intrinsic a part of my mental life, that I have to wrench it away from my own mixed-up inner world.

(I must have been a small child when I first heard it, the last time I was about 16. Between, she told it to me four or five times a year, as its turn came around, yet as far as I know few of the details changed with time.)

It was about a party which was being thrown in a house that belonged to the parents of a school-friend called Penelope. (There were other stories about Penelope, most of them pre-dating this one.) The houses, the grounds in which it stood, and its position in relation to the nearby town, were all described in great detail. Apparently, these people had a great deal of money. (My mother's background was more humble. Other stories of hers dealt with this.) Although she and Penelope had lost contact after leaving school, they had met again a few years later and they were now in their early twenties. The party was being held to celebrate the fact that another friend of Penelope's, a young man named Hugh, had returned from abroad.

107

Hugh was promised for Penelope and their engagement was due to be announced during the party. Both sets of parents were pleased with the arrangement, as it had been assumed for years that these two would eventually marry. Everything was satisfactory, from Hugh's education and prospects to Penelope's obvious wealth.

The point of the story was that my mother had known Hugh before he left for his sojourn abroad. In fact, both girls had had crushes on him at school, and there had been some kind of short-lived relationship between him and my mother. When she saw him again at this party he gave her the brush-off, pretending at first not to recognize her, then speaking to her in a way which my mother took as a final rejection. This made her extremely unhappy and angry, and after a while she left the main party in the marquee erected in the garden, and went into the house to be alone. She explored some of the upper rooms: my mother's account included detailed descriptions of the furniture, the paintings on the walls, the valuable trinkets she found in one of the bedrooms.

It seems that Hugh must have followed her into the house, because he came across her while she was still in the bedroom where she found the trinkets. A tearful scene ensued (my mother always cried while relating it). Hugh declared that he was marrying Penelope against his wishes, and that she, my mother, was the only one he loved. They hatched a plan, in which they would run away together and live abroad. This conversation ended with an embrace, which in its turn led quickly to a seduction. They made love on the bed. My mother described this part of the story in considerable physical detail. Her description of the coupling was exact; unlike other parts of the story these details never varied. (By the time I was old enough to understand what she was describing I was so

108

familiar with it all that I hardly listened.)

The only exciting part of the story came when she and Hugh, naked together on the bed and apparently still in the act, were interrupted by the sudden arrival of Penelope's father. Both she and Hugh were thrown out of the house.

The story ended here.

(Hugh was soon to die in mysterious circumstances. This was a later story, told archly – I was never clear in my mind about what happened to Hugh. Whether he died of some distressing illness or accident, or was killed by someone, I do not know, but his death was apparently unexpected and my mother was somehow involved.

Here her talent for detail left her, which was yet another distracting feature. Because so much detail was normally included, I missed it when it was left out.)

Another of her stories involved a pet dog. This was a stray mongrel that my mother adopted during the Second World War. It was an extremely friendly little dog, which my mother named Alex. (There was a reason for the name, which I now forget.) She used to take Alex for walks in a park - she was in London for much of the war - and passers-by used to comment on the tricks my mother had taught him to do. These included being able to walk on his hind legs, and wearing a woollen cap that my mother knitted for him. I loathed the stories about Alex.

Several stories were about my mother's schooldays.

One of the stories was about a disagreement my mother once had with a man she worked with. Both sides of the argument were included in the story, but I cannot remember the outcome.

Another dealt with an operation she had to have. (This had as much attention to detail as her stories about sex.) There

109

was another about buying some crockery. Another was about a plane that crashed. Another about the time she and my father moved house during the war. Another involved setting fire to a newspaper. Another was set on a boat. Another had a river in it. Another was at the seaside. Another was about shopping.

These are the memorable ones. There were hundreds of others.

What did my mother mean by these so-called explanations? I learnt nothing I wished to know about her, nothing that I did not know about myself or wanted to know about my life, and found out precious little about the world.

All I acquired was an abiding dislike of stories and of the people who tell them. I now have no patience with any kind of narrative form: I find most jokes unfunny, novels dull, and films entertaining only when they contain loud music, picturesque scenery or young women removing their clothes. All this I owe to my mother, who dominated my childhood with her endless tales.

And there was a consequence of them she did not know and never learned. I stole the stories from her and made them my own.

14

'ALICE? IS THAT really you? This is Lizzie!'
Alice was outside the house when the telephone rang.
She had at last decided to do something about the garden,
which had been growing wild all summer. Like everyone else,
she had obeyed the initial warnings and left it strictly alone,
but since then there had been nothing about this in the news
and she had been wondering what to do. Then, one by one,
the other people in the village had started cutting back the
wild growth, trimming the long grass of their lawns and
pruning the bushes, and the familiar autumnal smell of
bonfire smoke had been in the air for two or three weeks. She
knew she could leave it no longer. Winter had nearly arrived,
and if she didn't make a start the garden would look a mess
for months and be uncontrollable next year. In fact she was
lazy about gardening, and a part of her had been secretly
relieved when officialdom gave her an excuse to neglect it.
The only part of gardening she enjoyed was planting and
growing things. Pruning was just a chore.

She hacked back a part of the lawn, but stopped when she
realized how many skeletal remains of birds she was finding.
Then she moved to the largest flower bed, and had just
started to make an impression on it when she heard the phone
ringing. Glad of the interruption, she ran in to get it.

'Lizzie! Where are you?'

'I'm in London! I'm on a visit to see my parents. But where are *you?* I got your number from Bill. What's been going on?'

'We've split up... Bill and I are divorced. Didn't I write to you about this?'

'No. I was wondering -'

Lizzie's voice had a faint trace of America in it, intonation rather than accent: a rising inflexion. She had fallen in love with a post-graduate exchange student called Rolf when she was at Bath, married him before he went back to the US, and now lived in Pittsburgh.

'Bill didn't say where you were. I thought it was a bit odd.'

Alice sat down, feeling happy, letting the phone cord stretch across her desk.

'I'm a country mouse,' she said. 'I've bought a cottage in Wiltshire.'

'Are you on your own?'

'Completely. I've got a cat, though.'

'I thought you didn't like cats.'

'This one's different.'

They talked for half an hour, interrupting each other, exchanging fragments of news, catching up. Lizzie wanted to come and see her (she said 'visit with you'), and so they fixed up the following weekend.

Alice put down the phone and wrote 'L. Humbert' in neat lettering in the space on her wallchart. Afterwards, she looked wryly at the entry, surrounded as it was by white space and trivial reminders to pay bills. It was a long time since she had had a weekend visitor.

She was glad it was Lizzie. She hadn't been around last year to hear the gossip, and would therefore come without a freight of assumptions about what had gone wrong between

112

her and Bill. It wasn't that her other friends had taken sides. Most of them had gone to ground for the duration, and the rest had had their loyalties worn away.

She had been with Bill a long time. They had always acted like a couple and had been treated that way by the people around them. When the split came many of their friends seemed embarrassed, as if the assumptions they had been making over the years were mistaken and they were now expected to pretend that they weren't surprised to see them separately. During the bad months before she left London, Alice had simply wanted company. Several friends had provided that, and for a while it felt as if everything was going to carry on as before. But something intangible had changed: Bill had always been dominant, the part of their couple people wanted to see. He was the extrovert, the sociable one. It seemed to Alice that the people she thought of as her best friends were really Bill's friends . . . or else they were suddenly wrapped up in their own concerns, unwilling to let her open up too far.

Because that was what she wanted to do. Alice knew she must have been difficult in those months. Her long-suffering friends had grown tired of hearing about Bill's rages, Bill's selfishness, the infidelities, her own misery and feeling of isolation. She had wept a lot, poured out her troubles, talked until she was hoarse, endured periods of overcontrolled calm, and others of manic activity, all part of the obsession of trying to salvage something from the mess. Through this, she and Bill had remained inseparable in a different way: wherever she went Bill usually found her and telephoned her, or just turned up unexpectedly, bringing the endless tensions into other people's homes. There was hardly an old friend who had not seen or overheard some intimate bitterness or

113

score-settling, some intractable late-night impasse.

Lizzie had missed all this, thousands of miles away. It would be fun to see her again, show off her house and the countryside and the village life. It would be wonderful to have someone else staying in the house, using it, sharing it briefly with her.

This made her think more practically about the spare room and buying some new linen for the bed. And the room itself: she had been meaning to redecorate it. There was no excuse about money any more.

(But the money from Harriet was dribbling away quickly. It was ever thus: feast or famine. After the inevitable binge of minor extravagances, and the ritual paying of old bills, the chill of reality set in. Money was finite. It always ran out.)

She went back to the garden and carried on from where she had left off, but Lizzie's phonecall had shorted out her accumulation of energy. Soon she dumped all the cuttings on the compost heap, tidied away her tools and went inside for a cup of tea.

The local newspaper was delivered in the afternoon. Eleanor's murder was still in the news, and this week's edition had a lead story about the inquest. The jury's verdict was unlawful killing by person or persons unknown. The coroner had accepted the verdict, and formally requested the police to continue their investigations.

The telephone rang while she was reading this. By weird synchronicity it was the policeman in Ramsford, with a message for her from Gordon Sinclair. He (Mr Sinclair) had notified them that she was in possession of a key, and he was now notifying her that he (the policeman) knew, and she was now asked to notify him (the policeman again) if she came across anything that might assist with enquiries, or if he (Mr

Sinclair) returned unexpectedly to the village.

Alice untangled all this, agreed to everything, and hung up as quickly as she could.

She was still mildly surprised that Gordon had agreed to her request to go through Eleanor's books and papers. She supposed she hadn't thanked him sufficiently, but then he was not the sort of person she wanted to be effusive to. His manner made her understate everything, in case a display of warmth might produce an unwanted response.

This reminded her that if she was to go round to Eleanor's house she should do it soon. The weekend was approaching, and Gordon had told her that the weekends were the only time he could get away from his job. She didn't relish the idea of being alone in the house with him. Anyway, Lizzie would be staying with her at the weekend.

She started early the next day, and after waiting for the post to arrive (junk mail and a magazine; no cheques, no news from Granville) she walked along the lanes to Eleanor's house. As soon as she had opened the gate, and was walking up the short drive, she had a most peculiar feeling of being watched.

The paranoia about her book had receded recently, but this was a sudden reminder. Such feelings were alien to her. In the past she had always felt her life was so quiet, so hidden and private, that few people were even aware of her existence.

It was being with Bill that had given her this habit. Because he was so inexhaustibly sociable, she had fallen into playing the role of the bookish one. Anyway it had suited her to be always in her study, or reading, or taking notes quietly behind the stacks in a library. She knew that most of Bill's friends had probably thought of her as his mousy wife, loyally at his side, chatting to his friends' wives, smiling at his jokes. It was

115

a role that suited them both: Bill put his own ego first, and she valued what she thought of as her interior privacy.

She had paid for the privacy in the end. The marriage going wrong was her first experience of a badly wrecked relationship, and her habitual inwardness turned out to be no help. She discovered that when the inner life falls apart you need outward reserves to draw on: physical energy to deal with the changes, an outer shell to deflect some of the hurt, a brightness of manner to reassure those around you, and so on.

Well, she had changed from those days, but even so her sense of her own insignificance had never really left her. She had once relished the idea that no one really took any notice of her. She had had to adjust a little, once she realized that in a village everyone's life was of equal interest. Very little could be kept secret. And the Home Office had completed the process, making her feel not only picked on, but picked out.

As she slipped the key into the front door of Eleanor's house, Alice tried to shrug off the feeling. It was more particular than before: she sensed the presence of Eleanor's son, waiting for her inside the house, or lurking somewhere in the overgrown garden.

She closed the door quickly behind her, bracing herself to meet him, but the house was silent and stuffy, closed up with all Eleanor's possessions inside and no one moving around to stir the air.

It was unheated, too. Keeping her coat on, Alice went through to Eleanor's sitting-room, the only part of the house with which she was at all familiar. On her first visit Eleanor had taken her around the house and showed her all the rooms, but it had always been the comfortable kitchen-cum-sitting-room where they had sat together.

Alice's first priority was to locate her tape cassettes. The recordings had been made here, across this table, but there was no reason why Eleanor should have kept them in this room. Alice slid open the drawers that were part of the table, but these had been cleared of everything. Two stacks of paper were standing neatly on the table itself, but it was obvious the tapes were not among them.

She glanced briefly at the top few sheets and leafed through them. She hated the idea of snooping on Eleanor, even though she knew that was exactly what she was doing. Might the books still exist in manuscript form, and thus be buried somewhere with all the other sheets? There was nothing in the piles on the table that looked even remotely connected with books. There was a huge number of old bills, insurance policies, handwritten recipes, scraps of paper with telephone numbers, Eleanor's pension book, neatly folded sheets of used wrapping paper... all sorts of ordinary domestic trivia, full of poignancy, that Gordon had apparently put to one side for throwing away.

Alice looked for her tapes in the Welsh dresser, and in the other cupboards, but these contained some of Eleanor's crockery and cooking implements, neatly stacked, just as she must have left them on the night she was killed.

The room was beginning to depress her: it was too familiar, too firmly identified with the living Eleanor. When she knew the room it had usually been warm and sunlit, the windows open to the air, with a pleasant background smell of cooking. Now the house had already started to revert to an unoccupied state, the only smells being those of airlessness and damp. They reminded her of her own cottage, empty for so many months before she moved in.

She walked through the rest of the house, starting at the top.

This was the first village house she had been invited into. It was soon after she arrived. It had been spring then, with the fields around the house yellow with rapeseed, the trees almost subliminally sheened with green as their leaves began to break out of the buds. The house had been light, the curtains and windows wide open. The whole place seemed cheerful and cared for.

The bedclothes had been stripped from the bed in Eleanor's room, presumably by Gordon, and were in a neat folded stack on the end of the mattress. Eleanor's clothes were undisturbed in the drawers and wardrobe. Now feeling like a real snooper, Alice looked quickly for her tapes in all the possible places, then slid the drawers closed and hurried out of the room.

She disliked this. She could still feel Gordon's unfriendly presence in the house, a persecution. She paused on the landing at the top of the stairs, wondering if she were subconsciously transferring her own guilty feelings to her dislike of the son. Maybe she simply wasn't cut out to write a book about someone she knew.

Well. Then what?

She thought about Eleanor, trying to imagine what her opinion might be. A mental picture swam up unexpectedly: the amiable old lady smiling benignly, pouring tea, pouring benefaction. 'That's all right, Alice . . . you do whatever you think right.'

And that was another transference, another betrayal: Eleanor was not cosy like that. There had always been a hard individualistic wire coiled inside her. She was much more ambiguous and interesting. It was by no means predictable what she would say about this.

It was certainly wrong to summon up a false and sentimental image of her, then try to use it to justify what she was doing.

There were three more main rooms on the upper floor. Two were spare rooms for guests. The first was obviously the one Gordon had been using when he stayed in the house: the bed was made up but untidy, with the bedclothes thrown back in a crumpled heap. A small radio was on the bedside table, and a filthy handkerchief, balled up. Alice backed out, and looked in the other spare room. As soon as she saw it she knew her tapes would not be there. The twin beds were made up under their coverlets, and the furniture looked stiff and unused. Even so, Alice quickly opened the empty, paper-lined drawers in the dressing-table, just to be sure.

The third room was the one where Eleanor had stored her unused furniture, boxes and suitcases. Alice remembered it from her first visit, and it still looked much the same. She knew that Eleanor had rarely come into this room.

As she went downstairs again, Alice realized that there was no reason Eleanor should have hidden the tapes. It was much more likely she would have simply left them somewhere to be found again on Alice's next visit.

She went to the place where she should have looked first, Eleanor's workroom at the back of the house, and she found the tapes at once. They were lying side by side in their plastic cases on top of the piano, and the instant she saw them Alice remembered that Eleanor had told her she would keep them here, with her music tapes, until Alice wanted them. How could she have forgotten? The memory of Eleanor placing them here was suddenly vivid in her mind.

The police had apparently not touched them while

119

searching the house, because they were as dusty as the piano. But why should they? The tapes looked like ordinary music cassettes, and one of them even had an old scribble on the card inlay, identifying it as something by Liszt.

Alice picked them up and slipped them into her coat pocket.

Lying beneath them was an envelope, with her name written on the outside.

She slit it open, and found several pages inside written in Eleanor's neat hand. Standing there, with her backside leaning against the closed piano lid, Alice read the long letter Eleanor had written to her just before she died.

15

ELEANOR'S LETTER CHANGED everything. When she had read it, Alice sat down on the piano stool and stared blankly across the room, remembering her friend. It was as if Eleanor had been speaking directly to her, at a time when she had thought she would never hear from her again. Alice felt her emotions churning: happiness that she had found something so uniquely personal, relief that she had found it at all, renewed misery at her death.

It was pure Eleanor: the rebuke about her deviousness (which made Alice want to find her and beg forgiveness), the warm encouragement about her book, the deliberate setting of trails for her to follow, the coyness about her affair with the man called Hugh, the guarded giving of information. And children's novels!

If she had ever harboured any real doubts about what book she was going to write next, the letter dispelled them.

Alice read it again. Knowing how valuable it was going to be she returned it to its envelope and placed it in her pocket with the tapes. It resolved another, more practical, matter too. Eleanor unequivocally gave her permission for a biography, and assuming Gordon did not have serious objections she could surely now look through the papers with a clean conscience.

Would he object . . . or could he?

She tried to imagine what his reaction might be, but it was too difficult to anticipate him. He seemed uninterested in his mother's affairs, but as her only relative he might have some power of veto over a biography. After a few minutes' thought, Alice decided to go ahead and see if there was anything that might be useful to her for the book, then find some way of asking Gordon when she saw him again.

Eleanor had two filing cabinets, and her desk and the table next to it were both piled with papers. What should she look for?

Files, of course. Eleanor had told her once that she was scrupulous about keeping copies of everything she wrote. But what did she write these days: articles, letters to newspapers, notes of meetings? Tom Davie obviously knew her reputation. He had used the word 'doughty' about her, which seemed apt. It evoked a mental image of tireless, even cranky devotion, lodging protests about this and that, sending out fund-raising letters, lobbying politicians and pressure groups, never giving up or being discouraged.

Alice felt slightly envious of Tom's familiarity with Eleanor's work. She had spent so many years of her life wrapped up in herself: the first struggles to become a published writer, then meeting Bill and marrying him, and all that followed. The outside world had carried on in a blur of distant activity: events and disasters and political changes, glimpsed in the newspapers or on TV, passing by. She always measured her life by what she had been doing or writing, then later it came as a surprise to realize, for example, that she had written her first book during the time of the Arab oil embargo. But then, when she actually thought about it, she remembered having to synchronize her writing sessions

122

around the power cuts, and wasting time queuing up for petrol. But the outside world was always secondary in her life, distanced by the preoccupations of working and living.

In the same way, for most of her adult life she had been aware of popular protest, even feeling instinctive sympathy for it. Many people were against the arms race, against the presence of American bases in Europe, against government secrecy and interference, in favour of *rapprochement* with the Eastern Bloc countries, strongly in favour of protection of the environment, civil rights and liberties, the welfare state, freedom of expression and information. These were people she admired, but they made her feel complacent and irresolute because she had never found time actually to go on marches, or to demonstrate against important issues.

Instead she worked over her typewriter, and latterly with her computer, spent her spare time in libraries and second-hand bookshops, mixed with other apolitical writers and friends, researched other people's lives, drew on the events of history without involving herself with the idea that history actually had to be made.

Yet again she had doubts if she were the right kind of person to undertake a serious book about a woman like Eleanor. Her feelings of inadequacy loomed large.

But she had liked and admired her even if she had not really known her. Everything Alice had written in the past had enlarged her in some way, however minor.

Writing was a way of learning: you became or made yourself interested in a subject, learnt enough about it to think that there might be a book that could be written, then when you started researching you discovered, seemingly by accident, what the book might really be about. Usually it would be something completely unexpected. In this sense, books wrote themselves. Writing about Eleanor would undoubtedly be the same. It already was the same, when so much had happened since she first thought of doing it.

The letter suggested that she saw something of herself in Eleanor, which was percipient and true. Perhaps Eleanor had been telling her that it was time to write a book out of a sense of conviction, rather than just out of interest, or with the hope that a book might be found if you did enough research into a subject.

Then where to begin?

The same place any book begins, she supposed: here, in my head, in this room, inspired by a notion, looking for the real idea.

Alice opened the top drawer of one of the filing cabinets, and at once the scale of what she was undertaking was clear. Eleanor had not exaggerated when she talked about keeping everything. Paper was jammed into the drawer, separated by card dividers, labelled and categorized and sometimes dated. When Alice tried to lift out one of the sections she discovered it was wedged so tightly that the files next to it bulged up, and the papers in her hand threatened to slide out from her grasp. She wrapped an arm around them, pushed the others back into the drawer, then carefully placed the ones she had taken on one of the few uncluttered areas of Eleanor's desk.

The file consisted mainly of letters written to and from the Nuclear Freeze organization in the United States. The letters covered a period of about three years, the earliest being dated some seven years ago. Alice glanced through a few of the ones on the top, then returned to the filing cabinet for more. The next folder contained the same – these were dated more recently – but also had a huge collection of newspaper cuttings, pasted carefully and in date order on sheets of A4 paper. From another quick scan through, Alice found that these were reports of military spending, activities at US bases in Britain and Europe, and stories about the redeployment of warheads to other delivery systems after the INF Treaty.

Another cuttings file from the same drawer covered reports of the arms-reduction negotiations with the Soviet Union. Another was about terrorist actions in Northern Ireland, Europe and the Middle East.

In the next drawer down, Alice found more cuttings. These were newspaper reviews of children's fiction.

The desk was being quickly covered by these papers, so Alice moved most of them to the floor, careful to keep them in order.

With the first folders removed, it was easier to move about in the remaining files in the drawers, so Alice knelt down on the floor in front of the cabinets and began looking through them.

In half an hour she had several piles of potentially interesting material lying on the floor beside her. She stood up at last to stretch her back and legs, chilled through by the unheated house. Her hands felt dry and her fingertips were shiny with the cold. When she stepped back she realized just how much material she had already separated from the rest. Seen all together it looked a formidable pile.

She knew then that her squeamish feelings had been overcome. Rightly or wrongly, the book had started.

There were too many papers to be carried loose, so Alice went back upstairs to Eleanor's storage room, found a spare cardboard box and took it downstairs. She stuffed into it what she could, then let herself out of the house and walked back to her cottage.

After a warming cup of tea at home she drove the car to

Eleanor's house, and after three trips had transferred most of the papers to her office.

That evening, feeling as ill-equipped as ever to tackle this amount of research, and recognizing a pretext when she saw it, she telephoned Tom Davie.

16

I HAD TO visit London at the end of the week, which fitted in well with my plans, because I could drive from there to Wiltshire for the rest of the weekend. I already had a reason for being there – my mother's solicitor had called to remind me that the house had to be cleared of her possessions – but I wanted to see Alice again. She intrigued me. Did she remember me, or did she not?

I was delayed by fog on the M1. This, and road works and a multiple pile-up near Northampton, made me half an hour late for the meeting in our London office. I had no time to stop for lunch on the way, and because I suffer from the effects of low blood sugar, a form of secondary endogenous alcohol poisoning, I have to eat at regular intervals. If I miss a meal I feel disagreeable and light-headed, and find it difficult to concentrate. I was in this state for most of the afternoon.

I was already in a bad mood because of the current tension between myself and my partner, Guy Lawley.

Lawley and I had worked together for some fifteen years. I started the company on my own, but as it expanded I became unable to cope with everything. Lawley was an accountant, and I originally took him on to run the administrative side of the business. We worked together closely for many years, and the company expanded. We had been partners for a decade, and now co-owned the company. For most of the time there was little conflict between us, but the problem created by the *Morning Herald*, the subject of the day's meeting, had underlined our different priorities. We were both anxious to resolve this, but we had reached an impasse.

Our company is an information contractor, with a specialization in surveillance management. I began in the visual media, but had started to expand into the written media around the time Lawley joined me. We have diversified several times since, and now have separate divisions within the company for areas of specialist attention. In addition to media work, we are contractors to industrial and manufacturing concerns, we have a parliamentary consultancy division, and our most recent enterprise is in the lucrative field of defence issue marketing.

Media work remains our bread and butter, though. I still directly administer the written media division, and oversee the contracts with two national newspapers, a trade magazine group, and a handful of textbook and general publishers. I also have an interest in one of the cable television news networks, but this too is an area of growth which I am in the process of delegating to a separate division.

Since most companies working in the media are for one reason or another decentralized, our company also works from a number of regional centres. I remain in Manchester, where I began, but we have other offices in most of the major cities, as well as smaller monitoring bureaux in places such as Oxford, Durham and Milton Keynes. Manchester continues to suit me as a base, because I have lived there for most of my life, but also because several newspapers (including the *Herald*) have editorial offices and print-origination facilities there.

The *Herald* is one of the new-technology papers, entirely dependent on computers, satellite dissemination and news-gathering, cellnet and datanet access, and, of course, telephone landlines. Manchester happens to be a major nexus of this electronic net, and with the *Herald* offices near at hand we can keep in close contact with our clients as necessary.

The immediate problem with the *Herald* was, at base, extremely simple: they were withholding payment of our account. I happened to know what was behind this: it was a perverse and provocative kind of journalistic exercise, the point of which was not actually to default, but to stretch us financially to the point where we should be forced to act. Put simply, they wanted to see what we would do about it, then publicize our actions.

Guy Lawley disagreed with this analysis. He believed the newspaper was in serious financial difficulties, and that if we let it go on too long we would lose everything. He had already brokered part of the debt to one of our rival companies, and it seemed likely to me his next step would be to look for some kind of corporate amalgamation. I was vehemently against this. The sensitive nature of our work required maximum confidentiality, and this would be at risk if we became too large.

We had several means of redress against the newspaper. We could, for instance, simply employ an ordinary debt-collection agency to get the money from them. (Lawley continued to suggest this from time to time.) Then we had the usual kinds of legal redress: we could take out a civil suit against the newspaper's parent company, or against named directors. We could blacklist the datanet credit rating of the newspaper, the directors and most of the senior employees.

But what both sides were interested in was our final sanction. However much they may dislike our attentions, we have statutory powers against our clients to enforce payment. These powers are extensive: they include the authority to sequester land and buildings, seize assets, declare all directors bankrupt, and appoint a receiver to administer the dismantling of the business.

Lawley wanted the money. What I wanted was to find out how much the newspaper knew about these powers, and how far they would push us. If they took it too far, their business would be at risk. On the other hand, the essentially covert nature of our work would be finally exposed.

However, we too were subject to statutory powers, something that Lawley never let me forget. We were required by Act of Parliament to remain secret. If any of this became public, our own business would be in jeopardy.

We also had to take into account the kind of newspaper they published. The *Herald* was a popular campaigning newspaper, aligned politically to the left, with a history of successful investigations into bureaucratic corruption and industrial malpractice. They had, for instance, recently exposed a drug company for releasing a tranquillizer without sufficient testing, one which turned out to have dangerous side-effects on pregnant women and their unborn children. (By coincidence, our pharmaceutical division had been awarded the damage limitation contract when the scandal broke.)

The *Herald* took a high moral stand on most issues. Personally, I thought it was sensationalist and opportunist, ready to find conspiracies and base motives in more or less every human activity, but of course my own opinion was irrelevant in this. In spite of the rumours about the cash situation, the *Herald* had built up a wide circulation and carried a great deal of advertising. *Herald* journalists had won several press awards in the past year, and the paper was well known as a sponsor of major sports fixtures. They had an undeniable popular constituency.

Then there was the editor, a man called Stephen Ashbourne. He caused us trouble. He was always appearing on television as a press pundit, and showed unwelcome signs of becoming famous. In addition, and even more inconveniently for us, he was a personal friend to many politicians. He knew exactly what he was doing to us, and was an estimable adversary.

Whatever the background, the *Herald* had run up a debt to us that now exceeded half a million pounds, and something had to be done.

The meeting was the latest in a long series of similar meetings: in response to Lawley's most recent demand for payment, the newspaper management had proposed a meeting to 'discuss the issues between us'. We had to accede. Both sides were manoeuvring.

The others had assembled when I arrived. They were in the Balcony Atelier, a long narrow room with bare, white-painted walls and high ceiling, and a polished pine floor. Two computer terminals were mounted in wall alcoves, both permanently logged on to satellite databases, one in Los Angeles, the other in Tokyo. Four tall arched windows faced the balcony outside, and through these could be seen a panorama across the yacht basin and towards the Thames. Green vines grew across the balcony, sprawling over the parapet and already taking hold on the wall around the windows.

When I walked into the room Guy Lawley waved me towards one of the leather-upholstered posture chairs directly facing the distracting computer displays, and I sat down uncomfortably, feeling as displaced as I made myself appear.

(It was crucial that my true identity and position in the company should never be known, especially to the people we were with today. I had been introduced at an earlier meeting as Lawley's media consultant – his assistant, in other words – and held a low profile through all the proceedings. The pseudonym I used for this purpose was Peter Hamilton. I always felt that Lawley took pleasure from this deceit, and that his attitude to me at these meetings was revealing. In any event, I had a profound dislike of Lawley's taste in high-tech minimalism. I was happier in the plainer surroundings of my own office in a converted cotton warehouse in Manchester.) I was interested to see if Stephen Ashbourne was present. He was one of the few clients I had ever come face to face with. As I sat down he was talking about the fire that had recently occurred at their Manchester office.

'. . . we've sustained considerable losses. On the night of the fire a million and a half copies were destroyed. For all editions in the following week we lost an average of three-quarters of a million copies. Although we've made up the circulation since, our advertising revenue has fallen.'

'You were insured,' Lawley said.

'Our insurers think it was arson. We do too, as a matter of fact.'

'That has no bearing on the claim. Have you lodged it?'

'Why weren't we allowed to run the story?' Ashbourne said, glancing at me. I stared straight back at him.

'We've had an affidavit from the insurers,' Lawley said. 'This revealed that a loss of profits claim had been paid.'

132

'It was an interim payment,' Ashbourne said, still looking in my direction. 'Because it was arson the rest of the settlement has been frozen until after the police investigation. We haven't been allowed to print that either.'

'What makes you believe it was arson?' said David Mancowicz, Lawley's real assistant, and our head of client finances.

Ashbourne produced a thin sheaf of papers, and handed them to one of the members of his team. This young man left his chair, and solemnly handed us all a sheet. Just as seriously, we looked at it, then laid it aside.

'The loss adjusters found the remains of three incendiary devices. These had timing mechanisms set to discharge at the exact time we regularly take delivery of copies from our print works. The incendiary material was a commercial incineration chemical, of which we had never heard before this incident. The nature of this alone is something we feel entitled to publish. You of course will know all about it.'

'I hope that is not a suggestion we had something to do with it,' Lawley said. His PA, who was using a stenograph, paused and looked up.

'You know what I'm saying.'

'No I don't. It's almost certainly untrue that you did not know about this product before.'

'We concede.'

This was said to Ashbourne by one of the newspaper board members. I had met him once before, but could not recall his name. Our shorthand writer was still waiting.

'We always react to actionable allegations,' Lawley said calmly, using the usual formula.

The director spoke again. 'What Mr Ashbourne meant was that you were more likely to have heard of this product than

133

anyone on his staff.'

'All right.' Lawley nodded to his assistant, indicating that this should be left off the record.

The sub-text of this exchange was a controversial explosive called Tentertex. This was the proprietary name for a derivative of napalm. It was a volatile mixture of petrochemicals with aluminium and magnesium salts, alleged to release toxic gases, officially banned by the EC, but widely used in certain industrial waste-disposal sites. Two years earlier, one of these places had experienced a major disaster when several cartons of Tentertex ignited spontaneously. Our environmental division had won the crisis management contract. When the *Herald* started investigating this a year later, we had of course intervened. This is why it was untrue that Ashbourne had never heard of the substance.

We learned about the use of Tentertex at the *Herald* on the day of the incident. We had access to police forensic investigations, and it was plain to me that the fire had been started deliberately. Although it was clearly a case of arson, what was not so certain was the motive. The insurers pointed out that the newspaper had been intending to close one of the loading bays for some time, there was a planning dispute with Greater Manchester Council, and it seemed relevant to the insurers that after the fire the affected part of the building had not been reopened as a loading bay. The area was now in use as an archive and file store. This too was a sub-text.

Stephen Ashbourne called for a recess for consultation, to which we agreed. He and the others moved to an anteroom at the far end of the Atelier, and while the two record-takers met to check each other's notes, Lawley and I and the others from our side walked over to one of the windows for a brief discussion.

134

Lawley said to me at once, 'What about the Tentertex? Is there anything more?'

'No more than we had last week. It originated in Israel.'

'Do we know who was really responsible?'

'They were.'

'Are you sure?'

'No question.'

'Good,' said Lawley. 'Read this.' He passed me a sheet of folded paper which he took from a pocket inside his suit jacket. 'It's my current thinking on measures to gain settlement. Let me have it back when you've read it.'

I took the sheet to one of the chairs, and read it through as carefully as possible. It involved further brokering of the debt, this time linked to an exchange of share capital.

This, and the discussion I had just listened to, made me feel that something fundamental and alien was occurring, that the company I had built up was about to change in ways I could not halt. I would not accept this, and certainly was unwilling to discuss it with Lawley today.

The meeting resumed a few minutes later, with Mancowicz taking the initiative. He rehearsed the amount of the outstanding balance, and listed the statutory information management we had carried out on their behalf. He then repeated the familiar threats, and their likely consequences for the newspaper. Lawley took over, pointing out that as the sum increased so our information management was likely to become targeted more aggressively. It then fell to me to outline the areas in which our vigilance could be stepped up. (As usual, I had to keep to generalities. Too much detail from me might alert them. I was already concerned by Ashbourne's interest in me, and I knew that I should have to stay away from these meetings in future.) Mancowicz gave them yet

135

another copy of the section of our charter that dealt with their obligation to pay for our service.

The *Herald* team listened politely, then it was their turn. They repeated their accusations of censorship, of politically motivated intervention, of harassment of staff, of illegal wiretaps, of excessive use of our powers, etc.

So the meeting declined into the customary ritual, heading for the inevitable impasse. They agreed reluctantly to reconsider their position. We agreed reluctantly to hold off sanctions for another seven days. No further meeting was scheduled, although we all knew that another would have to happen.

I got away as soon afterwards as I could, and smoked a cigarette in my car. After this I went to the closest of the many restaurants that had sprung up around the concentration of new offices in Dockland.

It had only just opened for the evening and was almost deserted. If I hadn't been so hungry I should have tried to find somewhere else. I selected the least objectionable items from the menu. A cold watercress soup was followed by two undercooked miniature lamb cutlets in some kind of cream sauce; the vegetables were mangetout peas; the potatoes were tiny half-boiled spheres. The Château wine was sour and over-chilled. When I sent it back I was provided with a more expensive replacement. The waiter was a lout in white shirt and baggy trousers. The table was made of stainless steel, it was overhung by intrusive ferns, and whenever I used the knife and fork the table wobbled on the bare, sawdust-strewn floorboards. Before I left, a smirking halfwit in pre-war suit and spats began playing sentimental medleys on a pink-painted grand piano. The bill came to more than £45.

By the time I had driven across London and joined the M4

westwards, I was thinking again about Alice, haunted by my memories of her.

17

ELEANOR'S FILES DISTRACTED her from her real quest, but once she had started Alice felt she ought to finish. Because of the sheer quantity of material she became much more selective, but even so she accumulated several boxfuls of papers. The further she went the more she worried about what she was doing. The implication in Eleanor's letter was one thing, but it did not have the force of a will. Tom had warned her that if Gordon raised serious objections she would probably have to give everything back.

Trusting that he wouldn't, Alice carried on.

With everything transported back to her house, and arranged as logically as possible in heaps on her office floor, Alice at last turned her attention to Eleanor's books.

Most of Eleanor's collection was piled haphazardly on deep shelves built against the long back wall of the study. There had been some attempt to impose order: there were a few short runs of titles alphabetically by author, and one shelf was largely given over to poetry, but most of the books were crammed tightly against each other with dozens more lying flat on top. Novels were mixed in with biographies, histories, literary memoirs and letters, as well as an impressively wide range of practical books on subjects like gardening, travel, guides to stately homes, repairing cars, and so on. Nearly all the books were two-deep on the shelves, and none of the hardbacks had paper covers. All the paperbacks had creased spines.

At first Alice saw the collection as an incomparable treasure-trove, irresistible to someone like her because of the immense range of subjects. There were hundreds of books of which she had never heard, dozens more that she wanted to read immediately she noticed them, and many more that she would like to have on her shelves for possible future reference. Before she started going through them in earnest, Alice imagined herself filling box after box like a dedicated collector given free rein in a second-hand bookshop, but once she began browsing she realized she was going to have to be very selective.

For one thing there were practical considerations. Shelf space was strictly limited in her own house. Then there was the uncomfortable fact that many of the books appeared to be valuable. She came across first editions of pre-war novels by authors like Graham Greene, Evelyn Waugh, D.H. Lawrence and Christopher Isherwood, and collections of poetry by Thomas Hardy, Robert Graves and W.H. Auden. She knew books like these were rare and much sought-after, and because most of them were still in excellent condition they would fetch a decent price from a dealer, even without their dust jackets. To take away such books knowing what they were worth would be simple theft, even though no one else seemed to know or care about them. She felt the least she could do would be to tell Gordon about them, and, if he still showed no interest, to advise Eleanor's lawyers.

(There was one exception, though, which Alice seized without qualms: a battered copy of Rebecca West's book on treason. Dozens of scraps of paper had been slipped between the pages as markers, and marginal notes appeared throughout.)

Many of the less valuable books duplicated copies in her own collection. Alice was gratified by the discovery, thinking belatedly how much more in common she and Eleanor had had without realizing it. A great deal was explained by this, of course: the ease with which they had become friends, for instance, their shared tastes providing an unspoken background. They had never talked about literature as such, which was now both surprising and unsurprising.

She filled two boxes with books she felt she could in all conscience take away, then carried them out to her car. After another half an hour she had separated a second, much larger pile she would like to keep, and placed these on one side for later. The more she looked through the books the more of them she found she was taking for herself. For a while she dithered, putting some of them back, then taking them down again and returning others.

When she had picked out enough books to fill the back of her car she drove home, dumped them on the increasingly crowded floor of her study and returned to Eleanor's house.

With part of the deed thus done, it was easier to decide about the rest. She filled one more large box before declaring herself finished.

She had touched none of the books she thought were valuable; she had left any books of which she already had copies (she hadn't even been tempted to make a quiet exchange if Eleanor's copy was in better condition); and in general she had taken only those titles which she felt Eleanor herself might once have pressed on her as a loan.

A large number of the books were on subjects central to Eleanor's own concerns. Alice had filled the first two boxes with recent paperbacks about the arms race, the proliferation

140

of nuclear capability, and the effects of radioactive fall-out. Several of the books dealt with the dumping of nuclear and toxic waste, and the risks of accidents at nuclear power stations. Other titles were about the using up of natural resources, the pollution of the seas, the greenhouse effect, acid rain, damage to the ozone layer and the effects of multinational companies on the economies of poor nations.

These were all subjects on which Alice felt particularly ill-informed, without excuse. If any consolation could be found in Eleanor's death it was this. Even if she had not known that these books were necessary to a delayed understanding of Eleanor, Alice felt it was time to start learning.

When the last box had been stowed in her car, Alice returned to Eleanor's study and glanced around one more time, wondering if there was anything else she should take while she still had the chance. It was already Friday and she dreaded being in the house should Gordon turn up unexpectedly. She knew, or sensed, that this would be her last visit, that after this the house would be cleared.

She went through the filing cabinet drawers once more, but she had already passed over everything that remained. She closed the last drawer reluctantly, wishing she had started out with a clearer idea of what she was looking for.

A tall wooden cupboard, painted white, had been built into the corner of the room, next to one of the windows. Alice had never looked into it. From outside it resembled an airing cupboard, or the sort of place in which brooms might be kept. While Alice was thinking about the files and the books, it had never occurred to her to investigate. Now she did.

There were four deep shelves inside and they were all piled with books. Unlike those on the main shelves, these were stacked neatly and in even rows. The hardcovers still possessed their dustjackets. Alice took one of them out, and she knew at once what she had found.

It was a children's book called *Donnie at the Seaside*, and the author's name was E.S. Fulten. The cover illustration – rendered crudely in shades of blue and red – showed a small boy with curly hair, dirty knees and a cheeky expression on his face. He was standing on a beach with a pier in the background. A mouse was poking its nose from the pocket of his shirt.

There was another book called *Donnie Has a Party*, another, *Donnie Goes to London*, and another, *Donnie's Little Dog*.

Alice felt an extraordinary wave of relief and recognition. She knew these books! Eleanor's letter guessed she might have done. Years and years ago, borrowing the first one from her brother, who brought it back from the library one day, reading it through in an afternoon, then searching for the rest. The Donnie books were part of her childhood. E.S. Fulten! Why had she not recognized the name from Eleanor's letter?

She replaced the books she had taken down being careful not to damage them and to put them back exactly as she had found them. They were obviously stacked in the order in which they had been published, because the one at the far left-hand end was smaller than the others and more visibly worn. This was simply called *Donnie*, and was subtitled *A Tale for Children*. Alice opened it and looked at the copyright page. It had been published in 1945 'in complete conformity with the authorized economy standard'. There was no copyright notice. The paper, much yellowed, had the dry, acidic smell of wartime books.

The book next to it, *Donnie Again*, had also been published in 1945 but was produced to a higher standard.

A different publisher had taken over the series with the fourth title, and the uniform appearance of the books after this, and the sheer number of titles, bespoke their success. Alice recognized them like old, long-forgotten friends. More than thirty Donnie books had been published, sometimes with two or three titles appearing within a year. All of these later books were copyrighted to E.S. Fulten. The titles moved from the childlike and domestic to the more adventurous subjects that Alice had especially enjoyed: *Donnie and the Pirates*, *Donnie and the Mystery of the Moors*, *Donnie and the Flying Saucers*, and so on. The last book had been published in 1959.

The rest of the cupboard was crammed with different editions of the same titles: hundreds of translations, picture books, painting books, omnibus editions, hardbacks released with different cover illustrations, quiz books based on Donnie and his friends, and a few paperbacks. The most recent of these had been published in 1962. There appeared to be no American editions.

Alice went back to the first set of books, the editions she recognized, and carried them carefully across to Eleanor's desk. She sat down and started browsing through them.

All the books were illustrated with line-drawings, although some of the later ones used simple colouring effects with red or green overlays. The illustrator was the same throughout, identified only by the initials 'I.T.' Alice had no idea who it might be, although his or her drawings gave her a pang of recognition.

The later books, from about 1953 onwards, had brief introductions written by the author. Alice read them all, but there was much duplication between them. Each of the short

143

pieces began: 'To My Readers', or 'Dear Reader', and simply said that 'Donnie had asked' her to say thank you for all the letters, and that this book was the latest of his adventures, with several already available and more to come. A printed reproduction of a signature appeared at the bottom. It was recognizably Eleanor's handwriting.

The last few books in the series each had a black and white studio photograph of Eleanor on the inside back flap.

Alice shook her head, remembering. As a small child she had stared at this picture so often that the face seemed permanently imprinted on her mind. She had worshipped the lady who wrote these stories, and this kindly face, so wise and friendly, had seemed to smile directly at her. Now more than thirty years later the face was the same and her feeling was the same, but adult hindsight placed confusing screens around the memories. This was the Eleanor she knew, and the picture of E.S. Fulten – permed dark hair, black blouse, a string of pearls – was undoubtedly the same person.

How she had once wanted to meet E.S. Fulten! How she wanted to know Eleanor!

Everything connected. Reading the Fulten books at an early age had helped make her into the teenager who dreamed of becoming a writer, and from there into the adult who had actually started, and from there into the adult who had become the would-be biographer.

Alice sat at the desk for a long time, turning the pages of the books and remembering incidents from the stories, thinking about Eleanor and the chances she had lost without knowing they existed . . . and thinking too of the new chances that were opening up before her.

The light of the day was beginning to fail. Alice brought herself out of her reverie and looked at her wristwatch. Her time was up. The discovery of Eleanor's novels had decided their fate beyond argument. She found a spare cardboard box, put the books carefully inside, then carried them out to the car.

Back in Eleanor's study, knowing that this really was her last opportunity, Alice took a calm look around the room. There was nothing else. She let herself out of the house for the last time, and locked the door. She drove the short distance home, thinking about Eleanor, exhilarated by her discoveries, and already planning how she would start the book.

18

A LICE WAS TALKING to Tom when she began to feel ill, so she mumbled apologies at him, put down the phone quickly and ran upstairs to the bathroom. She was only just in time: bending over the toilet bowl she threw up most of her evening meal. She crouched there miserably, waiting for the spasm to return, but after a few minutes she began to feel a little better. Dread settled on her like a black cloak. She chewed two peppermint-flavoured antacid tablets, then washed her face and hands in cold water.

The telephone started ringing while she was towelling herself dry.

She combed her hair quickly, peered anxiously at her face in the mirror, and went back to her office.

'Hello?'

'What's happening?' said Tom. 'Are you all right?'

'Yes, I feel a bit better now.'

'What was it? Were you sick?'

'It was nothing . . . something I ate. It's OK.'

'Are you sure?'

'Yes... it's nothing.'

Tom was silent for a while. Alice chewed on her lower lip, felt traces of the chalky tablets there.

'Are you going to tell me about it?' Tom said in the end.

'On Sunday. You're still going to come, aren't you?'

'Yes. But tell me now. What's going on?'

The fear was still in her, one she could not face on her own, let alone talk about to someone else. Not even to Tom. Some things were made easier by ignoring them. It was no good talking about them, no point in worrying, nothing to say.

She was thinking: I hardly know you. Just that one evening, and all these long phonecalls, night after night. I know you feel the same about me as I feel about you, but we are still new. Your voice so far away in London, and you have Pamela, and for all I know she's waiting for you in another room even as we speak.

'Would you like me to come and see you now? Are you ill?'

'I told you. It just came on me suddenly. You've got to go to Wales, and I'll see you on Sunday. I'll tell you then. I'm all right, *really.*'

And she thought: How do I tell him I think I might be dying?

How do you tell anyone, let alone someone you've only just met, and when nothing's been settled, only that you both want to see each other again?

'Have you seen a doctor?'

'Yes.'

'What did he say?'

'There's a bug going around. A lot of people in the village have had it. He put me on a course of antibiotics, and I've been a lot better since. I ate some frozen fish for dinner this evening... it might have been bad.'

'You know what it is, don't you, Alice? It's not a bug, and it's nothing to do with food.'

Her eyes were closed tightly, so that she should not have to look at even the untidy desk in front of her.

She sobbed suddenly, and said, 'I don't want to talk about

147

it. I'm sorry.'

'All right, then.'

'Goodbye.' She put down the phone, then spread her fingers to watch them trembling.

He called back half an hour later. She would have telephoned him first, but she was always scared Pamela would pick up the phone if she was in his flat at the time.

She was still sitting at her desk, with the cat lying asleep in the pool of light thrown by her lamp. Tom apologized for having pressed her earlier, but she was feeling better. The nausea had left her, and for the time being so had much of the dread. Talking to Tom made it better.

They spent most of their evenings on the phone. They were both running up immense bills, but he was working on his book, and he had been offered a well-paid column by a magazine. He couldn't get out of London until the weekend. Until then they had only their one evening together to go on, and hour after hour on the phone. Alice knew what was happening, and that he must feel the same way, but they both left this unspoken.

Meanwhile, they talked about everything else: her plans for the book about Eleanor, his relationship with Pamela, the mystery of Eleanor's death, her missing manuscript, and Tom's political theories.

Tom's theories above all. She encouraged him to talk about them. It was the book he was working on, and she liked him to use her as a sounding board. Anyway, the only thing she knew for sure about politics was that she knew nothing. She had everything to learn, and Tom was a willing teacher.

She asked about his book, because he had asked about hers earlier, but also because she was interested.

'I turned up something this afternoon,' he said. 'I had lunch with an old friend of mine, a parliamentary researcher, and he told me about an off-the-record briefing he'd been to. He thinks MI5 is being run down.'

'By the Government?'

'Probably because Washington has never trusted them. I think they're getting rid of the secret service now!'

Tom's book was going to be about the loss of governmental power in Britain, what he called the winding down of central authority. He said it was an historical process that had begun after the Second World War, when NATO was formed and all defence policy was devolved to the USA. This coincided with the final dissolution of the Empire. The process had continued when Britain joined the EC, and since then had been accelerated by the privatization of formerly state-run industries.

In short, over the last half-century British governments had given themselves less and less to do, or at least had delegated authority to foreign powers or private enterprise within the UK.

Tom's theory was that this was ultimately a moral issue, because central authority was symbolic. Without it, ordinary people lost their own sense of centralized values and identity, and grew to accept that they had no influence over their own lives. This was an unconscious acceptance of reality, because in effect by devolving all power the Government had made it almost impossible to find out what was going on.

(Tom used Alice's missing manuscript as an example of this. He said it was likely the Home Office no longer knew where it was, that it had probably been passed to some specialist outside group. Alice felt privately that he must be wrong, but didn't argue with him. It was as plausible a theory as any.)

Another frequent subject of these evening phonecalls was Pamela, discussed at great length.

Alice felt she was in no position to make any demands about this, but Tom kept raising the subject. What he was saying, without actually using the words, was that he and Pamela had been drifting apart for some time, and that now he had met Alice he wanted to finish with her for good.

Alice was greatly torn by this. She couldn't help feeling pleased, but at the same time she felt sorry for the other woman, and identified with her. She also knew Tom was still seeing her, and presumably sleeping with her, and she didn't like that idea at all.

All she wanted was to see him again, as soon as possible. The telephone was no substitute. He had to go to Wales the next day, and would be calling in to see her on Sunday evening, on his way back to London. His name was already on Alice's wallchart, next to Lizzie's.

19

M Y MOTHER'S MAD storytelling continued all through the years I was at school. I started junior school in 1951, and after passing the eleven-plus in 1954 I went to the local grammar school. I left in 1959, when I was 16.

School was a distraction from life at home, but it made me no happier. I was not especially bright, I disliked many of the teachers, and I was unpopular with the other children. I was often bullied, called a mother's boy or an orphan, tormented because I was different from the others. However, I survived. I had enough intelligence to obtain average marks in most subjects, but never tried to do better. All I wanted was never to draw attention to myself. In the same way I got through the more physical side of school, being good enough at games to be able to join in with the others, but never to win at anything, or be picked for sides.

The physical appearance of the school was a constant presence in my life. It daunted me. It had been built in the nineteenth century by industrial and church philanthropists, and these influences showed in the architecture. It was tall, narrow and dark, like the old mills and warehouses in the centre of Manchester. It had sooty brick walls, steep slate roofs, heavy gables and, here the church influence, three spires; one small one at each end of the long building, and a high one in the centre. The main entrance was an imposing stone staircase leading to a vast door of carved oak with stained-glass inlays. Although this door was only used on formal occasions we had to troop past it every day, knowing that just beyond it was the headmaster's study, a place of dread.

This gaunt and depressing institution had originally been built in the countryside, but since then the suburbs had spread around it so that it now stood anomalously surrounded by pre-war housing estates. It had extensive grounds, so once we were inside the school area it was difficult to see out into the real world and we were subsumed into its heavy atmosphere of old times, past years. The school was strong on tradition, and used conventional methods of education and discipline.

More recent buildings had been put up in the grounds around the main block, but their architecture had been modelled on the original building, spreading the oppressive institutional feeling no matter where you were. Most of the classes took place in these smaller buildings, or in modern pre-fabricated huts, added to the school during the Second World War. The main school was used for assembly and prayers, the teachers' studies, the infirmary, the gymnasium, and so on, and for the dormitories used by the boarders. These residents, as they were known, were almost all from the Manchester slums, real orphans, taken in by the school under the terms of its charitable foundation. During the years I was at the school there were a great number of residents, many of whom had been orphaned by the blitz.

The events of the war were constantly in mind. Like all the children of my year, and those around us, I had been born while it was still going on. The country was enduring the aftermath for most of the time I was growing up. For instance, much of the centre of Manchester had been destroyed by the German bombs, and for many years my unconscious assumption about how any big city must look was that it consisted of acres of wasteland and rubble. Pieces of shrapnel were found so often in the school grounds that no one remarked on them. Several times while I was at school we were temporarily evacuated while an unexploded bomb found in a nearby garden was dealt with. A few miles away a kind of war continued: there was a US Air Force base in the neighbourhood, and the sight of bombers and heavy transports flying low over the houses was one we were all used to. Outside school, rationing of food, clothes and fuel went on well into the fifties, power-cuts were imposed every winter, and there was a general feeling of austerity, closed minds and horizons, drabness, restrictions.

Our culture, for what it was, was war-oriented too. War films were popular, and comics and books were often based on wartime exploits. Several of the teachers had served during the war, and would place much of what they taught us from within that perspective. I grew up believing that I had *missed* something by being born in it. Only three important times existed: the period before the war, the war itself, and the post-war years. Everything seemed to relate to one or another of these times. The war discoloured my childhood, an ugly stain from the past.

There was a known link between the war and the school that lent an extra edge to this preoccupation.

During the war many children had been evacuated from Manchester and the surrounding suburbs, but the school had continued to function. Because some of the buildings were not in use they were taken over by a detachment of the Guard

Volunteers, and they remained billeted there until three years after the war ended.

Although no one now seems to remember the GV, the school in my day was proud of its link with the force. The corridor walls were lined with photographs of GV training and patrol activities, the prefabricated buildings had been put up by the GV men (and made over by them into classrooms afterwards), and guests at school Speech Days were often high-ranking GV officers.

There was of course a GV Cadet Force in the school, which I joined like all the other boys. This taught me to march and drill, to dismantle and reassemble a rifle, and instilled in me a real sense of comradeship and self-respect. In general it made up for the bleakness of the rest of my life. I had no idea of the influence the GV was to have on me later, but the one evening a week when we drilled was the only time I was truly happy at school.

Regular GV members were still a common sight around the streets. I always saluted them and stood to attention until they had passed, but like all children I was half-afraid of them, knowing the playground stories about their weapons of torture, and so on. For me, the smart uniforms, the rifles, the neutral and disciplined faces, produced awe and admiration, not genuine fear.

The school is still there, its dark spire visible above the surrounding houses. I often see it when I have to drive through the area, but now it has become just a part of the background, a Victorian anachronism in prosperous suburbia. Otherwise the place has changed. Many new housing estates have been built, the roads are wider and better lit, there are electronics factories and shopping precincts and leisure centres. What used to be the USAF base is now an international airport. A

154

motorway runs through what was once the farmland a short walk away from our house.

When I was living there with my mother it was a dingier, grimmer place, full of disillusion, short of food, worn out and worn down by the war. The GV operated public transport, ran the auxiliary fire service, monitored elections, controlled the queues for food. And the physical environment was drab: the houses were shabby after six years' neglect, the roads were unmended, nothing worked properly and nothing could be repaired or replaced. Many brick walls still had the letters 'EWS' painted on them in large yellow letters, with an arrow pointing to the closest fire hydrant. The kerbstones were painted white, a wartime guide for traffic using the unlit roads. At the end of our street was the boarded-up concrete entrance to a public air raid shelter. Bomb-sites were found in almost every suburban avenue, the houses and shops blasted to ruin, their remaining walls and staircases shored up amidst the rubble. There were almost no distractions for someone of my age: the radio was full of adult talk, newspapers had no photographs, there was no television, very few people had cars, a holiday was time away from school.

And I sat at the centre, or so it seemed, surrounded by this bleak world, trapped in my mother's faded sitting-room, cut off from friends of my own age, very alone, powerless to resist her, listening to her mad and relentless stories, and clinging somehow to my own sanity.

There was only one possible refuge, and that was within.

One day, while my mother's voice droned around me, I realized that I was able to dream while I was awake.

It was like the moment when you recognize your own identity: the knowledge that you live, that you have lived, that it is all real. I knew suddenly that I could enter conscious

155

dreams, because I had been doing it all my life.

I can explain it now, looking back, but I could not then. It was a release, an escape, a search for essential privacy.

The only privacy I had was when I was asleep. Dreams were my sanctuary, but sleep-dreams were too unreliable, with their certainty of occurrence but their uncertainty of recollection.

I had a constant need for the oddness of dreams: the unexpected connections, the weird images, the seamless safety . . . but I also wanted to be able to enter and leave at will, hold the dreamworld intact and alive within my mind, a counterpoint to the real world.

I wanted all this *because I knew I could have it,* and I knew because I had always done it. It had grown in me and with me, my only talent. Somewhere in my childhood, without properly knowing what I was doing, I discovered that dream-images did not come from outside the mind, but were generated from within.

On the day I recognized all this I began training myself to produce then at will. All my life I had walked around with an instinctive pseudo-reality as alive to me as the external world itself, and as soon as I realized what I had been doing it was relatively easy to get it under control.

I knew the two worlds apart. One was of my own creation. The other was the one I had to share with everyone else, particularly with my mother who was at the front of everything. I never confused them, because I functioned adequately in them both.

How did it happen, and what did I do? There was no conscious method, although when I grew up and read books about the mind I learned that such phenomena were not unknown. When I read about self-hypnosis, and the summoning of pre-sleep hypnagogic imagery, I recognized that these were similar to what I had discovered for myself.

My dreamworld was at first childish, escapist. It began with my daydreaming about a general place, an idealized and improved version of the depressing suburb where we lived and of the countryside close by. The more I thought about this, and the better I could see it in my mind's eye, the easier it was to 'go' there. Because of past visits I already had most of this in my imagination, so when I wished to I could summon the dream in almost any idle moment: while sitting through a lesson at school, while pretending to listen to a radio programme, while I moved my eyes unseeingly across the pages of a book, and so on. Nor was it just when I was inactive. I could daydream while walking to school, while reluctantly following my mother around shops, or while playing with other children ... even while listening to my mother.

This last in particular. Once I had structured my entries to the dreamworld, it became the only true defence against her. I let her words drift unnoticed around me, circling meaninglessly while I wandered away in my mind.

And she never found out. The important thing, the overriding quality, was that I knew the difference between the fantasy and the everyday reality, and could sustain them separately and simultaneously. An hypnotic subject can open his eyes, talk, laugh, walk around, all without breaking the trance. So it was with me. I could exist on two levels of consciousness. I switched off, drifted away, but maintained an appearance of normality.

When I entered this place I was at last free to do whatever I wished. No one intruded, especially not my mother. I could think, say and do whatever I liked without fear of guidance or correction. It was therefore a happy place, aimless in its way, just a retreat from reality that no one else knew of or could enter. No one knew I went there, and I never told anyone about it. It was my only true secret, and it was the way I survived childhood with a mind of my own.

When I was actually there in my make-believe world the only things that mattered were the appearance and the feelings of the experience. But it is now more than thirty years in my past, and what interests me more is whether or not the experience was 'real'.

It did not survive into adulthood. When I was 16, and made my first conscious break with my mother, the dreamworld was replaced by the more immediate excitements that followed. I became unable to reenter the fantasy world. It's true that I sometimes hungered for it, but although I could *remember* it, I had somehow lost the mental key that opened the way.

I can still remember it vividly. My memories of these waking dreams are as strong as my memories of reality.

Yet the dreamworld was an unremarkable place. It began as a re-imagined version of the neighbourhood where we lived. All was familiar: places and streets I saw every day, or houses I had been into or patches of the local countryside I knew. In my version, though, the place was tidy, undamaged, free of the shabby after-effects of war.

Sometimes I would imagine the seaside, where I had been as a small child. Sometimes I went to great cities, still and beautiful. I learnt how to move around, discovering how to walk and run, or how to ride a bicycle. I went along empty lanes, past empty houses, across fields of lonely crops, or along deserted beaches where stark trees grew along the shore.

Sometimes I swam in silent seas.

I taught myself to fly. I could burrow into the soil, walk sideways on walls, grow tall, flatten myself like paper against the floor.

I hid.

(I also trudged to school, spent dismal winter evenings with my mother, fought with other boys, sat in classes, made and lost friends, went in for examinations, yearned for the freedom that was otherwise mine.)

Then hiding was no longer enough. I wanted to make something of the place I had found, and discover more about it. I began to explore, no longer content just to see, but to *see into*.

I chose to investigate one particular house, and went inside. There were people there, but they did not notice me. I watched them for a while, but I thought they were dull. They were static, silent, unreal, their bodies halted in the middle of mundane actions. I had mixed feelings about them: I resented them for being there in my private world, but they also made me curious. Why did they say and do nothing? What had they been doing before I arrived, and what would they do when I had left? Why could I stand in front of them without being seen?

I stayed away from the houses for the next few visits, because I was disappointed with the way I had created these people. It took me several more entries to the dreamworld before I realized that the solution was in my own hands.

When I next saw these people they were not confined to their house, and seemed to have lives of their own. I was scared of them, so instead I went to the seaside.

Here I rode on the giant wheel with my father, cuddling up against him while he snapped one photograph after the other, the cradle rocking excitingly in the breeze. We went round and round, ever faster, into the sky and down again. Frank stood alone at the bottom.

On another entry, feeling braver after I had been with my father, I went to visit the other people again. They still could not see me, so I followed them, listening to what they were saying and observing what they were doing. I heard their names. One of the men was named Hugh. One of the women was named Penelope. There was a dog, too, a mongrel called Alex who could perform little tricks.

I already knew them!

My mother's stories were taking life in my dreamworld!

During another entry I was sailing on a ship, when pirates suddenly attacked. In another, I saw silver-coloured disks hovering in the sky, and when they landed on bleak moorland I saw strange men in suits made of golden fibre. In another, I was in a shop that sold nothing but crockery. In another, the mongrel dog followed me wherever I went.

My mother's words droning in the background, her life infusing mine, her stories given shape in my mind. I could never escape her.

20

ALICE COLLECTED LIZZIE from Ramsford station, and after they had hugged and kissed excitedly they locked up Lizzie's overnight bag in the back of the car and went for a walk around the village.

Alice wanted to show off Ramsford to Lizzie, a kind of staking-out of sentimental territory. Almost none of her friends knew how she lived, and the simple pleasure of life in the village was something she badly wanted to share with someone else. But Ramsford was not a place for tourists. Its attractions were not obvious, and it lacked conventional prettiness. The shops and houses around the Market Place all had thatched roofs, but some of them had been built this century so the village did not have the picture-postcard look that a visitor might expect. Then there was a statue of King Alfred in the Market Place, but it was neither very large nor especially well executed, and Alfred had no particular historical connection with the village, so its presence was a minor mystery. The fact that it was there lent a certain eccentric charm, though.

Lizzie dutifully reacted to whatever Alice pointed out to her, but Alice sensed she was being polite rather than enthusiastic. She kept chatting away about what she had been doing and the people she had seen in London. After a few minutes Alice began to feel she had made a mistake. Lizzie probably wanted a rest after the train journey. She should have taken her straight to the house, and offered a walk later. She cut the planned route short, missing out the pleasant walk along the bank of the River Avon, and led the way back to the car.

But it was good to see Lizzie again, and hear her familiar laugh. She had put on weight since the last time they met, and her hair was shorter and curlier. She seemed very American in a way that was impossible to define; her clothes, perhaps, or her voice. The American sound to her voice was more obvious than it had been on the phone, adding to Alice's sense of disorientation, because they had grown up together.

'It's a beautiful village, Alice,' she said, as they sat down in the car. 'I bet you just love it.'

'It's home, that's all. Yes, I love my home.'

'I miss England.'

'Why don't you come back here to live?'

Lizzie laughed.

'They drove out of the village, climbing the gently sloping road that led out of Ramsford Vale towards the Downs. They caught up with a farm tractor, its rear wheels throwing small clods of mud high into the air. Alice slowed the car, followed for a short distance until she could see safely past it, then overtook. Because it was Saturday there was more traffic than usual on the road.

They approached Eleanor's house. Alice wanted to point it out to Lizzie, so she could tell her later about her new book, but as the house came into view Lizzie said, 'I saw Bill in London.'

Alice turned her face away in surprise, then had to jerk at the steering wheel to straighten the car.

'Was that OK? To see Bill, I mean?'

'I'm surprised. I didn't know you knew him.'

'I was at your wedding, Alice.'

'I know, but –'

But she had been there as one of Alice's own friends. She had flown back from the States specially to be there.

'I called your old number, trying to find you. I didn't know you and Bill had split up. I told you this on the phone.'

'You didn't tell me you'd seen him.'

'I didn't think it would matter. He was very friendly to me.'

'That's Bill,' Alice said.

Somehow during this exchange Alice had slowed the car, then negotiated the tricky right turn into the lane leading to her cottage. She hadn't been thinking about her driving, but must have gone through the motions because suddenly there was her house in front of them, Jimmy visible on the small lawn in front. When he saw the car he darted away around the side of the house.

Alice halted the car in the tiny drive, and switched off the engine. Lizzie was looking concerned and defensive.

'Have I done something wrong?'

'No . . . it's just that I didn't know you had been to see him.'

'When I called you up he answered the phone, and he invited me over. He told me straight away what had happened. But I thought he was just being polite. I couldn't see any harm.'

'It doesn't matter,' Alice said.

'It obviously does.'

'Did he tell you about us? Why we split up?'

'Some. I asked him, because you'd already told me. I wasn't there long. He was going out somewhere –'

'You went to see him *after* you called me?'

'I just said I did.' Lizzie had picked up her bag and was

groping deep inside it. 'There was some mail for you. Bill said he'd been meaning to send it on.' She pulled out a small bundle of envelopes, as if in proof. 'Some of it had been there quite a while, but he thought it wasn't important.'

Alice took the letters from her and held them loosely in her hand.

'Lizzie, I didn't want you to talk to Bill,' she said simply. 'Don't you understand why?'

'Yeah. Listen, he didn't say anything I shouldn't have heard. He hardly knew who I was. I was only there an hour, maybe two.'

'Then why –?'

Two hours to pick up mail? Alice glanced at the envelopes in her hand, flicked through them quickly. There was, as Bill had predicted, nothing important. She recognized three of the letters by their labels: one of the estate agents in Salisbury had a computer that was still sending her details of houses. A colourful window-envelope from a book club claimed that she was about to win £100,000, and a postcard from her old dentist reminded her she should make an appointment.

'I'm sorry, Alice. I guess I walked into something.'

'No, you didn't. It's just Bill.' She tried to make her voice sound light. 'He wanted to meet you in case you were unattached.'

'It was *nothing* like that.'

'It probably was, even if you didn't know it. Bill's always eager to meet new women.'

'Is that why you're angry? Because you think I went to bed with Bill?'

'No . . . and I'm not angry.' She tried to get Lizzie to look at her, but she had turned her head away, staring out at the hedge. Alice felt a helpless sense of despair, everything going

164

wrong from the start. 'Lizzie, you're the only one of my friends who wasn't around when Bill and I parted. All the others . . . well, they were caught in the crossfire.'

'You mean I'm the only one he didn't screw around with.'

'No, of course not . . .'

But it was that. She had never formed the actual thought before, but Lizzie had done it for her. When she found out that Bill had slept with two of her best friends, the sense of betrayal and humiliation was not only unbearable, but reached out to embrace everyone else. From that moment she had felt unable to trust anyone. Lizzie had been safely excluded from all that.

Alice stared miserably at her unwanted letters, still lying in her lap. How long would it be before the past was behind her? Permanently behind her? It was as if she lived here under sufferance, an illusion of a new life while everything she did was somehow influenced and judged by the context of the old days.

'Lizzie, I'm sorry,' she said. 'I didn't know what I was saying. Why don't we go inside? I'd like to show you round the house.'

Lizzie said, 'Bill was a real shit to you, wasn't he?'

'It was probably both of us.'

'No, I don't think it was. Listen, Alice, I never liked Bill. You know that? I didn't like Bill when I met him before the wedding, and I didn't like Bill *during* the wedding, and I didn't like Bill's friends, and I didn't like the things you told me about Bill in your letters . . . and I'm *glad* you've split up with him. OK?'

'Yes. I didn't know. Sorry.'

'Never mind.'

Lizzie opened her door and climbed out. Scooping up the

165

letters, and collecting her bag from the back seat, Alice followed.

Jimmy came into the house behind them. Lizzie made a fuss of him, and after a few moments of cautious hand-sniffing he responded affectionately. Alice filled the kettle to make some tea, then led Lizzie upstairs to the hastily prepared spare room.

Lizzie put down her bag, then went to the bathroom.

A long, unexplained silence followed the sound of the toilet flushing. Alice moved about noisily downstairs, getting out the cups and saucers and milk jug, pretending not to notice. When the tea things were ready she sat at the kitchen table, listening to the silence Lizzie was making.

At last she heard the bathroom door being opened, and the staircase creaking as Lizzie came downstairs. She was carrying a large envelope.

'I've brought some photographs.'

'Oh good . . . I was hoping you would!'

Lizzie took the chair from the other side of the table, and brought it round beside Alice's. They moved the teapot away, to make a bit of room, and Lizzie pulled out a thick wad of coloured snapshots. Alice put on her spectacles.

'You OK, Alice?'

'Yes. But I'm feeling pretty bad about all that.'

'Me too. It was crass of me to see Bill. I should have known.'

'Can we forget it?'

They spent the next hour companionably, sipping the tea, looking at the photos of Lizzie's children, her husband Rolf, their house, the two cars. Jimmy curled up heavily on Alice's lap, purring while she scratched his neck and ears. Lizzie talked non-stop, but Alice was happy to listen, fascinated by the glimpses of American life she saw in the pictures. Rolf was tall and shockheaded, and usually wore an amiable grin for the camera. He didn't seem to have changed much from the days when Lizzie and Alice knew him at university. The two children, seen at various stages of growing up, looked healthy and active. The house was white-painted, single-storeyed, vast by British standards. There were trees everywhere, smiling people, distant hills, large cars, big tables stacked with food. Alice could not help but contrast all this with her own life, but it made her feel closer to Lizzie, happy for her, wishing she had her own pictures to show.

When they had looked at all the snapshots, Alice led Lizzie around the house, showing off her tiny domain. The books and files she had removed from Eleanor's house were in great unmanageable heaps on the floor in her study, and they had to step around them ('I want to tell you about those later,' Alice said), but the rest of the cottage was cleaner and tidier than at any time since she moved in.

They returned to the kitchen and Alice brought out the quiche she had cooked the evening before. While they were eating, Lizzie told her more about living in the outer suburbs of Pittsburgh, the differences she had noticed when she went to live with Rolf, then how everything had changed when she became pregnant the first time. She had given up her job, but she was hoping to go back to it now both children were in school.

When they had washed up the dishes, and were drinking coffee, Lizzie said, 'Stonehenge is near here, isn't it?'

'Just a few miles away. Do you want to go?'

'I know this sounds weird, but I never saw it while I was living here. And Rolf would never forgive me if I didn't take back some photos. Would you mind?'

'Of course not . . . I love the place. But it's always full of Am –, I mean tourists.' Lizzie was grinning at her. 'Wouldn't you prefer to go to Avebury?'

'No, it's got to be Stonehenge. Surely it's not going to be busy at this time of year?'

'There's always someone there.'

Alice found her Ordnance Survey road atlas, and showed Lizzie where Stonehenge was in relation to the house. She also pointed out Avebury, roughly the same distance away, and in her opinion a much more interesting ancient site. But Lizzie wanted to go to Stonehenge, so she didn't push it.

They left straight away, because of the short daylight hours. Alice drove down the winding road towards Amesbury, passing the abandoned tank and artillery ranges, and the old Army camps. The clouds were low and grey, driven by a stiff wind from the south-west. A fine drizzle overlaid the countryside, softening the views of the modest slopes of Salisbury Plain, lying to either side.

They joined the main road. A short distance beyond Amesbury they breasted a hill and Stonehenge came into sight. Lizzie smiled.

'People back home said it would look smaller than I thought, and it does,' she said. 'But you were right about visitors.'

Several people could be seen around the stones, well wrapped up in anoraks and overcoats. Alice parked the car, and they walked past the souvenir shop and through the underpass to the stones themselves. Alice was able to get in free because she still belonged to the National Trust, so she shared the cost of Lizzie's ticket.

They spent twenty minutes at the monument while Lizzie took several photographs, but it was miserable out on the exposed Plain, the rain blowing into their faces, the cold wind

168

pressing their clothes against them. Within a few minutes one of Alice's ears was aching from the wind. She gamely followed Lizzie around while she tried to take pictures of the stones, but a guy-rope kept visitors at least thirty yards away from them. Sightseers arrived and left in a constant stream, heads turned away from the worst of the wind. Two resourceful Japanese walked in step, sharing a large sheet of transparent plastic as a windbreak. She heard a middle-aged couple speaking in German, and one of the children shouted something in Italian as she dashed past. Alice kept hoping to hear American accents, to vindicate her slip about tourists, but the only people who were obviously American were half a dozen US servicemen.

Lizzie was obviously disappointed that they could go nowhere near the stones, and after a slow circuit of the monument declared she had seen enough.

'What was this other place you mentioned?' she said as they hurried back to the car.

'Avebury. You must have heard of it.'

'I don't think so. I never did this kind of thing when I lived here.'

'It's a village with a stone circle around it. Want to see it?'

'Can we get up to the stones?'

'That's the whole idea,' Alice said.

The windows of the car steamed up as soon as they were inside. Alice took off her rain-soaked jacket and threw it on the back seat. She put on the heater, and for the first two miles drove one-handed, with the other cupped over her sore ear.

21

HALF AN HOUR after leaving Stonehenge they were in Avebury, still exposed to the blustering wind and rain, but sheltered from time to time when they moved through the deep earthworks that encircled the village, or passed in the lee of one of the great sarsens.

When the rain suddenly worsened they sheltered behind one of the largest standing stones, hands thrust deep into their pockets, scarves wrapped around their necks and ears. No one else was in sight.

Alice said, 'We can go to the pub if you like. It's just across there. Or there's a souvenir shop.'

'This is OK.' Lizzie's nose had turned bright pink. 'This is what I came back to England for, I guess. Lousy weather, muddy fields, old stones. Now I know I'm home.'

'It's all right in summer,' Alice said defensively.

'Yeah, I know. I'm only kidding.' She stared towards the misty horizon. 'It's so bleak here . . . I'd no idea there was still so much open space in England.'

'It's not as empty as it seems. Swindon's just a few miles away, below the Downs. At night you can see the glow of the streetlights from here. And Marlborough's only about five miles away.'

'Will you come visit us? We'd love to have you.'

Alice's ear was hurting again. 'Thanks . . . I wish I could say yes. But you know. I don't have much money these days.'

'You should get away from here.'

'I'm only just settling down! I don't want to move house again.'

'Yes, but the danger. All that.'

Alice stared at the muddy ground.

'All what?' she said.

'The fall-out. Don't pretend you don't know what I mean.'

'The worst is over now.'

Lizzie was pressing her back against the overhanging stone, but the wind was whipping around the side, blowing strands of hair across her face.

'Do you believe that?' she said.

'It must be. The accident was months ago.'

'Do you know what Rolf made me promise, when I said I wanted to visit with you?'

'What?'

'That I wouldn't stay longer than a day.'

'Lizzie, I don't want to talk about this. Not now.'

'I had to get a special permit from the US Government to come to England. They only let me have one because my parents are here. Most people aren't allowed to travel anywhere in England.'

'That's ridiculous,' Alice said, and moved out from the stone's shelter to give herself an excuse to turn away. The wind cut at her. 'I know the US protects its citizens, but that's going a bit far.'

'How many Americans have you seen recently?'

Alice was going to make a glib reply, then suddenly remembered the non-existent hordes of American tourists at Stonehenge.

'Oh, hell,' she said. Rainwater was dripping down the lee side of the sarsen, and daylight was fading fast. 'Come on, let's get out of the weather. I'm freezing to death.'

'Have you had a medical check-up lately?'

'I'll survive. We get used to the cold here.'

'You know what I'm talking about.'

'I started getting symptoms. Nothing much. A bit of diarrhoea, and I missed a couple of periods. Then I cut my hand, and it wouldn't heal up. I saw the doctor, and he said it was a bug. I said I thought it might be . . . you know, radiation poisoning. He said I was worrying too much, and prescribed me some iodine tablets.'

'Did you ask him for an examination?'

'Yes.'

'What did he say?'

'Come on, Lizzie!' Alice moved out from behind the shelter of the stone, and started across the field towards the pub. Lizzie caught up with her, and linked a hand into her arm.

'Well?'

'He wanted to put me on a waiting-list.'

'So you found another doctor?'

'It's not as easy as that. There's only one practice around here. What he said was that there had been a lot of people wanting check-ups, and he'd used up his budget. It's the system now. Doctors can only spend so much in a year. The only way I could avoid waiting was to pay to see a specialist. I just didn't have enough money for that. The doctor made me feel I was over-reacting, making a special case for myself. He said only a few other patients had been in about it. He was trying to make out that the majority of people weren't concerned.'

'Like all those other people on the waiting-list.'

'I know. You're right.'

Lizzie was making her feel stupid and ineffectual. It was

her own fault, she should have insisted on proper screening. But it was different when she went to the doctor, six weeks after the melt-down. Everything seemed to be getting better. Not at first, though, when there was the big scare, the terrible warnings and advice, the experts on the radio talking about what precautions people should take. If she'd gone to the doctor then – But within a few days it had begun to die down. Politicians made reassuring speeches, the wet summer was supposed to be washing it all away. News about Cap la Hague slipped further down the order of priorities. Other events took precedence in the news. Within two or three weeks of the accident it was barely mentioned anywhere. Life, as she had said to Gordon Sinclair, went on.

'Alice, I've been worried about you,' Lizzie said, squeezing her arm.

'I'm worried too.'

'Are you still having symptoms?'

'Yes.' Her voice sounded small, childlike.

'What are they?'

'Not much, if you take them one by one. I still suffer from diarrhoea, and I throw up sometimes. My periods are all over the place. Some of my hair fell out, but it grew again.'

'Have you lost weight?'

'A little . . . but that could be caused by all sorts of things.'

They had reached the edge of the field. Access to the road was through an old wooden kissing-gate. There was nowhere to walk except along the grassy verge. A truck went by, billowing muddy spray at them.

'You've got to get out of here, Alice. Move to somewhere else in England. Go back to London, or up north. Anywhere away from all this.'

'I'm all right,' Alice said, thinking how feeble it sounded,

173

but knowing it was the only thing she could say. 'I don't want to move. I like Ramsford, I like my house, I'm starting to meet people around here. And my next book is going to be about someone who lived in the village.'

'You used to say a writer can live anywhere.'

'Did I?'

They plodded on in silence, heads down against the wind. It was noisy when vehicles went by, and trying to talk against the noise and the cold wind was making Alice's bad gum hurt. Her ear was throbbing again. She always suffered in winter.

The pub was open, but when they went inside the bar was empty and they had to wait at the counter until a woman appeared from the back. She looked surprised to see them. Alice ordered two half-pints of lager, but cancelled hers when she noticed that coffee was available. They went to a polished oaken table next to the fireplace, and sat facing the fire, warming their hands.

They took it in turns to visit the toilet, but when Lizzie returned she said she was going outside again. Alice waited, sipping her coffee and feeling warmth spreading through her body.

When Lizzie came back she was carrying two newspapers, the *Daily Mirror* and the *Morning Herald*.

'Do you mind if I look through these?' she said. 'I miss the British newspapers.'

'Go ahead. I don't suppose they've changed much.'

'Has this been coming out long?' Lizzie said, indicating the *Herald*.

'A year or two. I don't read it'

Lizzie spread the papers on the table and scanned through them. She looked at most of the headlines, read one or two of the shorter items, skipped the business and sport sections,

174

then folded them up.

'Do you want these?' she said.

'No, I've got the *Independent* at home.'

'OK.' Lizzie pushed them to the centre of the table. 'Like you say, they haven't changed. Royalty and soap operas and sex. The *Herald's* not bad. A lot of foreign news, though.'

'Were you looking for something?'

'Just being curious.'

'They drove back to Alice's cottage through heavy rain. Lizzie went upstairs to change her clothes while Alice fed the cat, then the two women sat together in the warm kitchen while the chicken cooked slowly in the oven. Lizzie seemed tired and uncommunicative, even when Alice asked more questions about Rolf and the children. She wanted to watch the evening news on TV, but Alice explained about the old set breaking down. They listened to Radio 4.

Afterwards, Lizzie said, 'I can't understand why there's no news about the nuclear accident.'

'It was all over months ago.'

'That's what you keep saying. But it's still a big story in the US.'

Jimmy was asleep on the floor beside the cooker. Alice was peeling the potatoes.

'You'd better tell me,' she said.

'OK. I was just about to get a ticket to come over here when the accident happened. It was a major story in the US ... like Chernobyl, but bigger because it was France and Britain. It was the only thing they talked about on TV, and it was all over the papers. So Rolf got me to hold off on the trip for a while, until it was safer. I called my parents and they agreed. They're in Norwich, so it wasn't too bad there, but we all thought it was best just to hang on for a while until it settled

175

down. Then, like you said, it slowly started getting better. We heard they'd capped the leak and closed the reactor down. It got so it wasn't on the news all the time. There was some kind of political scandal in France, something to do with the Communist Party, and who had caused the accident. I didn't follow all that. Then my father called, said things were all right here and why didn't I make the trip anyway. Rolf said it was OK, and I still wanted to come, so I went ahead and booked a flight. I then found out all the stuff about needing a permit, but it didn't affect me too much so it didn't seem important. But after I'd got the ticket there was all that other news.'

Lizzie was interrupted by the cat leaping up on the table and standing in front of Alice, butting her face with his. She picked him up and placed him on her lap, stroking him. He turned around a few times before settling.

'Do you know what I'm talking about?' Lizzie said.

'No, but I'm interested. Go on.'

'The first thing that happened was that the Pentagon started pulling a lot of troops out of the bases in England. They said it was because of the background radiation levels. Did you hear about this?'

'No.'

'There was a political row again, this time about NATO. So in the end they sent a lot of the troops back.'

'When was this?'

'About six or eight weeks ago. Around the same time, we started hearing that the contamination was worse than anyone thought. The reactor in France wasn't an ordinary one, the sort they use for electricity. It was a breeder reactor, and when it went up it spilled a lot of plutonium. Last week they did a special on *60 Minutes* about this. They said

176

England had a lot of real hot-spots, and that people didn't know about them.'

Alice put down the potato-peeler amongst the scrapings, and looked down at the sleeping cat on her lap. She leaned forward, pressing her stomach against his warm back.

'Was this true?' she said.

'I think so.'

'What are you saying? Is this one of the hot-spots?'

'I don't know. They didn't identify places. But there's something else. I came over with Pan Am. A few minutes before we landed, the captain came on the public-address system, and gave us the usual information. You know, what the weather was going to be like in London, and all that. Then he read something out, which he said had been issued by the State Department. It was a warning not to travel in southern England. Hampshire, Wiltshire and Dorset were all specifically mentioned.'

'What am I going to do?' Alice felt helpless, scared, confused. She bent low over the cat, stroking him fiercely, making him purr. 'I'm stuck here. I've no money, I can't go back to London. And what about Jimmy?'

'Would you like to come visit us? We have a spare room. Could you afford the fare?'

'I don't think so. Anyway . . .'

Anyway, there was the cat, and the need to write a book, and to try to get her last book published. And now there was Tom.

They sat silently for a while. Alice finished preparing the potatoes, but she wasn't hungry.

'Would you like me to fix the rest of the vegetables?' Lizzie said.

Alice came out of her gloomy thoughts.

'No, you stay put,' she said. 'You're a guest. I like cooking for other people.'

'OK.'

Alice transferred Jimmy to Lizzie's lap, then went to the fridge and took out the courgettes in their sealed polythene bag. She held them up for Lizzie to see.

'You're not eating local food, in case you're wondering. These were imported from Italy.'

Lizzie grinned. 'I'm glad you told me. I didn't like to ask.'

'The chicken's from Germany. Tonight we have *das Geflügel*. I don't know where the potatoes are from.'

'So somebody does know something about what's going on.'

'We all do. What we don't know is if it's dangerous or not.'

Lizzie said, 'It's dangerous.'

'All right.'

Alice got to work on the courgettes, slicing them, then washing them in bottled water.

'When were you planning to go back to London, Lizzie?'

'Tomorrow some time. Whenever it suits you, really.'

'There's only one train tomorrow. After lunch.'

'OK. That's the one I'll get.'

'I was wondering . . . you wouldn't like to stay one more night, would you?'

She glanced back at Lizzie who feigned horror. It was a glimpse of the old Lizzie, who had rarely been serious for more than five minutes at a time.

'I shouldn't really. I promised Rolf.'

'You see,' Alice said, leaning over her cooking again. 'There's someone I'd like you to meet. I haven't had a chance to tell you yet, but I think I've got a new boyfriend. Well, a friend, really. I haven't known him long. He's calling in to see me. Tomorrow evening.'

178

'Alice, that's wonderful! You sure you want me hanging around?'

Alice knew she was reddening, and kept her face turned away.

'He won't be here long. I don't know him very well yet.'

'What's his name? What does he do?'

'He's called Tom, and he's another writer. But not like me. He's a political journalist, who writes for weekly magazines. He's working on a book at the moment.'

'Why are you blushing, Alice?'

'Because I'm a thirty-nine-year-old divorcée, and I find him very attractive.' She flashed a smile over her shoulder, then swept the courgettes into the pan. She began chopping the tomatoes and onions. 'What about it? Will you stay?'

'OK. Are you sure you wouldn't prefer to be on your own? When's he arriving? Just after you thought I'd be leaving?'

'I didn't plan it that way. We only arranged it a couple of days ago. He's visiting friends in Wales this weekend, and he's going to call in on his way back to London. You see, after what you've been talking about, I thought maybe he should hear it too. I don't think he knows about the American troops, for instance.'

'And I wouldn't be in the way?'

'I *told* you.'

Just then, Jimmy suddenly leapt down from Lizzie's lap, scratching her leg. He dashed into Alice's study. They both heard a noise outside the house.

'You expecting visitors?' Lizzie said, rubbing her leg.

'I don't think so.'

Someone rapped on the door.

'Maybe that's Tom now,' Lizzie said.

'It couldn't be.'

But Alice took off her apron, and ran her fingers quickly

179

through her hair. She switched on the outside light, and eased the door open.

Gordon Sinclair was standing there. The rain, illuminated by the house lights, drifted around him.

'Oh,' said Alice. 'Hello, Gordon.'

'I was going to ring you,' he said. 'But the phone's been disconnected at my mother's house. I wondered if you'd be free for dinner this evening?'

He smiled, trying to look appealing.

'Um, well . . . the thing is, I've someone staying with me. It's not –'

Feeling the cold draught from outside, seeing the rain, she had been instinctively inching the door open, conventional politeness overriding her more conscious wish to get rid of him.

Gordon stepped forward and peered in.

'So I see.'

'This is Lizzie. She's visiting from the USA.' To Lizzie she said, 'This is Gordon Sinclair.'

'Good evening,' Gordon said.

'Hello.'

'Would you like to stay and have a drink with us?' Alice said. 'But after that we'll be having supper.'

'Thank you.'

As he passed in front of her, Alice grimaced wildly to Lizzie from behind his back, a gesture of exaggerated despair. Her friend stood up, and shook hands politely.

'This is a pleasant surprise,' Gordon said. 'But since there are two of you, perhaps we could all go out for dinner?'

Alice closed the door against the rain, felt the warmth from the oven, saw the steam rising from the vegetable pan.

'It's almost ready,' she said, trying to keep a note of

resignation out of her voice. 'Why don't you stay and eat with us? There's plenty of food.'

'If you're sure I wouldn't be intruding.'

'No,' said Alice. 'Of course not.'

She went to her study to find a spare chair. When she returned Gordon was sitting in the one she had been using.

(Later, while Gordon was upstairs using the bathroom, Lizzie whispered, 'Why didn't you tell him to go away?' and Alice said, 'Because I couldn't think how to,' and Lizzie replied, 'You ought to come live in the US for a while, and learn to talk straight.')

22

AS SOON AS I arrived at the party I knew it was a
mistake to be there, but Gavin Rawnshaw spotted me
as I walked in, and I was trapped.

Rawnshaw was in fact the only reason I was there. He was
a rising young spin doctor, highly skilled and ambitious, who
at this time had been working for me for some eighteen
months. I had him earmarked to take over control of our
cable TV division, but for in-house structural reasons it could
not happen for a few months. Meanwhile, I was worried in
case he was head-hunted by one of our competitors.
(Rawnshaw later moved to Strasbourg, where he now heads
crisis strategy and damage limitation ethics for the European
Parliament.)

It turned out that apart from one or two people from the
office, there was no one I knew at the party. Rawnshaw's
friends appeared to be young and moneyed, with loud voices
and expensive cars. The men were opinionated young louts,
and the women were shrill and over-dressed and jealous of
each other.

Rawnshaw's house (or, as I later discovered it to be,
Rawnshaw's parents' house) was a Victorian mansion standing in its own grounds on the edge of an old mill town in the
part of Cheshire that nestles beneath the Pennine range. The

early stages of the party had been held in a marquee erected in the garden, but as the evening grew colder most of the guests drifted indoors. This had been my chance to slip away, but I somehow missed it and found myself the passive third party in a loud conversation between two men about a business deal. I felt prominent, ill at ease and different from the others, if only because they were all so much younger than me. Like everyone there I was drinking steadily, but my mind stayed chill and clear. I remained on the outside.

When I escaped at last from the conversation, I tried to get away, but Rawnshaw saw me in the hall and drew me back to the party. I took another drink, then wandered around the rooms, looking half-heartedly for a woman to pick up. I noticed one possibility.

Unlike the other women she seemed unattached to any particular male, but moved around from one group to another, chatting noisily, with much eye-contact and touching of hands. She was pretty, had long dark hair and looked available, reckless and sexy. She was also drunk. Her dress was made of thin material, and whenever she passed in front of a light I glimpsed the outline of her breasts. Once, when she bent forward to pick up a drink, I noticed that her panties could be seen through the flimsy fabric.

She saw me staring at her, but pretended not to notice.

Just as I was about to move over and talk to her I was buttonholed by one of Rawnshaw's friends. He was a parliamentary image adviser and gesture coach who had worked for us during a recent general election campaign. He also knew who I was, and was intent on letting me know. He rambled at me interminably, airing an old grievance. I saw the girl leaving the room. I did my best to get away from the man, but he cornered me and was obviously determined to pick a fight with me. When he began prodding his finger against my chest I brushed his hand aside angrily and pushed him away from me. He took a violent swing at me, and missed, but immediately we were scrapping and punching at each other. We were soon pulled apart, wheezing and cursing each other, red in the face, jackets half off our shoulders.

I got away from them all, and went to stand outside in the hall to calm down. I was too drunk to drive home, too full of resentment to return to the party.

I looked up the main staircase and noticed that very few lights were on in the upstairs rooms. Thinking that I could find somewhere to sit down by myself, and sober up in my own time, I went upstairs. Moving quietly, I opened one or two doors on the first landing, looking around. I stumbled against furniture in the dark, but I turned on none of the lights.

On the next floor I saw a narrow corridor leading off to one side. At the end of this I came to a second landing, where I found a small group of party guests, sprawling on the floor with bottles and glasses all around them. Two of the men lurched drunkenly to their feet, looking aggressive. I backed away into the corridor. There was one door leading off this, so I opened it and went through. I closed the door behind me.

The room had muted acoustics, indicating heavy curtains and carpets. It was hot and there was a pungent smell. From somewhere in the dark a woman said, 'Is that you, Gavin?'

She sounded extremely drunk, verging on hysteria.

'No,' I said, without identifying myself. 'I'm sorry . . . I didn't know there was anyone here.'

'Stay with me!'

I stood awkwardly by the door, not sure what to do. The room was totally dark.

'I need a drink!' the woman said. 'Do you have one?'

184

'Only this.' I held out my glass in the dark uselessly.

She came towards me, colliding with me. A bare arm rubbed against my hand. I smelt her, and recoiled. She found my hand and arm, and prised the glass away from me. I heard it click against her teeth.

'Whoareyou?' she said indistinctly, putting the glass down somewhere, but knocking it on its side. It must have rolled against the wall, because I heard it clink quietly.

'You don't know me,' I said. 'I came in the wrong door.'

'What's your name?'

'It doesn't matter.'

'What's your goddam name?'

'Peter Hamilton.'

'Do you wan' make love, Peter Hamilton?'

'You're drunk,' I said.

'So're you.' She grabbed my hand in the dark, gripping it tightly with her long fingernails sinking into me. She thrust my hand against the top part of her legs. I felt naked flesh, a prickle of hair. 'I don't have my clothes on,' she said.

I jerked my hand away and tried to find the door-handle: my eyes had adjusted to the gloom and I could see dim light around the door. The woman forced herself against me, pushing me back against the wall.

'Kiss me!' she said. 'Come on!'

I tried to move away from her, but she got her face up to mine and kissed me full on the mouth, forcing her tongue inside. She tasted vile, and I turned roughly away from her. Her skin was sticky and hot. No woman had ever disgusted me as much as she did.

'Leave me alone!' I shouted. I could still taste whatever it was, and I wanted to swill out my mouth.

She released me, and moved away. She said something so

quietly I could not hear what it was, but it was in a very different tone of voice. The drunken aggression had left her. Now she sounded subdued.

'What?'

'I said help me.'

'I'm leaving. Help yourself.'

'Hugh's dead. Help me . . . *Please!*'

I reached along the wall until I found a light switch. As light flooded into the room I turned to look at her. She was backing away from me, shaking her head in a confused way, dazzled by the sudden glare, her arms stretching out behind her.

It was the pretty girl I had seen downstairs, but she looked shockingly different.

She was not entirely naked, because she was still wearing her dress, but it had been cut or torn all down the front, and pulled back from her so that it now hung from one shoulder. She had no underclothes on. Her dark hair was a tangled mess, wet and matted. A leather belt was tied around her throat. Her eyes were dilated, staring madly around the room. Her mouth was drawn back in a ghastly inverted rictus, showing her teeth. Her face, hair and stomach were covered with thin streaks of blood, mixed with smears of yellow. I could see her chest heaving.

She retreated from me as far as the bed, then when the backs of her legs made contact she turned and threw herself face down on the top of the bed.

I said, 'What's going on? What the hell is happening?'

She started to shake and groan, clutching at the bed sheets and pulling herself in anguish across them.

A man lay stiffly on the floor at the side of the bed, face-up. He was naked, and he too was covered in blood and slime.

186

I stumbled across the room and stared down at him in horror. I knew he was dead. His face was turned to one side, and his jaw sagged open. A lumpy and disgusting pool of bloodied vomit lay thickly on the carpet beside him. His eyes were wide open, staring horribly. His penis was erect, and a trickle of semen ran down his stomach to the carpet.

I wiped my hands across my lips. They were sticky where she had kissed me. I wanted to throw up.

'What happened?' I shouted in panic. 'Is he dead? How did it happen? What did you do?'

She ignored my inane questions, and began letting out a terrible moaning noise, broken by violent and noisy intakes of air. Her face was turned towards me on the bed, her eyes unseeing. She writhed in the tangle of the bedding, then rolled on her back and screamed. It finally broke the spell of stupidity that had taken me.

I leant over her and slapped her face as hard as I could.

She shrieked, and curled up into a foetal position . . . but her breathing steadied. She began crying, a sustained wailing and sobbing.

Two young men rushed into the room. They looked in amazement at what was going on.

'Get an ambulance!' I shouted. 'There's been an accident!'

They paused a moment longer, then one of them hurried out of the room. The other lingered by the door, staring helplessly at me.

'Get out!' I yelled. 'Get help!'

The man left. I turned back to the girl on the bed. I touched her shoulder, and although at first she huddled more tightly, the wailing noise stopped.

I said, 'Calm down . . . calm down.'

She slumped, all resistance gone from her. I rolled her on

187

her back, then helped her sit up. She lolled forward, her head dangling.

'Hugh's dead, isn't he?' she said in a dull voice.

'Yes. How did it happen?'

'We were doing it. He was inside me, there was nothing wrong. Then his face seemed to burst open . . .'

'What caused it?'

'I don't know, don't know . . .' She looked at me with unfocused eyes. 'Who are you?' she said. 'Why are you here?'

· The bed was awash with his blood and vomit. She sat in the mess, her body greased with the debris of his death. I was overcome with disgust, felt myself starting to faint, and turned away from her. As I lurched towards the door, Gavin Rawnshaw appeared. Another man was behind him, taller, much older.

Rawnshaw grabbed my arm, and pulled me out into the corridor.

'The police are coming, Mr Sinclair. We've got to get you out of here.'

'All right,' I said.

'You weren't here, you saw nothing.'

'Right. OK. I'm leaving.'

I left the house and went to sit in my car. I was still too drunk to drive, so I closed my eyes and breathed deeply, trying to relax. I was aware of much activity around me, but I sat silently in the shadows. I must have dozed, because the next thing I knew was when I woke up some hours later. I was chilled through and my neck was cramped from lying at an awkward angle. The driveway, which had been crowded with cars when I arrived, was empty. The house showed no lights. I drove home.

I could not forget what I had seen in that room. Above all,

I could not forget the sight of that young woman. It seemed that only a few minutes had passed while the man downstairs picked a fight with me, but in that short time she had been transformed from a pretty young woman, lighthearted and gregarious, into the embodiment of depravity and wretchedness.

Both images of her stirred a deep response in me.

Three weeks later I was sitting at my desk in the office when the telephone rang. I picked it up and said, 'Yes.'

'Is that Peter Hamilton?' a woman's voice said.

'Yes. May I help you?'

There was a short silence, which should have warned me.

Then she said, very quietly and calmly, 'This is Alice Hazledine. I was the one at the party. In the room.'

I had been thinking about the report I was reading. Someone was waiting in reception to see me. I had another meeting in an hour's time. That evening I was due to have dinner with a chief under-secretary from the Home Office. I stared dumbly at the wall in front of me.

'Are you there?'

I said, 'What do you want?'

'Can I see you?'

I sat in silence, holding the telephone, looking at the papers on my desk. Then I hung up.

She called me at home that night. I had just returned from the dinner with the government official, feeling tired, a little drunk. Thoughts of her had dominated the evening. The first thing I heard when I picked up the receiver was, 'Please don't put down the phone again.'

I knew at once who it was, but I said, 'Who is this?'

'Alice Hazledine.'

189

I said coldly, suppressing a sudden surge of sexual excitement, 'How did you get my number? This is unlisted.'

'Gavin Rawnshaw gave it to me. He said it would be all right.' I said nothing. She added, 'I want to explain what happened that night.'

'I thought you had already.'

'No. There was more to it. It wasn't how it looked.'

'Everyone had been drinking too much,' I said. 'Including you, and me.'

'It wasn't that. I must see you again . . . when can it be? Just a few minutes. As long as it takes to explain.'

'I don't think that's possible.'

'I'll telephone you at work tomorrow.'

She was about to put down the phone, so I said, 'Don't come through the switchboard. I have a private line.'

I gave her the number of my desk phone, the one known only to Guy Lawley, Home Office officials and the staff in the Commissioners' office in Brussels.

What impressed me was her voice: it was low and pleasant, very calm and assured, unhysterical. It was impossible to reconcile this with what I had seen that night.

She called me shortly before lunchtime the next day. I had been obsessed with thoughts of her all morning, very aware that if she did not telephone me I could not get in touch with her except through Rawnshaw. She suggested meeting that evening in the centre of Manchester. We chose a busy public place, where we were unlikely to be noticed.

She was already waiting at the rendezvous when I arrived. I went past her without recognizing her, and she had to follow me to catch me up, touching me on the elbow.

What I saw when I turned came as another surprise. My mental image of her consisted of contrasts, the duality of her.

There was her drunken wretchedness in the foetid room, but behind that was the earlier sight I had of her: the party image, the light dress, the flirting and smiling and inadvertent revelations of her body. Since she called me I had deliberately suspended this intoxicating duality in my mind, the depraved and the innocent. Now, unexpectedly, I saw her in a third light.

She was wearing a navy-blue tailored business suit, with a demure cream-coloured blouse and silk scarf knotted at the throat. Her hair was combed back in a tight bun, but a feminine touch was added by a small coloured ribbon. She was carrying a leather attaché case. My office staff included several young career women who looked and dressed similarly. I always found their studied sexual neutrality irresistible and forbidding.

I had not expected Alice Hazledine to look like them.

It was a warm, dry evening, and we strolled slowly through the streets, mixing with the crowds of people heading home from work.

She would not say why she wanted to meet me, and did not give the explanation she had promised. We went through a lot of small-talk: I asked about her job, and she about mine. (She said she was an author; I lied about what I do.) She knew Gavin Rawnshaw through her husband.

I glanced at her hand, where she wore the ring.

She said, 'My husband's a bastard. That's why I was at the party. Are you married too?'

'No.'

'I don't sleep around,' she said. 'You've got the wrong idea about me.'

'You wanted me to make love to you that night.'

'Did I? I don't remember.'

191

She lived in a dormitory town several miles to the south of the city, and she had to cut our meeting short. I walked with her to Piccadilly Station, and, as she was about to board the waiting train, I said, 'Can't you stay a little longer?'

She shook her head. 'My husband's away at present, but I ought to be at home in case he telephones.'

'Why did you want to meet me this evening?'

'Because you saw me that night. I don't remember much about it now, just fragments. All I knew about you was that you were the man who came in after Hugh died. And that Gavin Rawnshaw worked for you. You didn't mean to but you helped straighten me out afterwards. One of the few things I remember is when you hit me. I saw the expression in your eyes, and afterwards I kept remembering that.

'I had to give evidence at the inquest, and I thought you'd be there too. I was counting on seeing you. Well, you weren't in court, but by then it didn't matter because the idea that you might have been was enough.'

'I'm sorry I hit you,' I said. 'I was trying to calm you down.'

'I needed it. But when you did, I realized you were as scared as I was. But I was frightened of what had just happened, and you were scared of *me*. That's true, isn't it?'

'No, I didn't know what else to do.'

'You were scared of me,' she said again. 'You're scared of all women. I discovered that when you hit me across the face. No man has ever hit me as hard as that. You get off on hitting women like me, don't you? There's real fear in you, Peter.' The train was about to leave. 'I have to go. I'll telephone you again.'

I said, 'Why don't I come back with you now?'

'To my house?'

'You said your husband's away.'

192

Down the platform the guard blew his whistle, and shouted a warning about the automatic doors.

'I don't think you're ready for it yet,' she said.

The train pulled out of the station a few seconds later. She had taken a seat by the window, and had a magazine on her lap. She turned the pages, and did not look up as the train moved away.

I continued to be obsessed with thoughts of Alice Hazledine in the days that followed. She now fitted three distinct stereotypes of female sexuality, and tempted me with a fourth. Each contradicted the others. I still could not reconcile the party girl with the wretched debauchee in the room, and neither would match with her crisp and daunting career woman image. Now she had exposed her knowledge of sexual fear, making me writhe with excitement and anticipation.

She telephoned me a week later, and this time she must have judged I was, in her terms, ready, because she willingly made a firm assignation. On the Saturday evening of that week she would come to my house alone. We prepared the encounter like two businessmen making an appointment, calmly agreeing what it was we each required and how it would be done. Her quiet voice was full of promises, and hidden threats.

Much to my fury I was summoned to Brussels for an urgent meeting, and in the short time I had I was unable to contact her. I flew to Brussels on the Friday morning, and did not return until the following week. I found a note from her in the pile of mail by the door.

It said: *I came but you were not here. I was wrong about you. This has to stop. The risks are too great. Alice Hazledine.*

Her handwriting was clear and confident, with large, well-shaped characters. She wrote her name in the same style, without making it look like a signature.

I did not hear from her again for nearly a month, and for the first two or three weeks I could not stop thinking about her. I was frustrated with myself for having broken the arrangement, but I was also disturbed by her cryptic note and her failure to contact me again. I saw it all as a shallow attempt to surround herself with intrigue.

She telephoned me at home one evening, when I had all but given up hope of hearing from her. She sounded breathless, and did not introduce herself. Because I was not expecting her to call me, and because her voice sounded different, I did not realize at first who it was.

She started the call by saying, 'I could come and see you now.'

'Who is this?'

'Alice. I could be there in twenty minutes.'

'What do you want?' I said.

'The same as before. How about you?'

'I thought you said I wasn't ready. And the note you left when I was away. What did you mean by the risks?'

'I don't remember that. I think I must have been upset because you weren't there. I have to see you.'

She arrived half an hour later. I heard a taxi driving away just before my doorbell rang. I hesitated before opening the door, but when I did she came in quickly, glancing behind her as if to see if anyone was watching. She was wearing her career woman's clothes.

I offered her something to drink, and while I was washing the glasses in the kitchen I could hear her moving around in the other room. When I returned she was sitting on my sofa with her legs tucked under her. She had slipped off her shoes, and her attaché case was on the floor beside her. I poured

194

her a whisky and soda, while she complimented me on my house. I answered her conventional questions: yes, I lived here alone, no, I wasn't lonely, and yes, I often had visitors. She drank the whisky in one. I offered her another, which she accepted, but she put it aside without touching it. She sat silently, staring into her lap. I waited for her to break the silence.

Eventually, I said, 'Why are you here, Alice?'

She shifted position, to pull the hem of her skirt lower down over her knees. 'I want to talk about Hugh, and how he died.'

'I thought the coroner's verdict was natural causes.'

'Yes. But the coroner was wrong. I killed him. I lied when I gave evidence. I said he had been complaining of chest pains. But it wasn't true, because I killed him.'

She was fingering the loose end of her silk scarf, rolling it to and fro between her fingertips, staring directly at me.

'How?' I said.

She picked up her glass, but did not drink from it. 'I don't know. I only know I did.'

'Then you're imagining it.'

'Have I imagined the others?'

'Which others?'

'The four other people I've killed.' She leaned towards me earnestly. 'Tell me something, honestly. Why do you think I'm here this evening?'

'You said it was to talk about Hugh.'

'What do you think is the real reason? Or, if you like, what do you *hope* is the real reason?'

'I assumed we would go to bed together,' I said.

'Then you will be the sixth to die. Listen to me. I was a virgin when I married my husband. I had my first affair with someone three years after we were married. Since then, I've

195

slept with four other people. I only ever slept with any of them once . . . because they died. All of them. Three of them died while we were actually in bed, one died an hour later, and another was dead within a week. The man you saw me with was the fifth.'

'Are you being serious?'

'Yes.'

'Are you lying?'

'No. I'm telling you what happens to people who have sex with me.' She loosened the scarf, slipped it from her neck and laid it on the sofa beside her. 'I said I thought you weren't ready. Do you understand what I meant?'

I turned away from her steady and disconcerting gaze, and reached for the bottle. I wanted to smile.

'How about it, Peter?' she said. 'Want to try? Is it worth the risk?'

When I looked back at her she was pulling at the slides which held her hair in place. She shook her head, loosening her hair.

'These five men. Who were they?'

'One was a woman. She was the one who lasted a week. None of them was anyone you would know. Except Hugh, perhaps. Did you know him?'

'No.'

'They were all people who looked at me the way you did, when you hit me. People who were scared of me. I'm always turned on by fear, and I don't care whether it's me who's frightened or the other person. The first one to die was just a boy. I hardly knew him. I met him somewhere, and he said he wanted his first sexual experience with an older woman. I was twenty-five at the time, and he amused me. I liked the way I could intimidate him. When we went to bed, he died of

196

fright before he had even entered me. The next one happened a couple of years later, and this time it was a man of my own age. We made love only once, I went home, and the next day I found out he had died the same night. The other three happened later.'

'What about your husband?'

She shook her head.

'Is this a joke?'

'I told you I was being serious.' She swung her legs to the floor, and stood up. She unzipped her skirt at the side, and let it fall to the floor. She was wearing a white slip underneath. She removed her jacket, folded it carefully and laid it across the back of the sofa. She sat down again, and resumed her position. 'What about it? Do you want to go to bed with me?'

'No.'

'Of course you do.'

'No, I'm certain.'

'Then why don't you tell me to stop what I'm doing?' She was undoing the buttons of her blouse, one by one.

'Stop what you're doing, and get out of my house.'

When the last button was undone, she hooked her hands together behind her head. The blouse fell open, revealing her bra.

'Stand up, Peter,' she said.

'Why?

'Do it.' I stood, and the moment I did she glanced at my crotch and grinned at me. 'You do want this, don't you? You've wanted it ever since the party, and you want it because I scare you. Here's your chance.'

I stared at her discarded skirt. She was right; she knew about me. Her face was flushed, her lips had a new gloss.

She moved her legs again, crossing one over the other, keeping her knee high so I could see along the inside of her thigh.

'How do you like to fuck?' she said. 'What are the rules?'

'No rules.' I sounded hoarse, and I cleared my throat.

'It's just people you don't know. Am I right? No rules, no limits, so long as you think you don't know the person.'

I said, 'So long as they don't know me.'

'Are you willing to die for this, Peter?'

She stood up suddenly, surprising me. She shrugged off the blouse, then pushed the slip down her legs. She was wearing a white bra and pants, both garments made of opaque material and fashioned for comfort, not sex-play. She had nylon tights on over her panties.

She stepped towards me, crossing one wrist over the other. She thrust them towards me.

'You know what to do. Get on with it!'

I removed my necktie and wound it around her wrists, attempting to constrain them, but she easily pulled free. She swivelled around so that her back was towards me. Again she pushed her crossed wrists towards me.

'Use your belt. Do it so I can't see how. Make it tight!'

I did as she said, and wrapped the belt around her wrists, crossing it twice before buckling it. She struggled briefly, and again got a hand free.

She knelt down on the floor crouching low so that her arms were raised high behind her. I tied the belt again this time winding it around her wrists in a figure of eight and connecting the buckle so that the metal clasp dug into her flesh.

I pulled her to her feet, dragged her tights off, then from behind I hooked a foot around her shins and pushed her to the floor. She fell heavily, and yelled.

'Cut it out! My shoulder . . . you hurt my shoulder!'

'Shut up!'

Before she could stand up I stamped my foot on her loose hair, wrenching her head around. She gasped, and her mouth was drawn back in pain, but she said nothing. I used the necktie to secure her ankles.

She said, 'You hate women, don't you?'

'Sometimes.'

'I thought you were frightened of women, but you *hate* them. You hate me.'

'Not yet.'

I left her trussed up on the carpet, then ran upstairs and took two more leather belts from my wardrobe. When I returned, Alice had managed to roll over on to her back, and was trying to crawl awkwardly towards her clothes. I pushed her over on her side, then dragged her across to the bottom of the iron staircase. I hauled her to her feet, then used one of the belts to tie her roughly to the banister.

I tried to use the second belt as a gag across her mouth, but she jerked her face to one side.

'Leave my mouth free, you bastard!'

I fastened it instead around her throat, as tightly as I dared, remembering what I had seen of her in that room where Hugh had died. I slapped her face, twice, three times. Her head fell forward, with her long dark hair hiding her face. I heard the noise she was making in her throat, so I went to the kitchen and found a sharp carving knife. I made sure she had seen it by lifting her hair with the blade, then placed it on the carpet before her, pointing at her. I took off all my clothes and folded them neatly while she watched.

I picked up the knife, stroked her bare stomach gently with

its flat side, then slipped the blade beneath the strap of her bra and cut through it. She turned her face away. When her breasts were bare I used the knife to cut away her panties.

I collected the rest of her clothes and took them to where she was.

'I hate these clothes,' I said. 'Why do you wear them?'

She said nothing, staring at me in horror as I began carefully cutting the clothes to shreds. I made sure she could never wear them again.

Perspiration was glossing Alice's forehead, and running down from her armpits.

She said, 'You'll die for this.'

'No, I won't. You were lying.'

'You saw what happened to Hugh. He did this. He tried to humiliate me. He was younger than you, healthier. He died. You saw it.'

'I know what I saw. I don't believe the rest.'

I went behind her on the stairs, and dragged her bonds down the vertical banisters, forcing her to sag at the knees. Her legs parted. I moved around in front of her and thrust my cock between her legs, sliding the tip over her natal cleft. She was moist. Her face was up against mine.

Whispering, she said, 'Push it in. Push it all the way. See what happens when you fuck me.'

'Not yet.'

I freed her from the staircase, then used the belt around her throat to drag her back to the sofa. She gasped, drawing breath with difficulty. Her face was red. I arranged her body so that she lay supine, with her head lolling backwards over the edge of the cushion. Crouching before her I moved my cock to her mouth, and teased the end of it across her lips. She flicked her tongue at me, and thrust her face forward as best she could, trying to take me inside. I pulled back from her.

'Get it in!'

Instead, I hit her again. I swung the flat of my hand violently against her face, thighs, breasts, buttocks, reddening the skin, making her cry with pain.

I moved back from her, to stare at her, to relish the sight of her at my mercy.

Then she said, 'I know who you are, Gordon Sinclair.'

'That's not my name!'

'I know everything about you. I know who you are, what you do, and I know why you do it.'

'Keep quiet, or I'll gag you!'

'They sent me to kill you. Fuck me and you die.'

I had warned her, so I gagged her with the belt. I pulled it as tightly as it would go, forcing her jaw open, the thong biting back into the flesh of her cheeks. Her eyes were wide with terror.

I released her ankles first, then her throat, then her arms. I left the gag in place. She rolled on her back, spread her legs, raised her arms above her head.

I said, 'Do you want me to stop?'

She grunted and shook her head, so I climbed on top of her and mounted her at last. When I had finished I removed the gag from her, and we did it again. She stayed with me all night, and in the morning I drove her back to her house.

I saw Alice Hazledine four more times before we tired of each other. As she had done on this first occasion, she always brought a change of clothes in her case. I did not die.

23

('I'M SORRY, ALICE,' Lizzie said, as they sat together on the edge of the bed in the spare room. 'I know I'm abandoning you, but I can't stay awake any longer. I've still got jetlag.'

'How do I get rid of him?' Alice whispered.

'Tell him you want to go to bed, and show him the door. If he doesn't take the hint, be rude to him.'

'I can't do that. He's Eleanor's son.'

'Who's Eleanor?'

'A friend of mine who was murdered. I'll tell you tomorrow.'

'He doesn't come on like the son of a friend.'

'I know,' Alice said. 'He's giving me the creeps.'

'You'll be OK. Be firm with him. Listen, if my light's still on when he's gone, come in and tell me about Eleanor. Who murdered her? Was it Gordon?'

'Sshh!')

Alice went to use the toilet, then returned to the kitchen. She found Gordon sitting at the table, a freshly-lit cigarette in his fingers. While she was upstairs he had moved the dinner plates and stacked them beside the sink. The coffee filter machine was gurgling.

'Did you start a fresh pot?' she said.

'I hope you don't mind. I drink a lot of coffee in the evenings.'

'I'm about to go to bed.'

'I'll leave as soon as I've drunk the coffee.'

'All right.'

Alice sat down opposite him, then stood up again to empty his saucerful of cigarette ends. She no longer possessed ashtrays. In the first zeal of being a non-smoker she had thrown them all away. Now the familiar old smell of smoke and dirty ashes was making her crave for a cigarette.

'I like Lizzie,' Gordon said. 'Have you known her a long time?'

'Many years. We were at school together.'

'That can't be such a long time,' he said.

Alice recoiled inwardly, but she said, 'It's more than twenty years.'

She added a few harmless facts about Lizzie, looking past him at the coffee machine. It had not finished filtering, but enough had trickled through to the pot, so she went over to it and poured two cups. She couldn't resist coffee when she smelt it brewing, although it always kept her awake if she drank it after nine o'clock. She put extra milk in her own cup, hoping it might somehow dilute the caffeine.

As she sat down again Gordon stubbed out his cigarette and immediately took another from the packet. Alice watched him tapping it on the table-top, then deftly applying the lighter-flame to it. He made her think of Bill when she first knew him. They had both been heavy smokers, and seemed to spend most evenings in a crowded club somewhere, sitting jammed at a table with all their friends, shouting above the music, drinking coffee sometimes or beer mostly, filling ashtrays. Those were her happy memories of Bill.

'I'd like to hear more about the books you write,' Gordon said.

203

Alice had been staring at the end of his cigarette.

'I didn't think you were interested,' she said.

'I am. Very interested. What are they about?'

'That's an awfully hard question to answer quickly.'

'Then take your time.'

She said, 'Gordon, I don't want to be rude . . . but I really would like to go to bed very soon.'

'While we're finishing this coffee. Just tell me briefly.'

(If you give me one of your cigarettes then you can stay as long as you wish.)

'I write about women, usually historical women. About their lives, what they made of themselves, and how they influenced other people.'

'What was the last book called?'

'The one I've just finished, or the last one I had published?'

'Either of them.'

'The one I just finished is called *Six Women*. It's about . . . well, it's about six women who were overshadowed by the men they were with.'

'When will it be published?'

She made a vague gesture, not wanting to go into all that. Not with Gordon.

'It's a bit complicated,' she said. 'I only finished it a couple of months ago, and these things take a while. It usually takes about a year before a book comes out.'

'What's next? Are you writing another?'

'Yes.'

'More historical women?'

'Just one this time.'

She felt an extraordinary sense of power, *because he did not know*. The book was going to be about Eleanor, and Eleanor was the real subject, the actual subject. But there was another subject too, a sub-text. Books had levels, explicit and implicit. No whole picture could be drawn of Eleanor without attempting to explain why she had never admitted to having this son.

Gordon, sitting here at her table, had to be the sub-text, buried in the text she intended to write, made implicit by Eleanor's secrecy, yet eventually to be revealed by the book.

And she realized then her duplicity. She was with Eleanor. Whatever Eleanor's reasons had been for rejecting this son, they would have to become hers too. Setting everything else aside, starting from the basic fact that she just did not *like* him, her text would have to reject or deny Gordon for the same reasons Eleanor herself had done so.

Eleanor had censored this man from her life. Alice's book could not avoid the fact of his existence, but when she was writing it she could distort what he had meant to his mother. Not because of what he was or what he had done, but because Eleanor had done the same.

While this was going through her mind she had been giving routine answers to more questions about her writing, but now he was getting interested in money. Alice had noticed that when anyone who wasn't a writer talked to someone who *was*, the subject always turned sooner or later to money.

She felt she must have explained how authors' royalties worked to everyone she had met in the last ten years.

'– so the writer gets a percentage of the cover price,' she said. 'It's not much . . . ten per cent, usually.'

'But doesn't the publisher pay a lump sum too?'

'An advance against the royalties. You have to sell all the copies covered by that before you get any more royalties.'

Gordon ground out his cigarette. (Alice thought: Tomorrow I could collect all his stubs and make a roll-up with them . . .)

205

'If you don't mind my asking, how big is this lump sum?'

'Not very,' she said, feeling uncomfortable. 'It varies from book to book.'

'Well, how much? Twenty pounds? Twenty thousand pounds?'

'There's no rule. It does vary a great deal.' He was staring at her expectantly, so against her better judgement she said, 'Well, for my last book I was paid five thousand pounds.'

(Actually, it had been £5,500, and very glad of it too, had she been. Damn Gordon! Why should she tell him this?)

Alice looked at her watch.

Gordon said, 'That's more than I thought it might be. The way some writers complain, you'd think they were paid in peanuts.'

'It took me a year to write that book.'

'Even so, it's a lot of money.'

'Could *you* live for a year on five thousand quid?'

'Not if you put it that way,' Gordon said.

'Is there another way of putting it?'

He shrugged, as if it didn't matter.

'Why don't you apply for a subsidy?' he said. 'I don't have much sympathy for writers who go around grousing about money.'

'Gordon, I hadn't even mentioned it until you asked!'

'Since I've known you, you've told me in at least three different ways how short of cash you are. The solution is a subsidy from the intervention fund. I happen to know something about this. The fund was set up for people like you. If you don't make use of it then it's your fault.'

'What fund is that?'

'The European Repository of Knowledge. Haven't you heard of it?'

'No.'

'For the last two years there's been a whole range of Common Market subsidies for writers. Why don't you know about them?'

'I've no idea.' Alice felt provoked, intrigued and defensive, all at once. 'I'm out of touch. I live in the country. I've been busy.'

'Don't you belong to any writers' organizations?'

'I used to be in the Society of Authors, but my membership lapsed.'

'You can get an application form from the public library or the post office.'

He looked officious and earnest, rather like a minor civil servant dealing with a recalcitrant member of the public. Alice thought: That's what he is! A bureaucrat, a functionary of some kind!

She knew him only as he had appeared to her, as Eleanor's son, but this was the most tenuous of links, implicit as it was in Eleanor's deceits. She had never really wondered about him, his own life outside Eleanor. She knew he wasn't married, but had he ever been? If so, did he have children somewhere? And what about his job? A civil servant was too easy. Maybe he managed a post office. Or was a caretaker at a school. Or ran a grants scheme for writers?

That didn't fit any better than the others.

He bored her, and she wanted him to leave.

'Well, do you want to know more about the subsidies?'

'Yes,' Alice said. 'Of course.'

'As it happens, they're indirectly connected with my job. I'm surprised you don't know about them. Someone like you would have no difficulty obtaining one.'

'I did try for a grant a few years ago. I didn't get

anywhere . . . and I've never heard of a grant that was anything like as much money as writers actually need.'

'These aren't grants, they're subsidies . . . and the money's good. How much do you say you need?'

'Are you serious about all this?' Alice said.

'Tell me about this last book of yours, and I can give you a rough idea what the subsidy for it would be. How long was it?'

He had taken a calculator the size of a credit card from his top pocket, and he laid it on the table. He lit another cigarette.

'It was about eighty-five thousand words, I think.'

'That's not what I meant. How many pages?'

'I can't remember.' Alice tried to visualize what the book had looked like in manuscript. That was the trouble with using a computer: the words were on the screen until the very end, and the manuscript was something you printed out to send to the publisher. 'About three hundred pages, I think.'

He pressed a few keys. 'Non-fiction?'

'Yes.'

'How many books had you written before this one?'

'Four.' (Three and a half, Alice thought, remembering the first one, which had been written with someone else and published by the university press in Bath.)

'And it was original?'

'Pardon?'

'No one had written it before. You made it all up yourself.'

'Yes, Gordon.' Alice fought down the temptation to throw a plate at his head. 'It was original.'

He did a few swift calculations, then said, 'You say you were paid five thousand pounds by the publisher. If you'd applied to the intervention fund, you'd have received more than three times that. About fifteen thousand one hundred pounds.'

Alice jolted with surprise, in spite of having prepared herself not to react to whatever the result might be.

'I could have got a grant for *that* much?'

'I keep telling you. It's a subsidy, not a grant.'

'What's the difference? It's all money.'

'You'd have to pay tax on it. That's part of the difference.' He put the calculator away. 'Another difference is that it's not an arbitrary amount: you calculate exactly how much it's worth before you send in the application form. It's the number of pages, scaled against the subject-matter, with an increment for the number of books you've written in the past. The library will have all the details.'

'I can't believe this! How could I have not known about it?'

But the last two years had been the worst of times, Bill and everything. Then the later feeling of self-imposed isolation, hiding away from old friends and other writers, with just the house and the cat and the need to get *Six Women* finished.

Fifteen thousand pounds. It seemed like a small fortune, even after tax: a surplus amount, free money. A trip to visit Lizzie in the USA, a better car . . . maybe even enough for a move back to the London area.

And she had the book about Eleanor to come. Could she qualify now for a subsidy for that, if she sent in an outline? Free from worries about money she could concentrate more on her writing and produce a better book. It was like a great easing of unnecessary pressure: she could easily expand to fill the extra space that having more money would allow.

'Gordon, I'm very glad you told me about this. Thank you.'

'My pleasure.' He stubbed out his cigarette and leant towards her across the table, putting out a hand in her direction. She moved her own hand away just in time.

'You seem to know a lot about all this,' she said, trying to sound chatty. 'Did you say this was your job?'

'No, it was set up through one of our associate companies,' he said vaguely. 'I had nothing to do with it.'

'What sort of job *do* you do?'

'Nothing very interesting. I run an office in Manchester.'

'What kind of office?' Alice could hear that her voice had taken on a false bantering note. 'What does it do?'

'Administration . . . that sort of thing.' He lit yet another cigarette.

Alice shook her head firmly. 'No that's not good enough! You've been asking me a lot of questions. Now it's my turn.'

She squirmed inwardly at the lightness of her voice, but it was difficult to break out of it once she had started. Why had Gordon suddenly become mysterious about his job in response to an innocent question? It intrigued her for that reason alone, but she was also thinking that any information she could get out of him might eventually come in handy when she was writing her book.

He inhaled smoke deeply, then expelled it in her general direction. He grinned, and again Alice sensed that beneath his awkward manner lay a sincere but ineptly expressed wish to be liked.

'I was asking about your writing because I thought the subsidy might be useful to you,' he said. 'But asking questions about me isn't allowed.'

'Why not? Is your job secret?'

'Not secret. Shall we say, sensitive?'

'Do you work for the Common Market?'

'Indirectly. Not exactly.'

'Do you or don't you?'

'I work for a private company that operates under contract to the European Commissioners.'

'All right. What does your company do?'

'I'm a sort of . . . media consultant.'

'You don't give anything away, do you, Gordon?'

'Why should I?'

'Why should I have told you what I earned from my last book?'

'There was a reason for that. I told you.'

'Come on, what does a media consultant do for the EC? And why is it sensitive?'

'You know I find you very attractive, Alice.' He stood up, pushing his chair so far back that it collided with the wall behind him, then moved around the table towards her side.

'The hell you do!'

'It's true. All evening I've been thinking –'

'Why won't you talk about your job?'

'Because it doesn't interest me, and you do.' He was next to her now, and his hand was resting on her arm. 'You're so distant from me, Alice. Why won't you let me –?'

'Gordon!' Alice moved back from him, but she was hemmed in by him. She pulled her arm away. 'Please don't!'

He stood over her for a few more seconds, but he seemed clumsy and uncertain, not at all threatening.

He said, 'I could get you some work to do. Editorial work. Would you be interested?'

'No. Thank you, but no.'

'It's extremely well paid.'

'I wouldn't have time. Gordon, please . . . I'd like to go to bed. It's time we said goodnight.'

'Alice –?' Bending towards her again he put his hand on the side of her neck, tried to lift her face towards his.

'No! I'm sorry!' She pushed him away fiercely. It was almost a relief that he had at last made an overt physical move. She brushed him aside, and stood up. 'Not that, Gordon. I mean it.'

He did not seem too disappointed by her response. He stood beside the chair she had been in, reached across the table to where he had left his cigarette smouldering, and picked it up. He drew on it, and where the paper had burned unevenly while the end was resting in the saucer a red flame briefly flared. A fragment of ash fell to the carpet.

'Alice, I know you feel uncomfortable with me. I don't want to rush you, but unless – Well, after this weekend I won't be coming to my mother's house any more. I'd like to think we might be able to see each other again. Would that be possible?'

'I don't know.'

'I often have to visit London. We could meet there . . . but if you didn't want to, it's no trouble to drive here.'

'I'm sorry, Gordon. It's not possible.' She had been thinking: At least I know how to deal with an unwanted proposition. But when it came to form the words it was as difficult as ever. 'I find you very interesting, and I'm grateful for the help you've given me, and the offer of work, and everything . . . and I'm especially grateful to you for letting me look through your mother's papers. But I don't want to . . . commit myself.'

'Is there someone else, Alice?'

'No. Not really. Since my marriage ended I've just wanted to live alone for a while, and not get involved with anyone.'

He said, 'You didn't say you had been married.'

'I'm divorced. So, you see –'

'All right. I understand.'

He left soon after that, apologizing to her for having embarrassed her, then stumbling on the step below the door, trying to make the best of an undignified exit. Alice would have felt sorry for him if he had been anyone else, but she'd had enough, enough.

She waited until she heard his car driving away, then she closed and locked the main door. She moved all the dirty crockery to the draining board, ready to be washed first thing in the morning. She left the plates and pans to soak overnight, then put down food for the cat.

Upstairs, no light showed beneath Lizzie's door. After a quick bath (lukewarm, because she had forgotten to turn on the immersion heater) she went to bed and turned out the light immediately.

She shouldn't have drunk coffee so late in the evening. She lay in the dark on a mild caffeine high, her thoughts circling. Common Market grants, radioactivity, Tom arriving the next day, Stonehenge and Avebury, a new approach to her book about Eleanor, Lizzie's photographs, Gordon's blundering advances, £15,000 . . .

She was still awake an hour or so later when she heard the cat-flap clicking to and fro. A few minutes later Jimmy jumped up gently on the bed beside her, purring and treading down a patch in the crook of her legs. He smelt of cat-food.

24

THE SECOND REBELLION against my mother came soon after my sixteenth birthday, when, in defiance of her wishes, I joined the Guard Volunteers.

Why should an introspective and lonely adolescent, living half in a world of fantasy, be drawn to the rough discipline and violent doings of a paramilitary law-enforcement corps? At the time, I neither asked the question nor saw the paradox. I simply wanted to do it and so I followed my instincts. I was far too young to see myself in any objective way, and the arbitrary nature of my dreamworld had created the mental habit of not questioning actions. Sometimes you have to do something to find out *why you are doing it.*

Adult hindsight suggests that the two might not be as different from each other as they seem.

My flights into the dreamworld began as escapism, but as I grew older the attraction was the power I had over events in the imagined world, and how this helped me relate to the real world. I used my experiences there to *reshape* what little I knew of life.

My time with the GV had much the same effect, although not at first, and not all at once.

The GV was a part-time civilian force which had come into being during the early years of the Second World War.

Several similar groups were formed at around the same time: the Home Guard, who relieved the regular Army of domestic defence duties, the Auxiliary Fire Service, the Air Raid Wardens, and so on. The GV was intended to supplement the police, and, unlike the other groups, it continued in existence for many years after the war had ended.

The GV was constitutionally similar to the police, in that it had civilian status and was funded by local authorities, but it operated under the ultimate control of the Ministry of Defence, rather than the Home Office. It had an independent command structure, extensive powers of search and arrest, and a different law-enforcement role from that of the police. For instance, GV members were all trained in the use of firearms, which in those days the police generally were not. The intention during the war had been to free the police from defence and air raid duties so that they could concentrate on civil and criminal matters. Dealing with looters was a major problem during the blitz, and the first GV operations took place in the cities which suffered the worst of the bombing.

Although this support role continued throughout the post-war period, at least in theory, many peacetime GV operations involved straightforward police work. The GV were most frequently called in for traffic duties at holiday weekends, crowd control at football matches, monitoring strikes and demonstrations, and so on.

I joined the GV only just in time. By the time I was 16, in 1959, recruitment had been cut back to a minimum. Out of my own group of about twenty-five applicants only three were admitted, and all of us had belonged to the GV cadet corps while still at school.

(During the time I was involved with the force the GV was gradually run down, its independence and responsibilities undermined by parliamentary committees, Ministry of Defence intervention and political rivalry between the M.o.D. and the Home Office. It was finally disbanded early in 1963, just before my twentieth birthday.) Because the GV was regionalized on a county basis, I joined the North Cheshire GV. Our area covered part of the Manchester suburbs, and a number of important industrial towns including Stockport, Birkenhead and Warrington.

My three and a half years in the GV were amongst the happiest of my life. They enabled me to grow up, to mix freely with people of my own age who shared my interests, to discover what I might be good at and what I wanted to do with the rest of my life and finally to move away from under my mother's influence. I found myself at last, I learnt something about the political world, developed a strong sense of self-discipline, and discovered what it meant to be part of an effective and highly trained team.

The GV, though, was only a part-time force. I bitterly regretted that I had joined too late for full-time service, and accordingly envied and admired the few regulars under whom I served. They were efficient and admirable men, motivated, disciplined and brave. I was always a very junior member, given the dullest assignments and lowliest tasks for most of my service. The pay, too, was negligible, part of a deliberate government policy of ensuring that the GV remained a part-time service. I had to get work at a local engineering company, and became a trainee clerk in their payroll office. Although I wore a cheap suit from a chain-store outfitters, and I was called 'Mr Sinclair' by everyone from the department head to the copy-typist, I was still in essence a schoolboy. I drifted through my days at work, half in and half out of my dreamworld, just as I had done at school.

216

I lived for the evenings and weekends.

Then I would hurry home from the office, put on the smart dark-green uniform, and report for duty at the local HQ. I never knew until we had been mustered where we would be sent or what we would be expected to do. I liked the rules, the barking orders from the NCOs, the constant emphasis on order and obedience, the knowledge that this was a job worth doing. The uniform gave me anonymity and a feeling of power. I was a dedicated Volunteer: reliable and committed, and willing to do whatever I was told, whether it was to stand guard-duty for hour after hour, or pace the city streets, or even sweep the barracks floor. Memory puts a gloss of excitement over this time.

In my last twelve months with the GV my work actually did become much more interesting, making my final discharge the harder to bear.

I was promoted at the end of my first year, then again at the end of the second. Promotion was nominal, a way of maintaining morale, and in theory my status as one of the last recruits (and thus, for ever, one of the most junior) meant that I could never really advance anywhere.

However, with the rank of VFC (Volunteer First Class) I became eligible for specialist training. I had to make repeated requests to my platoon leader before anything was done, but at last I was ordered to appear before a training board and was offered a few rather vague options. I selected crowd control from the uninspiring list, mainly because I had always enjoyed the physical rough-and-tumble (one of the things I was good at was breaking people's fingers when restraining them) and the sense of comradeship with my mates afterwards.

Crowd control turned out to be a wise choice, but not for

the reasons I had thought.

The country was going through a period of industrial turmoil, with many big companies virtually at the mercy of the union bosses. Strikes were no longer the weapon of last resort. Workers walked out of their jobs on what often seemed to be the flimsiest of pretexts, bringing production to a halt and in many cases having far-reaching effects on the wider economy. Political destabilization was behind it, of course. The unions were run by communists, seeking to bring about the downfall of authority by creating social instability and unrest.

The GV was routinely called out to keep such protest meetings and strike gatherings under control. I often took part in these actions, and teaching these workshy troublemakers a short and painful lesson was one of the duties I liked the most. But although the GV had the material means to control such rowdy events, it was obvious that to deal with the problem effectively we had to identity the ringleaders and obtain enough evidence against them to be able to prosecute.

New surveillance units were being set up throughout the GV divisions, and as part of my specialist training I was ordered to join the one being set up by the North Cheshire GV.

This was my first experience of information management, as it later became known.

After basic familiarization in surveillance and interception techniques I was given a 16mm Bell & Howell camera and taught how to use it. The camera was ex-Army equipment dating from the war years. It had a hand-wound clockwork motor and its spools held only 100′ of film, so by the standards of modern video camcorders, say, it was very primitive. Even so, I found it convenient and unobtrusive to use, and because it had a turret with three different focal-length lenses it was actually very versatile. I got the hang of it quickly, and with a bit of practice I was able to take some effective footage. I was soon in my element, quite content to leave the physical side of GV work to others and move quietly in the background, filming the ringleaders through the telephoto lens.

The camera framed the action, isolated it, focused the eye and concentrated the mind on selected moments. Seeing through the lens gave me a new insight into the way people behave. In the confusion of a rowdy demonstration, or in a running battle with the GV men, the real troublemakers blended with the others. When careful use of the camera removed them from their context, or part of it, and placed them centrally in the frame, they could be seen more clearly, and their actions could be better understood.

I learned how to anticipate events, where to position myself, how to turn the camera away quickly if I thought I was about to be spotted. I had an instinct for the work, and I knew the footage I obtained was valuable to my superiors. One short sequence that I filmed during a CND protest march was later sent to GV headquarters in London, where it was used in the training of other riot-control cameramen.

At the very end of my GV service, only a couple of months before I was discharged, I was sent on a more advanced course in surveillance work, this time to learn film editing.

Although I was at first disappointed to have the camera taken away from me, I soon discovered that editing film was even more rewarding.

I was taught how to select crucial shots from a mass of raw footage, and then how to assemble them so as to make what appeared to be a coherent piece. While I was actually

219

shooting the film it had seemed important only to take a clear shot of whatever it was that was going on. In this sense, film itself was a medium of record. Much footage is wasted, or repeats other shots, or by its own camera-imposed continuity seems to create a whole or meaningful sequence. This is of course misleading. No cameraman can capture everything that happens through a single lens.

It is the work of a film editor to convert raw footage from record into meaning.

He does this by selecting different shots, then joining them to other shots, and finally by carefully examining what he has brought together he produces what appears to other people to be one continuous and seamless sequence.

I became adept at this almost at once, and completed the test sequences in what the course instructor said was record time. When I returned to my unit I quickly applied the skills to the job in hand.

The GV was trying to prove that a certain union organizer in a local firm was behind a series of damaging strikes. When I looked at the footage we had already shot it struck me that we could prove this more quickly by using film from other contexts, and thus incriminate the man.

To prove my point I used a piece of old film that showed our suspect grinning at the camera. In fact I had shot the sequence myself: I'd caught the man in an off-guard moment when someone told a joke. But when I took this clip and joined it to another scene, one that showed one of our GV men being hit by a stone, not only did the man's grin seem callous, it made it appear as if *he* had thrown the stone.

This crude experiment, simple and effective, was a great success. I was given the use of an editing suite, and three more Volunteers were put in my charge so that we could construct

220

a library of useful film footage.

But we had been in operation only a few days when, almost without warning, the GV was disbanded. A general election was due, and our political masters were under attack from the left-wing press. The Guard Volunteer Force was sacrificed. Along with everyone else I was returned unwillingly and precipitately to full civilian life.

It was a major frustration to me, and left me once more unmotivated and inner-directed. While I had been in the GV, my dreamworld had receded, and I had at last started to integrate fully with the real world.

From being a miserably introverted boy I had grown into a successful and ambitious young man with a very clear idea of what I wished to do and how I intended to do it. Film editing had given me an outlet for talents that I had not known existed; everything that had happened to me in my life until then was given shape and meaning by surveillance work.

This was not mere vanity. On my last day on duty I was summoned to the office of our commandant, where he gave me a personal commendation for what I had achieved in such short time. He informed me that I had been singled out for further promotion, and that had the GV been allowed to continue I should certainly have moved quickly to the higher echelons.

However, this praise was academic. Like the commandant, I was once more a civilian by the same time the following day.

I had no idea what to do next. Many of my former GV buddies, feeling equally rejected, joined the armed forces or went into the police; a few of them went to work for private security firms, the first of which were just then starting up. None of these appealed to me. I felt I was different. Much as

I had enjoyed the routine law-enforcement work, those last two or three weeks had shown me what I really wanted to do.

I quit my job in the payroll office, and started to look for work in the communications industry. This was far from easy, because although in those days jobs were not hard to come by, like all ex-GV personnel I was forbidden from revealing my experience in the force.

To my potential employers I had to present myself as a youth of 20 who had left school at the age of 16, and had worked in a payroll office ever since but had a great deal of potential as a film editor. I was interviewed by Granada Television and the BBC, and then by an independent documentary film company, but all without success.

Casting my net wider I travelled to London in search of work, and here at last I was in luck. I landed a job as a junior trainee film editor with a small company who made television commercials. Although the job description sounded right, in practice my daily tasks were not much more interesting than those in the payroll office. I was sent on errands to film-processing laboratories, I made the tea, I typed invoices, and I sometimes answered the telephone. When at last I was given some film to edit, the material (an advertisement for a breakfast cereal) was so uninspired I barely knew what to do with it.

But it was all a beginning, and within a couple of years I had learnt the trade, and I transferred to another company as a film editor in my own right. A few years later I had advanced to the point where I won several industry awards, and was working for a major advertising agency in London.

I found in advertising the medium I had been seeking: the kind of campaigns I was best at created a fantasy world from elements of reality, heightened the fantasy to induce

222

uncertainty and discontent in the audience, then satisfied those negative feelings with the advertised product.

Advertising used all the techniques I had discovered in those early efforts with the GV. It narrowed the frame, it filtered out the confusions of context, it selected clear targets, it emphasized its message with telling images, it rearranged reality to heighten reality.

But advertising turned out to be yet another transition. I did not find an outlet for my real skills until, in the early seventies, I formed my own small information management company. With this I finally discovered what I had been aiming towards all my life, and as the company grew and our influence spread, I receded to the heart of it, absorbed in what I was doing, narrowing the frame, removing from context, heightening the fantasy, and in doing so fabricating a new reality.

25

ALICE WOKE UP to a delicious but momentarily unidentified smell, one that reminded her vaguely of childhood. She propped herself on her elbows and looked around for the cat, normally found on the end of the bed in the mornings. There was no sign of him.

She rolled out of bed, pulled her dressing-gown over her shoulders and sat looking groggily at the carpet, inexplicably thinking about sending off to buy a new ribbon for her computer printer, then at last identifying the smell as a mixture of fresh coffee and frying bacon. She went to the bathroom, peed, splashed water on her face and brushed her hair.

As she went downstairs she heard the tinny sound of pop music rising from her transistor radio.

Lizzie was at the kitchen sink, washing the dishes from last night's meal. The coffee filter machine was popping and growling in its familiar way, while bacon fried in the pan. Jimmy, munching at the brown sludge of his tinned food, looked up at Alice in surprise, then scuttled outside through the cat-flap.

Lizzie said, 'Hi!'

'Hello. Oh, you shouldn't have started the dishes. I was going to do them first thing.'

'I don't mind. I like doing them. Would you like a cup of coffee?'

'Yes, please. I suppose you have a dishwasher at home.'
Lizzie grinned at her.

'I hope you don't mind but I fed the cat,' she said. 'He heard me down here, so he came and rubbed my legs.'

'That's adultery, that is!' Alice tried to make it sound like a joke, but she actually felt a twinge of jealousy at the realization that Jimmy would accept food from someone else.

Lizzie made her sit at the table while she finished cooking breakfast. Alice used a Kleenex to clear a circle in the condensation on the window, and glanced outside. It was a blue, cold day, the trees and grass still spiky with frost. The sun was slanting down at a shallow angle through the branches on the other side of the road. The light was begging to be photographed, foreshadowing the sort of luminous day that would probably convince the most determined city-dweller of the joys of country living. In cities an icy morning like this was just chill and inconvenient, but here the light added a quality of new seeing, fresh discoveries.

Lizzie had cooked the bacon to a crisp, and Alice noticed she ate it with her fingers. When it proved impossible to use a fork – bits of bacon shattered on her plate – she did too. She wasn't sure whether or not she preferred it overcooked. It tasted better, but was harder to eat.

When they were sipping the coffee afterwards, Lizzie said, 'I was wondering if I could borrow your car for half an hour this morning?'

'Oh. Yes . . . but why?'

'Well, I'd like to take some photos of Ramsford. I should have taken them yesterday, while I had the chance.'

'I wouldn't mind coming with you.'

'If you don't mind . . . I'm not very good with a camera. I get self-conscious. I like going around on my own. You wouldn't be offended, would you?'

'No. But don't be long. I've so much I want to talk about, and we never seem to find the time.'

'Tell me about last night. Did Gordon get fresh?'

'I think he was about to try. I fought him off. What did you think of him?'

'Not my type, Alice. He's all yours.'

'Thanks. He did tell me one thing that's going to be useful. A grant I'm eligible for. I'm going to find out more about it tomorrow.' Lizzie was looking fairly blank. Alice added, 'I haven't had a chance to tell you what's been happening to me recently. Can I talk at you later, before Tom gets here?'

'Talk at me?'

'You know . . . aggressive stuff.'

'OK. Let me go take these pictures. It's so *pretty* out there today. I must have something to show Rolf . . . he's convinced this place is a radioactive desert. I won't be long.'

Fifteen minutes later, when Lizzie had driven away towards Ramsford, Alice washed up the breakfast dishes, put everything in the cupboards and tidied the room. She took a long hot bath, then shampooed and dried her hair. She dressed in jeans and a thick pullover, thinking that she and Lizzie could go for a walk after lunch, and be back in time for her to change into a blouse and skirt before Tom arrived.

While she sat in front of her mirror, despairing as usual of her face, she thought again about the European subsidy. If Gordon was right about the £15,000, then it was an undoubted bonus. But it so happened that £15,000 was roughly what she had been hoping to get from her American publisher. That advance, plus what Harriet had already paid for it, would be most of what she could expect to earn in the first twelve months . . . the two sums together producing a

226

reasonable income for a year's work.

So although the subsidy would be welcome, its real effect would be to top up her income to what it should have been in the first place.

On the other hand, if she had known about it three months ago she could have applied for it then and would be living on it now, instead of spending her way at alarming speed through the rest of the British publisher's advance.

If the subsidy was going to make any long-term difference to her, it would be as an income supplement, not as a replacement for real sales.

Alice walked into the spare room, looked through the window to see if Lizzie had brought back the car yet, then went downstairs to her study. During her long night of half-sleep, an intriguing fragment of memory had come back to her.

When Gordon mentioned the subsidy it had taken her genuinely by surprise, but as she tossed and turned in bed she realized that she had already been dimly aware of the intervention fund. She had read something about it in a newspaper, or heard about it on the radio . . . but the news had passed her by, like so much else, because it had never occurred to her that she might be affected.

More recently than that, though, Eleanor had been talking about the fund.

She found the cassettes at the bottom of one of the cardboard boxes she had brought back from Eleanor's house, and clattered them out of their cases. She had not bothered to number them and they looked identical. She slotted one into the tape machine and pressed the Play button. The machine started, then immediately stopped again. Alice turned the cassette over and tried again.

The tape started with a lot of background noise: banging and rustling and an inexplicable scraping noise. Then her own voice came on, far too loudly: 'Eleanor Hamilton, tape 2, side 1.' This crude attempt at identification was followed by more background noises, making the tape sound as if it was recorded in a room that was full of cars, collapsing furniture and people stamping around wearing large boots. It had been summertime when she recorded this, with the windows open. The simple microphone picked up all sounds indiscriminately. Alice had been straining to hear for several seconds before she realized that her own voice was part of the raucous background, asking Eleanor a question.

She wound the tape back to the beginning, turned up the volume, muted the treble tone, and tried again. She winced at the sound of her own voice, simultaneously so familiar and strange. Her intonation surprised her. She seemed to put emphasis on all the wrong words and syllables.

Eleanor's reply was clearer, presumably because the microphone had been pointing in her direction, but the noise made it difficult to follow everything. Eleanor sounded older than Alice remembered her. She kept clearing her throat, and at times her voice faltered so that some of what she said became inaudible.

But to hear her voice again brought Alice a vivid mental picture of her friend: the way she used to sit with a straight back and how she held her head, her iron-grey hair, still wavy and with flecks of dark brown, her fair skin and delicate hands. The comfortable room seemed to build itself around her, replacing Alice's last memory of the house when it had been cold and dark and about to be emptied.

In this part of the recording Eleanor was talking about her husband Martin, describing how he had suffered his first heart attack soon after they both retired. Alice listened, remembering the day this conversation had taken place, but also feeling as if she was listening to the answers for the first time. She believed she knew Eleanor rather better now than she had at the time.

Eleanor began talking about her feelings after Martin died, the loneliness, the difficulty of adjusting to life without him.

Alice's voice cut in with a question, lost in the crackle, and Eleanor replied, 'No, it was the first time I'd ever gone through anything like this.'

Alice hit the Stop button. She wound back the tape for a couple of seconds, then started it up again. When her voice cut in she leaned closer to the speaker on the machine and tried to hear what she had asked.

On the second attempt she heard, 'Had you ever been married before?'

'No,' said Eleanor, 'it was the first time . . .'

Why had she said this? What about her first husband, Peter? Her letter had described how she and Peter had married. Why did Eleanor say this?

Alice turned off the tape, and tried to make sense of it. Assuming that Eleanor had not deliberately lied to her, why should she deny she had been married before?

The context was ambiguous, though. Alice's question had asked if she had married before, but Eleanor had been talking about how Martin had died. Maybe she misheard the question, and meant that her first husband had not died, that they had been divorced.

Alice glanced at her wristwatch. Lizzie had been gone for more than an hour, and would surely be back soon.

She pressed Fast Forward and began halting the tape at random, to see if she could find what she was looking for.

It didn't appear to be on the first side, so she flipped the tape over and scanned through the second. Once or twice, as she listened in, she heard Eleanor laughing. She had liked Eleanor's laugh; it was deeper in tone than her voice, a knowing, sincere chuckle. Listening to her on the tape it was again difficult to credit that she was dead.

Alice felt her planned book changing again in her mind. She suddenly realized that it should not be an historical account, a testament to Eleanor. A biography was a *life*.

Halfway through the second side she jabbed at the Play button to hear Eleanor saying, '– imagine anything so silly?' She laughed.

Alice rewound the tape and listened closely.

Eleanor said, 'I've been thinking of writing my memoirs. Do you suppose anyone would want to publish them?' (In the background, somewhere in the noise, Alice heard herself saying yes in an emphatic way.) 'I'm not worried about being published. I've lost that urge. I suppose the money might be useful . . . but these days you don't even need a publisher to make a living out of writing. I'd be able to get one of those Common Market intervention grants, wouldn't I? Can you imagine anything so silly?'

She laughed, and it wasn't her sociable chuckle. This was higher pitched, more of a giggle. She thought the grant was ridiculous, and this was her response.

(And in the background Alice could hear herself laughing too, although she supposed that when she laughed she did not really know why. Nor did she now.) Alice put away the tapes, first numbering them both, and writing 'Death of Martin' and 'grant' on the labels on each side of the tape she had listened to. After going to the front of the house to see if there was any sign of Lizzie, she went back to her office and picked up

230

one of Eleanor's novels. She sat at her desk and began reading.

A few minutes later she heard her car stopping outside the house, but when she looked she saw Lizzie had gone across to the other side of the lane and was now photographing the house from the elevation of the grassy bank.

Alice went out to join her.

'How did you get on?'

'Alice, it's lovely here. I'm sorry I was gone so long. I drove down into Ramsford Vale, nearly as far as Devizes. I used up two whole films!'

'There's some coffee ready.'

'Great . . . but go stand by the house. I want a picture of you.'

Their breath was making thin white veils of condensation, drifting around them in the windless air. Alice picked up the exuberant feeling from Lizzie and posed happily while her friend took a few more photographs. Lizzie kept apologizing for her slowness in framing the shots and getting them into focus. Alice didn't mind and said so, thinking suddenly how everything seemed to be all right, and was turning out in her favour. Jimmy emerged from beneath a hedge, and sat in the middle of the lane, watching them.

When Lizzie had finished, Alice picked up the cat and hugged him to her.

'Come on, Lizzie. I'm starting to feel cold.'

'OK . . . I want just one more. I'll be right in.'

Carrying the cat in her arms, Alice went into the kitchen and poured two mugfuls of coffee. Lizzie followed shortly, her face pink and beaming.

'I'm going to tell Rolf he's got to find a job here in England.' Lizzie stripped off her quilted jacket and hung it on one of the hooks on the back of the door. 'I didn't realize how much

I've been missing the place.'

'Days like this are the best of it. The worst was yesterday.'

'We can't change the weather. I know.'

'Do you think Rolf would want to move back to England? I mean, really want to? And what about your children?'

Lizzie looked serious. 'That's something else. I don't know. Rolf's job pays well . . . I guess he earns about twice what he could hope to get here. And the kids have friends, they're starting school. And there's the radiation. I don't think I should bring them to this.'

Alice said, 'But you've spent most of the morning driving around in it!'

'All right . . . it's not logical. But just because you can't see it doesn't mean it's harmless.'

'I know. Look, don't start on me again. I feel a lot better today. We can talk to Tom about it this evening, if we must.' Lizzie looked regretful, so Alice said, 'Can I tell you about my book now? I'm dying to talk to you about it.'

'Is this where you talk at me?'

'Yes.'

'All right.'

'Are you sure? There's an awful lot I have to tell you.'

Lizzie grinned at her, so Alice went to her study to find the copy of the novel by Eleanor she had been reading while waiting for Lizzie. It was on the desk where she had left it. She stood there for a moment with the book in her hand, trying to organize her thoughts.

What was it she actually wanted to tell Lizzie? About Eleanor, or about her death, or about the biography she planned to write? They were all mixed up together in her mind, as yet unscrambled from the momentum of everything happening.

But she knew exactly why she wanted to talk. When she was writing, or planning to write, she liked to talk out her ideas. It was her way of discovering how to think. It wasn't an inner need to show off, or to get other people to contribute ideas, although she had sometimes supposed that these might inadvertently come into it. The real reason was that she always felt trapped by ideas. They lacked shape. To talk about a book helped her assemble it verbally, and give it structure.

Over the years the need to talk about her books had become a part of her working method. Bill had never been any good at that. He was the worst kind of listener, with his bored expression, restless movements, and the grudging questions at the end that revealed he hadn't taken in more than a few words. So her friends had been drafted, and some had learnt how to humour her.

Living alone in the village had isolated her from this, especially now that Eleanor was no longer around. In her heart of hearts, Alice knew that she had earmarked Eleanor as her working audience. Selfish, yes, and perhaps even ruthless, but she knew it was vital to her.

And she knew she had now virtually press-ganged poor Lizzie into the role.

When Alice returned to the kitchen with her notes, Lizzie said she wanted to use the bathroom before they started, so while she was upstairs Alice took some cooked meat and salad vegetables from the fridge, and put them on the table within easy reach. She opened her last bottle of wine. When Lizzie returned, Alice made her sit in the only armchair, then turned one of the hard kitchen chairs to face her.

'OK,' she said. 'You're being buttonholed. Do you mind?'

'Do I have a choice?'

'No, but do you mind?'

'I want to hear this. Truly! What do I have to do?'

'Listen for as long as you can. Kick me or throw something at me if you get bored.'

'Can I interrupt with questions?' Lizzie said.

'Say anything you like. Something's going on, you're the only person I can tell, and you *must* listen!'

'All right. I'm ready.' Lizzie pretended to shrink back defensively into her chair, then went to the table and poured them both some wine.

Needing no further encouragement, Alice launched herself straight in and started talking. At first it came in no particular order: her missing manuscript, then the news about Eleanor's death, the introduction to Tom Davie, the arrival of Gordon Sinclair, going through the files, and the letter from Eleanor, the children's books.

('Was Gor*don* the *Don*ny of the novels?' Alice scribbled on her pad.)

Now the interesting contradiction about Eleanor's first marriage ('CHECK THIS: does Eleanor's letter actually *say* that she and Peter got married?') and what seemed to be a denial when Alice had asked her outright. ('Does the letter say she and Peter divorced, or does it say that Peter died?')

Someone broke into her house, and it was something to do with her computer disks, she told Lizzie (but she wrote in her notebook: 'Was this actually somehow connected with ELEANOR'S DEATH?').

Lizzie said, 'Was this after you met Gordon?'

'Yes.'

(Alice wrote: 'Compile a DIARY of the events as they happened, before I forget what order they came in.')

Gordon had turned up in the village less than twenty-four

hours after Eleanor's death. This was a mystery, because no one in the village knew about him, and Eleanor had never mentioned him and perhaps even denied he existed.

('Play the TAPES through, transcribe them. Is Gordon mentioned anywhere? Or anyhow? Does Eleanor at any point actually DENY having had CHILDREN?')

Yet someone, presumably the police, must have known about him to tell him the news, because he had turned up a few hours after her body was discovered.

'When did you find out?' Lizzie said.

'The day she was murdered. No, the day they found her body.'

('How long was it before Eleanor's body was DISCOVERED?')

Then there was Eleanor herself, and why she was someone she wanted to write a book about. This interest was not connected with the dramatic way she had died.

('A Dramatic Way To Have Lived' Alice wrote down, but then she immediately crossed it out again.)

She began to describe Eleanor to Lizzie, recalling the first time they had met, and the impression she had made at the time. As she spoke, Alice realized that this must be the true beginning of any book she might write. The formal facts about Eleanor could emerge as and when they were needed, but to give the biography its structure she must tell it autobiographically, or at least begin it in that way. Her personal knowledge of Eleanor came at the end, in the weeks just before she died.

(She wrote down: 'Tell it from the end.')

It was after all her book, and a first-person narrative would give it shape; everything in Eleanor's story would fit naturally.

(She added: 'Explain how I met her; explain how she lived; explain how we talked; explain MYSELF and thus explain

235

Alice knew she was talking too much, leaving bits out, leaping from one subject to another, letting sentences hang unfinished while she scribbled her notes. But the chemistry was working for her, because the more she spoke about the book the more enthusiastic about it she felt. Several times she had to go back on her impromptu narrative, contradict or correct herself, then pause while she made another note.

Lizzie sat patiently through it all, maintaining what at least appeared to be an expression of great interest, but a calmer part of her mind told Alice that the poor woman had suffered enough. To finish as soon as possible, Alice went to her study and came back with two or three of Eleanor's children's books, and thrust them into Lizzie's hands.

Then she realized that she could not remember what point she had been meaning to make with them. While Lizzie stared in a bemused way at the books, Alice began to giggle.

'That's it,' she said. 'I think I've finished!'

'OK.' Lizzie looked wry, and put the books on the floor beside her. 'Is that how the book's going to end?'

'No . . . I've run out of things to say. What do you think?'

'I think you've got to write it all down, and make it into a book.'

'I will, I will. But do you think I ought to? Is it good enough?'

'I just said so.'

'I've been boring you!'

'No, honestly. It was fascinating.'

'Oh, shit!' Alice said, with all the energy suddenly discharged from her. The house seemed very silent now she had stopped speaking, and it made her realize just how much talking she had been doing for the past hour. Lizzie had seemed to be interested, had seemed to ask the right

236

questions, had seemed to be encouraging her to keep going . . . but now she was yawning, trying not to show it, keeping her jaw steady. Alice remembered how she had practically brow-beaten her at the beginning. 'I'm sorry. I should have stopped ages ago! I can't imagine what all that must have sounded like. But I had to tell you.'

'It's OK, Alice.'

'I feel ridiculous now,' she said.

She really did, and to cover her embarrassment she went across the room to fill the kettle for tea.

'You weren't boring me,' Lizzie said. 'It's just that I'm not sure I followed it all.'

Alice filled the electric kettle from the bottle of water, then plugged it in. She stood over it, glaring down at it. It wasn't as if Lizzie had even *asked* about the damned book!

But then, through the withdrawal feelings, a bright thought: It had helped. Talking about the book had made it take shape. She knew, if not how to write the whole thing, at least how to begin.

On an impulse she pulled the plug from the kettle before it boiled, and said, 'Would you prefer to go out for a drink, Lizzie?'

'Yes. What about you?'

'I'd like one. There's a pub down the lane. Let's go there now, come back here and eat the rest of this food, and this afternoon we'll go for a walk. Then I want to change before Tom arrives.'

Lizzie was grinning. 'Do you always structure your days so exactly?'

26

I FOLLOWED HER car through Ramsford, then out of the village and down the main road towards Devizes. A couple of miles outside the village she turned right along a narrow side road leading towards the steep hills of Marlborough Downs. I continued to follow, hanging well back so that she would not notice me.

When she reached the crest of the Downs and started across the bleak, undulating moor, I let her put even more distance between us. In this remote area there were very few other cars using the roads, and I would rather lose track of her than have her realize I was following.

After another mile or two she turned on to a wider road. When I reached the junction and drove after her, I saw the road sign and realized that this must have been the stretch of countryside where my car had broken down in the night and I had seen the black cylinders.

I drove more slowly, trying to orient myself. Of course, the whole area looked completely different in daylight, but I felt certain the circular impressions in the ground must still be visible. I had temporarily lost my bearings, and wasn't sure if I was heading in the same direction as I had been that night, so as I drove along I looked at the landscape on both sides of the road, hoping to see some trace of that terrifying event. I was not paying attention to what I was doing, and so I did not notice her car slow down.

I was almost abreast of her before I realized she had stopped, and the door on the driver's side was opening as I went past. I moved a hand up to hide my face, and accelerated, but rather to my surprise I realized it was not Alice who had been driving the car, but her friend from America.

I drove on, using the rear-view mirror as long as possible, just in case Alice had been travelling unnoticed in one of the passenger seats. But I saw that the friend, Lizzie, was by herself. She was leaning against the car, resting her elbows on the roof to steady a camera. As my car went over the brow of a hill, and I lost sight of her, she was turning around to take a photograph in the other direction.

I followed the winding road down into Ramsford Vale again. When I came to the next village, I saw a pub with a large car park so I drove in and switched off the engine. On the off-chance that there might be a cell sub-station somewhere close at hand I turned on the terminal, and was surprised when the acquisition came through. I used the directional aerial to get the best signal, and a few moments later I was logged on to my computer in the office.

I first checked to see if there were any messages for me, and when I had downloaded these I hooked into the evaluation computer that interfaced with the datanet.

Because of my immunity under Data Protection legislation I had access to all areas of the datanet. Nothing was closed to me. The datanet was the basis of all our work, and we referred to it constantly.

I accessed Alice Stockton's file, but during the week I had ordered a complete update and unless my staff had been working over the weekend this would not be ready for a few more days. Sure enough, Alice's file consisted only of header and identity data, which was all that was normally left in place while an update was in progress.

I ran a search from this file's headers for Lizzie Humbert, without much hope of success, and duly found nothing.

I tried again, using 'liz' and 'lis' as the criteria, and was immediately referred to Epping Forest Educational Authority. I dumped the Stockton file, and accessed the new one.

This time I used 'liz' and 'alice' as the criteria, and was given a list of seventeen schools within the educational authority's area, all of which had pupils with both names or variations of the names. I narrowed the search to 'alice stockton' and 'liz', and the result was Chingford Grammar School for the years 1966-1970.

Her name was Elizabeth Julia Thaw. She began attending Chingford Grammar in 1966, when her parents moved into the area. With four A levels she gained entry to Bath University (local authority grant £1,100), where she eventually gained a degree in social sciences in 1974. Married Rolf A. Humbert (US citizen) in 1975, and emigrated to the USA in the same year. No further entries. I deleted her from the record.

27

TOM ARRIVED JUST before six-thirty, apologizing for being late, looking tired after driving from Wales, and bringing two bottles of wine and a rather bedraggled bunch of freesias. He hurriedly dumped everything on her kitchen table, then put his arms around her and kissed her. Alice put up token resistance, thinking she should, but five minutes later they were upstairs in her bed together.

(During an interval, Tom said, 'I didn't mean to leap on you as soon as I arrived,' and Alice said, 'I didn't mean to let you.' But they did it again soon after.)

Time passed. By nine o'clock they were downstairs again, and because they were ravenous for food and didn't want to wait while something cooked, Tom drove into Ramsford and brought back some fish and chips. They ate these with some rather stale French bread, and left-over salad.

When they had finished eating, Tom said, 'By the way, I've brought you that material about Eleanor Hamilton. It's in my bag.'

It was on the floor beside her so Alice passed it over to him. Tom pulled out a thin card folder containing several sheets of paper.

'There's not much,' he said. 'A few letters she wrote to CND, and some newspaper cuttings. There are probably copies of the letters in the files you have, but the cuttings might be useful. One's a profile from the *Observer* about two years ago.'

Alice took the folder from him. The profile was the first sheet. There were about four half-columns of newspaper text, with a small head-and-shoulders photograph. The headline said: *The Quiet Campaigner,* and Eleanor's name had been printed under the photograph.

While Alice was skimming through it, Tom said, 'She'd been in the news that week. You'll see in some of the other cuttings. She was arrested several times for blocking the entrance to one of the US bases. She'd turn up on her own and sit in the road until they moved her on. Apparently she had quite a job getting them to arrest her. They kept moving her away but she went back again and again until they were forced to charge her. One of the newspapers picked up the story and the others followed. There's a lot of duplication in the file.'

Alice glanced through the rest of the cuttings, reading quickly enough to get sense from them but thinking she would have to go through them properly later.

'The most interesting piece is at the bottom.'

Alice slipped it out. It appeared to be a photocopy of a photocopy of a carbon-copy, a mass of blurred single-spaced typewritten text, with a few almost indecipherable notes in the margin. A few passages had been circled, apparently by the person who had written the notes.

'What is it?'

'A Home Office internal memorandum. I found it in a pile of other material. CND receives a lot of leaked papers, and that was among a batch from about six months ago.'

It was more biographical material about Eleanor, but

242

written with a nastily suspicious and accusing tone. Again, Alice skimmed through it, but read the emphasized passages. One said: 'It is known that she is in possession of restricted copyright material, and that the usual steps could be taken to retrieve this.'

The handwritten marginal note said: *Too public now.*

'Is this genuine?' Alice said.

'Sort of.' When Alice frowned, he said, 'It's obviously not the original, and someone took a copy of a copy. In forensic terms, no, it's not genuine. But I don't think anyone has actually changed what it said.'

Another circled passage said: 'She has been under surveillance for several months with only partial result. She does not use the telephone very often, has no fax or telex facilities, and does not have access to public on-line datanet services. Most of her communications appear to be by Royal Mail, which makes interception time-intensive and fragmentary.'

The marginal note said: *Does she know about surv'ce?*

Alice turned the sheet round for Tom to see, and prodded her finger at that.

'Can you credit it?' she said. 'They think Eleanor was trying to avoid being bugged! She sent everything by post because she couldn't afford anything else.'

'It's a very suspicious act not to use a fax machine these days.'

'These people live in another universe,' Alice said.

'Have you seen the comment at the bottom?'

It said: 'The house has been wired for the last twenty-three months, but she receives very few visitors. Recordable conversations not worth reporting. Subject often mumbles to herself when alone (nothing has been deciphered). A woman who appears to have moved to the neighbourhood recently has started calling in the last four weeks. Shall we follow this up in the usual way?'

Next to it: *Yes.*

'That answers a lot of your questions,' Tom said. 'For instance, that's almost certainly why your manuscript was seized. And you don't have to be a genius to work out why Eleanor was killed, and who did it.'

Alice pushed the report to the bottom of the folder, feeling dirtied by it. It was a glimpse into a world of secrecy and distrust, suspicions and investigations, bureaucratic paranoia, with reports written by one anonymous official to another with a third making unsigned comments on the side. It gave her an unpleasant, uncomfortable feeling to read it, reinforcing everything she had thought about since her manuscript vanished. As Tom said, it was obvious now what had been going on.

But did it follow that the people who were behind this report were the same people who had murdered her?

Alice had always found conspiracy theories unconvincing. Civil servants wrote reports because that was what they were paid to do. Politicians tried to keep things quiet, because that was in the nature of being a politician. Yes, they might have been watching Eleanor, but no, it didn't mean they killed her, or even arranged for her to be killed.

She stared at the folder without focusing on it. She was thinking about the book she was planning, and everything she had been discovering about Eleanor. Talking about the book, working out the story, feeling the structure of it building up.

Structure was like an ideograph. It formed a shape whose purpose was to contain or enclose an idea without expressing it overtly.

Her book was to *tell* the story of Eleanor's life, but it was *structured* around her death. Writing about the life was a way of describing the death, because one was the ideograph that described the other. The structure contained not only the death but also its explanation.

The death was caused by that which Eleanor had omitted from her own life, that which she had censored out of existence.

'The murder was nothing to do with the Home Office,' Alice said. 'I know who killed her. I worked it out this afternoon. It was her son.' As she said the words she knew that she had not made the connection until that moment, but as soon as they were out she knew she was right.

Tom looked startled.

'I didn't think she had children,' he said.

'She had a son.'

She was thinking: Gordon did it because I know he did it. Only this makes sense, even though I don't yet know why.

'Alice, I've read everything there. Eleanor was married, but there's no mention of children.'

'No, the profile's wrong. There was an earlier marriage, to someone called Sinclair. She had at least two sons, one of whom is called Gordon. He's the one I've met. I told you about him. The interesting thing is that Eleanor never admitted to having had any children, until she wrote me a letter about herself, just before she was killed. And I think that letter's something to do with it. I think the fact she told me about him was why he killed her.'

'You can't actually prove this, I assume.'

'Not in the usual sense.'

Tom shook his head slowly, grinning at her. 'What's the son like?'

'I think he's a creep.'

'So you think he killed his mother because you don't like him?'

'For that reason too.' In fact her only case against Gordon was irrational. Nothing apart from her dislike of him incriminated him, or even hinted that he could or would have killed his mother. 'I think he identifies me with his mother somehow. I'm not sure why I think that. There's something about him I can't understand . . . the way he looks at me. He stares at me as if he's adoring me, then when he says something I feel he's about to attack me. Not physically . . . you know, criticize me, or tell me I'm stupid or something. That's most of why I don't like him. He puts me on the defensive all the time.' She knew she wasn't explaining this at all well. 'I'll have to write the book,' she said. 'That's the only way I can find out what I mean.'

And she remembered the note she had written: to explain Eleanor she had to explain herself.

She felt her head beginning to spin in a familiar way, when she was writing, things going round so fast in her mind that she couldn't write them down quickly enough. It made her want to rush away to her study, spend the next six hours in front of the word processor, working it all out.

And there was Tom, grinning at her as if to humour her, and all she *really* wanted to know was whether or not he was going to stay the night . . .

'I'd like a cup of tea,' she said. 'How about you?'

'I think I'll have some more wine.'

'You shouldn't drink and drive,' she said.

'I don't intend to. Drive, I mean . . . not tonight.' He was watching her for her reaction. 'Is that OK with you?'

'Yes.' She stood by the kettle, as she did so often, watching it while it boiled. It always induced a pleasantly blank feeling in her mind, a pause in the day. Now, though, Tom came up behind her, slipped his arms around her and held her, pulling her against him. His hands, crossing in front of her, cupped her breasts. When they had left the bedroom all she had put on was her thin dressing-gown, and she felt her nipples hardening against his fingers. He moved his hands to and fro, and she felt the gown starting to work loose at the front. He pressed his face against the side of her neck. She wanted to turn to face him, and kiss him properly, but he held her in that position.

He said, 'Can we be serious for a few minutes?'

'Not if you do that to me.'

'All right.' He stopped moving his hands around, but kept them in the same general area. 'Now can we?'

'I thought we were being.'

'Yes . . . but this is about something else.'

The kettle started to boil, so she pulled herself free from him, and poured the water into her cup. She let the tea-bag infuse for a few seconds, then lifted it out and plopped it into her rubbish bin.

'What is it?' she said.

'Come and stay with me in London. Move in with me for a while.'

'Why Tom?'

'You know why. I want you out of this place. It's not safe, and you shouldn't be here. You keep saying you've nowhere else to go, so I'm telling you that you have. You can move in with me for as long as you like.'

'You wouldn't have room for me, with all my stuff.'

'You don't have to bring it all. Keep most of it here. Just bring what you need.'

247

'Including my cat? I can't leave him here.'

'Bring the cat. He'll be all right.'

Alice shook her head, as if she were trying to argue her way out of something she didn't want to do. 'He's a country cat. I couldn't keep him cooped up in a flat in London.'

'There's a garden at the back. He can get all the freedom he needs out there.'

So she summoned the final argument. 'You don't know me, Tom. Just a few days . . . we've made love once –'

'Twice.'

'All right . . . but we've only been lovers once. And what about the unmentionable subject?'

'Pamela? I won't be seeing her again. It's all straightened out. It's over.'

'Maybe so. But you still don't know me.'

'And you don't know me. What I do know is that for the last week I've spent every waking moment thinking about you, missing you, wanting to be with you, counting the hours until I could get away to see you. I thought you felt the same way.'

'I do . . . but I've been like this before, and I've been wrong before.'

'I'm not asking you to move in permanently. I just want you to get away from this area for a while. Keep the house, go on paying the mortgage, use it as your main address. We can drive down here at weekends, pick up the mail. And what we'll do in the mean time is try to find out just how bad the fall-out levels are, and when we know we'll make a real decision about ourselves.'

She said, very seriously, 'I don't want to make plans like that. My life goes wrong when I make plans.'

'Then let me make plans for you.'

Tom took her in his arms again, kissed her, and pressed,

the side of her face against his. She closed her eyes. His hand slipped inside the loose opening of her gown, and he fondled her breast again. She felt exposed in the brightly lit room, and suddenly wanted the intimacy of darkness. She could feel Tom aroused and hardening against her. She was thinking, randomly: I hardly know him, is it true about Pamela? I want him, how would Jimmy survive in the city? I just want to fuck then fuck again then sleep, I hardly know him, nothing else matters at the moment, does he feel the same way about me . . .

Then she heard the sound of a car in the quiet lane outside, driving slowly towards the house. It halted and the engine was switched off; she clearly heard the ratchet of a handbrake.

Alice moved back from Tom.

'I don't believe it!' she said. 'Not now!'

'Are you expecting someone?'

'No.'

'But you know who it is.'

'I've a damned good idea. You're about to meet Eleanor's son.'

'Get rid of him,' Tom said, and kissed her again.

When the doorbell rang she jumped, because it was so loud. 'What shall I do?'

'You'd better find out what he wants. We can't pretend we're not at home. He can see the lights are on.'

She said softly, 'Tom, he could be here for hours! I can never get rid of him.'

But she pulled her dressing-gown tight across her, and tied the sash in front. She went to the door, opened it sufficiently wide to peer around. Gordon was there, and he was carrying a bottle of wine.

'Alice . . . I know it's late, but I wondered if you would care to have a nightcap with me?'

'I'm sorry, Gordon. It's not convenient. Maybe some other –'

She started to close the door on him, but he stepped forward quickly and pressed the flat of his hand against it. He pushed at it, and she leaned forward to prevent him opening it any further. She saw him glance at her breasts, ill-concealed by her thin gown.

'Won't you even invite me in?' he said.

'Not now. I'm sorry.'

'Is Lizzie still with you? I see there's a car outside.'

'Lizzie went back to London. Now, if you'll excuse me . . . '

Something changed then. He had been holding the wine bottle slightly towards her, as if to emphasize the conviviality of his visit. Now he lowered it, and it hung in his hand like a weapon.

He said, 'I want to talk to you about the material you've stolen from my mother's house. You'd better let me come in.'

'Stolen? But you gave me permission –'

Tom came up behind her, and put a hand on her shoulder. 'Do you need any help, Alice?'

Gordon looked at him, and started with surprise. Alice felt Tom's hand tighten on her neck. She sensed danger.

In the same instant, two things happened.

Gordon said, '*Fuck you!*' and Tom slammed the door in his face.

From outside there came a heavy thudding noise against the door, as if it had been kicked, or hit with the bottle.

Tom took Alice's hand and said urgently, 'Turn out the lights, then let's get upstairs.'

'What happened, Tom? Why did he say that?'

Tom looked shaken by the encounter. 'Do you know who that is?'

250

'That was Eleanor's son, Gordon Sinclair.'

'His real name is Peter Hamilton.' Tom pushed the bolt home with a loud noise. 'Eleanor Hamilton! Of course . . . I didn't make the connection before.'

'You already know him?'

'Sshh!'

They both leaned against the door, listening to Gordon's movements outside. They heard the door of his car slam shut, then the sound of the engine starting and revving up noisily. The car manoeuvred, grinding the loose dirt of Alice's drive as it turned around in the narrow lane. Then it accelerated away.

Alice was trembling. She had no idea why.

'Tom, do you already know Gordon Sinclair?' she said again.

'Yes. Do you know who he is?'

28

THE VDUs IN my office were permanently hooked into our evaluation computer, enabling instant access to any part of the information network. There were three terminals I used most often, all of which were operated from my desk: these were for corporate, political and personal data. Naturally, full data intervention was possible.

Eleanor Seraphina Hamilton, formerly Sinclair, née Fulten
Dead file. All the political data was now redundant, but I had reactivated the personal data.

Thomas Graham Davie
Davie's personal file was one of the largest in the British section of the datanet. He also had a political file, which although not as extensive as those for some of the trade union leaders, anarchists, journalists, lobbyists, etc., was one of the most comprehensive for someone not formally allied to a political party.

Much of his file was familiar to me, because his activities were routinely scrutinized in the office. After my final weekend in Wiltshire I therefore did not spend too long on his files, but I did make one necessary new intervention. His links with Alice Hazledine were previously unknown, so I concatenated both of his files to hers. All new data was then cross-referenced to Hazledine's, and vice versa.

Alice Hazledine

Hazledine's file had at last been updated by my staff, so when Davie's data had been brought across I concatenated everything from my mother's file. I issued sort, comparison and contact parameters, then got to work.

Alice Stockton took William Hazledine's name on marriage. According to the file she had not gone through any subsequent formalities to change back to her maiden name. She could of course call herself anything she liked, but it seemed strange to me that she should use one name in her private life and write her books under her former husband's name.

This was more or less the extent of the personal information I had about Alice before I knew she was connected with Davie. Until then I had not been unduly interested in her background, although it's possible that at some later date I or one of my staff might have run a routine scan of her file.

Alice Hazledine, née Stockton, had been born in Chingford, Essex, and educated first at Endlebury Road Junior School, then at Chingford Grammar. She obtained nine O levels, and three A levels. Sport poor, extra-curricular activities good, discipline good. At the age of 18 she went to Bath University (local authority grant total £1,450, with contributions from her father), and left after three years with a second-class Honours degree in social anthropology. During her time at college she became vice-president of the University of Bath Literary Society, and did voluntary unpaid work as assistant librarian, indexer and cataloguer.

In her final university year Alice Stockton's name was

linked with the death of another student: David Andrew McLennan, 22, of a barbiturate overdose. The coroner recorded a verdict of suicide while the balance of the mind was disturbed. Alice had been engaged to McLennan for four months, and on the night of the overdose had been in an argument with him.

After leaving university she returned to her parents' address.

Passport records showed that between the age of 21 and 24 she travelled abroad several times, usually for short visits in the holiday season to France, Greece or Spain. She had not been abroad since the age of 24, although her passport remained valid. During this period she had a number of jobs, mainly as a junior assistant or trainee: she had worked for a council rates office, two magazine publishers, an artists' agency and for a short while had a research job with a regional television company. When she was 25 she joined a book publisher as a secretary, but later became a proof-reader, copywriter and assistant editor.

Known or suspected sexual contacts at this time were David Andrew McLennan, Bath; Antony Alan Havers, London; Harry Laurence Minden, South Croydon; William Bush, Wimbledon; Paul Timothy Brode, London; Frederick Julian Hamilton, London. (All except McLennan were still alive. Havers was currently receiving radiation therapy for cancer of the liver; Minden was HIV positive.)

She married Hazledine when she was 26. They lived at a number of temporary addresses in London before moving to a ground-floor flat in West Hampstead (where Hazledine continued to live). The mortgage with the Halifax Building Society had not been in default, although Hazledine took out a second mortgage at the time of the divorce. Her present bank account, at the branch of Midland Bank in Ramsford, was under the name Alice Stockton, although a small joint account with Hazledine still existed at Barclays Bank in West Hampstead. (No transactions for more than two years, and the remaining balance was less than £2)

Alice Hazledine started earning income from freelance writing at the age of 29. Her tax records showed no serious defaults, although there was a persistent history of late declarations and delayed payments. Her file had been marked 'TT': troublesome taxpayer. Class II National Insurance contributions were correct, and paid by mandated bank direct debit. She had voluntarily registered for Value Added Tax as a freelance writer, but registration had been withdrawn by Customs & Excise after two years because of insufficient income.

She had applied for Supplementary Benefit shortly after her divorce, but had withdrawn the application before any money was paid over.

Numerous visits to a marriage guidance counsellor took place in the weeks leading up to and following the separation from Hazledine. These visits were initiated by consent. Among William Hazledine's complaints noted on file were: Alice's sullen nature, her unwillingness to make visits to friends, a constant preoccupation with work to the detriment of their relationship, infrequency of sexual intercourse, and her refusal to perform oral sex. Alice's complaints were: William's regular bouts of drunkenness, insensitivity to her work, the playing of loud music and the presence of his friends while she was working, persistent sexual infidelities, and unreasonable and excessive sexual demands, including one alleged marital rape after separation. The counsellor had entered personality appraisals against each party. William was judged to be extrovert, impulsive and immature; Alice was said to be uncooperative, selfish and sexually inhibited. (William had made one subsequent visit to the counsellor on his own; during this he said that Alice had started an extra-marital affair with one of his friends, who had revealed to William that oral sex was regularly performed. The counsellor noted that William's interest in this kind of sexual activity was disproportionate.)

The divorce was uncontested, although the original suit had been filed by Alice against her husband, citing mental cruelty. When Hazledine filed a countersuit, alleging adultery with a certain John Lucien Nolan, Alice withdrew her claim and the divorce against her was granted. Costs were shared, and property was divided on an equal basis. There were no children.

Alice's credit rating was poor, following a mistake by a mail-order company. The debt was cancelled after investigation, but the credit data had never been corrected. She held Visa and Access credit cards, but because of her credit status was allowed only low maximum-borrowing limits. The outstanding balance on each account was generally close to these limits, but small regular payments were made, with no serious default. She had been refused an American Express card, but held cheque guarantee and cash-withdrawal cards, which were used regularly.

Her account with Midland Bank was frequently over-drawn, although currently in credit.

She was presently mortgaged to the Nationwide Anglia Building Society to the extent of £47,500; no defaults, although there had been occasional late payments. Because of her credit rating she was being charged one half per cent interest above the standard rate.

She belonged to the Royal Automobile Club, the British Film Institute, the National Trust, the Jane Carlyle Society and the Arts Cinema Club, and until two years before had belonged to the London Library and the Society of Authors. She was a Friend of the Wharf Theatre in Devizes. She held a British Library reader's ticket. She subscribed to *Literary Review*, the *London Review of Books*, *Granta*, *Publishing News* and the *Bookseller*. She had a full driving licence (no endorsements). Her car was insured against third-party damage, fire and theft only. The contents of her house were insured for £15,000, and she had a life assurance policy for the sum of £5,000; William Hazledine was still the named beneficiary. She had made no pension arrangements.

The Police National Computer revealed no criminal record, although there were seventeen recorded parking offences over a period of eight years; two of these had been prosecuted, and the fines paid on time. She had been interviewed following the death of my mother; Superintendent Bowker, Wiltshire Constabulary, interviewing officer.

From her medical records I discovered that Alice Hazledine had had a tonsillectomy in childhood, and an appendectomy while at university. No other surgery was recorded, although over the years she had consulted her GP about numerous minor ailments: a cracked rib after a fall, painful and irregular menstruation, problems with sinusitis, migraine, rectal inflammation, mammary cyst, conjunctivitis and suspected radiation poisoning. Her blood group was O Positive. She had been a smoker until the age of 37, but had no record of alcohol, solvent or drug abuse. (The marriage guidance counsellor noted suspicions of drinking during one visit.) She had been vaccinated against polio, TB, cholera, para-typhoid and tetanus. She was HIV negative. At her last full medical examination she was 5′ 7″ tall and weighed 142 lbs. She had requested a kidney, heart and corneal lens donor card from her GP, and was assumed to carry it.

Her teeth were natural, although the four third molars and the upper right first molar had been removed, and her lower left first pre-molar was crowned. There were numerous cavity fillings. She had suffered four reported gum abscesses and one minor attack of gingivitis. She was due for another dental examination in three weeks' time.

No fax or telex facilities. No access to public on-line datanet services. Most communications were by Royal Mail.

Since the installation of the British Telecom-approved listening device all telephone and in-house conversations had been logged. Most of the outgoing telephone calls were in the neighbourhood of her village, but there were three with her literary agent and one with her publisher, all of which concerned her impounded manuscript and associated matters. Two were with William Hazledine, acrimonious in tone. Fifteen calls had been made to Thomas Graham Davie, all of which included: (a) discussions of the subversive work with which my mother had been involved; (b) discussions about the nature of literary freedom; (c) the exchange of theories of a political and subversive nature; (d) discussions of health, and, related to this, (e) discussions about the extent of possible radioactive contamination. All the calls to Davie contained remarks of a personal nature, and these became increasingly intimate. Of the incoming calls, one was from her literary agent, one was an unidentified call from the USA, and seventeen were from Davie; the remaining calls were from local traders, etc.

In-house conversations were infrequent because there were few visitors. (I deleted the parts of the record where I

258

appeared.) While alone, Alice frequently spoke to her cat, and sometimes talked in her sleep. None of this was of any interest.

She had published four books, the first being a collection of historical literary reminiscences produced with another writer called Annette Sumpter. The remaining three were solo efforts. Her maiden name was used on the first book, her married name on the others.

Facsimiles of newspaper and magazine reviews were reproduced graphically on the VDU. The first two books had been well reviewed, although the third had been heavily criticized. The fourth received a mixed press. The second book, her first solo effort, had been about a small group of (presumably real) women, describing their lives over a period of years, from childhood to adulthood. This was commended by several reviewers for its frankness about sex. The *Daily Mail* had published a feature interview with Alice, putting considerable emphasis on the sexual nature of the book. A photograph of Alice was printed beside the interview: she was several years younger, had long hair, and was wearing a low-cut summer dress. The caption said: *Alice Hazledine: 'Permissive'*. (When I saw this I used digital enhancement techniques on the photograph, then locked the door of my office and masturbated.) This book had later been released in paperback, where it was a success. It was still in print in this form, although the hardcover had been remaindered. The book was also published in the USA, France, Germany, Italy, Spain and Holland. Her distributions from Public Lending Right for the last three years amounted to £54.90, £56.65 and £62.80 respectively.

Her most recent book was the one that had been impounded. For this reason it was as yet unpublished, and existed only in typescript form.

I read the précis prepared by my appraisal staff, then had the typescript and computer disks delivered to my office. The book dealt with the lives of six women, concentrating in more or less equal part on their sexual proclivities and their professional careers. I first read the passages my staff had objected to, then I read the whole thing. It seemed to me unlikely that it would ever be published, being firstly of no interest in itself, and secondly in breach of Crown copyright in the section dealing with the common-law wife of a career diplomat wrongly alleged to have been an undercover agent for a foreign power.

There was no question but that Alice Hazledine had deliberately inserted this controversial and illegal material, because her research notes had been on file for more than a year, and these were incorporated into the typescript.

I was still evaluating all this information when my office received a request from Alice Hazledine for a personal interview.

29

WALKING THROUGH THE streets of central Manchester Alice felt again that subliminal sense that here, in this industrial city with its grey sky and soot-darkened buildings, the air was cleaner than in the countryside around her house. Her sense of transition was clearly defined, because she had not stopped anywhere on the long drive up the motorway, not even to buy petrol. This was the first time she had been out in the open since leaving home. The air was noticeably colder, too, and she wished she had put on warmer clothes.

She walked quickly, anxious to be finished with this.

Gordon Sinclair's office was in one of the square, red-brick cotton warehouses that still clustered around the streets just away from the central plazas. Tom had warned her that the office was not identified as such in any way on the outside, but when she found the address the main entrance led directly to a conventional reception area. The man behind the desk had apparently been warned to expect her. After making her fill out an index card with her name and address, she was given directions to take the lift to the fourth floor. An electronic security gate had to be passed through before she could leave the reception area.

She was met on the fourth floor by a sharp-looking young

man in a striped shirt, who greeted her by her professional writing name, then led her along a wide corridor with painted brick walls. The interior of the building was not modern and open-plan, as she had expected, but old, unattractive and not well heated. She seemed vulnerable to the cold these days.

She was shown into the office at the furthest end of the corridor, and Gordon stood up to greet her. The young man left them, and closed the door.

'It's good to see you again, Alice,' Gordon said. 'Did you have a pleasant drive up here?'

'Yes, thank you.'

'Take a seat.'

Still standing, and feeling herself tremble, Alice said, 'I should like a third-party witness present during this interview.'

'You don't want that, do you?'

'I most certainly do,' Alice said. 'I've been told my rights. I should like a third party present in the room.'

'I presume this is Thomas Davie's influence?'

'It doesn't matter who told me.'

'Whoever it was, you've been misinformed. A third party is not allowed when it's a matter of state security. This conversation will be tape recorded. If you wish, I can arrange to have a transcript or a copy sent to you.'

'All right.'

Tom had warned her that she might have to settle for something like this. The rules had changed recently, and he hadn't been able to find out exactly what was different.

Alice sat down in the chair Gordon had indicated. His office was not at all large or imposing. She had been expecting either Victorian drabness or high-tech chrome and glass, but Gordon's office was neither of these. If anything it reminded her of a small schoolroom, with its tall sash windows, painted brick walls and metal radiators. Although there was a thick carpet, and the windows were curtained, the office was almost bare. There were just three more spare chairs, apart from the one she was using, and no cupboards or filing cabinets. Gordon's desk backed on to the long corridor wall, standing away from it at a slight angle. Thick cables sprouted from the base of the wall, and branched up to three computer consoles arranged along a table set beside his desk. She could not tell whether or not the computers were in use, as their screens were turned away from where she was sitting.

'You asked to see me,' he said.

'Yes. I've come to request the return of my manuscript, Gordon.'

'While we are in this office, you have to call me Mr Sinclair. To which manuscript do you refer?'

'The manuscript of my book.'

'I don't know which one you mean. You will have to describe it.'

'It's called *Six Women*.'

'And why do you think I might have this manuscript?' he said.

'Because it was impounded by the Home Office.'

'Then you should take your search to the Home Office.'

'Are you denying you have it?' she said.

'No, I'm saying I can't help you. I must point out that personal interviews of this sort are granted exceptionally, and I agreed to see you only because we have happened to meet socially and, if I may say so, under very pleasant circumstances.'

'Gordon, I know you've got it,' she said. 'Don't play games with me.'

'I don't play games, as you put it. Your manuscript has been judged by three independent assessors. They say it is subversive and in breach of Crown copyright. I too have read it, and I agree with their opinion.'

'So you do have it!'

'In a manner of speaking.'

Alice gestured impatiently. 'What does *that* mean?'

'I don't have it in my personal possession.'

'But you know where it is.'

'Yes.'

'Then may I please have it back?'

'No. That's not possible.'

Tom had said, You have to satisfy yourself he's got it. You have to be certain the Home Office is no longer involved. He's agreed to see you . . . this might even mean you'll get it back.

But all through the long drive northwards, Alice had been tense and depressed. This interview was just wastefully going through the motions, like appealing to a corrupt judge against a wrongful conviction, so that afterwards the only satisfaction was that everything had been tried.

'Why is it not possible?' she said.

'Because you are a professional writer, Mrs Hazledine. If I were to give it to you, you would undoubtedly try to have it published. Even if that were technically feasible, I wouldn't allow it. Any attempt to have it published would cause it to be seized again.'

'My name is Stockton, and I am now unmarried.'

'You write professionally under your husband's name. This concerns your professional life.'

Alice felt her self-control beginning to slip. Tom had said, Don't let him goad you. He knows you dislike him.

'What if I were to give an undertaking that I wouldn't have

264

it published?' she said.

'Then why should you want it back?'

'Because I *wrote* it! I spent more than a year working on it. I'm not even allowed to keep a copy of it for myself!'

'That's correct. The book is subversive and in breach of copyright.'

'But it's completely innocent! How can biographies be subversive? And the book is completely original ... are you implying that I plagiarized it?'

'You don't know your copyright law, Mrs Hazledine. The latest Act, taken with the Official Secrets Act, establishes that Crown copyright will be breached by any work which a minister of the government decides infringes security.'

'But you're not a government minister!'

'I'm an appointed agent of the Home Secretary. I take these decisions on his behalf, and in this case my decision is final. The interview is concluded.'

'Please, Gordon ... can't you explain? All right, I've done something wrong. I accept that. I can't get it published, and I can't even have it back. But won't you tell me *why?*'

Rather than answer, he turned to one of his computer screens and typed something at the keyboard. He stared at the monitor while a response appeared; Alice could see the green glow reflected in his spectacles.

He said, 'Apart from its subversive nature, which is to be found in the section on the unmarried companion of Sir Percival Arnold-Smythe, the book is extremely badly written. It's too long for its subject matter. The depiction of the characters is sketchy, and only the most shallow of motives are attributed to them to explain their actions. Your storytelling ability is not strong. The text changes direction unexpectedly. You do not acquit yourself well in the writing, and as the narrator of the book you portray yourself as indecisive and weak, easily manipulated by others. Your vocabulary is restricted, and there are many repetitions. Parts of the story appear to have been left out. There are implausible coincidences. You seem anxious to explain many things, but the reader is left unsatisfied. Where you are not sure of facts you become imprecise. The reported dialogue is unrealistic and unconvincing. More research should have been conducted before you began work. At the end of the book there is a feeling of dissatisfaction, a sense that the book has been leading nowhere, that it is an artificial construct with no adequate purpose.'

He looked up from the computer monitor.

'Is that your own opinion?' Alice said.

'It is the judgement of the assessors. I substantially agree with what they say, otherwise I wouldn't repeat it to you.'

'But those are *literary* judgments! Apart from what you said about Mary Tessot, this is nothing to do with the book being subversive. I don't give a damn what you think of the writing! That's nothing to do with you.'

'If you say so.'

He sat facing her, staring impassively. His lips looked thin, and his cheeks, and the flesh around his eyes, had grown pale.

'*Why*, Gordon?'

'I'm not obliged to explain anything.'

'I've come here because I want explanations.'

He stood up suddenly. 'I never *explain!*' he said, raising his voice. 'I detest explanations! I owe no explanations to ANYONE!'

Five minutes later she was out in the street, giddy with rage, fright and frustration. Above all, she wanted to talk to Tom and tell him what had happened, so she went in search of a

266

callbox. She found one in a shopping arcade in Piccadilly, but Tom's phone rang without being answered. She waited a few minutes before trying again, but Tom was still not there. She found a coffee bar and bought a *cappuccino*, but when she sipped it she scalded her lip, and she left without drinking it. She walked around in the rainy streets, knowing that the anger was still blinding her, making her irrational.

An hour later, when she felt she was safe to drive, she returned to her car and began the long journey home. She drove slowly, still furious with Gordon Sinclair, loathing his impassive face, his bland recitation of the verdict on her book.

She stopped at one of the motorway service stations, and at last managed to get through to Tom. They talked until she ran out of money for the telephone, and when she carried on with her journey she drove more quickly, depressed now, no longer angry, just hungry for home and a fond greeting from her cat.

Soon after leaving the motorway, when she was driving along the main road between Cirencester and Swindon, she saw a large sign on the side of the road, briefly glimpsed in her headlights. It carried the international radiation symbol at the top, and the words 'RADIATION HAZARD AHEAD - DO NOT PROCEED EXCEPT IN EMERGENCY.'

Thoroughly depressed, she continued on home, and her cat was waiting for her by the door. He crawled all over her neck and shoulders while she forked his food out of the tin, then he gobbled down the unpleasant-smelling slurry with relish. He slept beside her, his small weight pressing into her back.

Tom turned up the next morning with a rented van.

30

WHILE SHE WAS buying some stamps in the post office in Old Brompton Road, Alice remembered to ask about the intervention fund. The woman behind the counter waved her pen vaguely at the rack of leaflets attached to the wall. After a brief search, Alice found a pamphlet entitled *European Repository of Knowledge* - LITERATURE SUBSIDY - *How To Qualify*.

She glanced through it to make certain it was what she wanted (the back page was an application form for money, so it was), then tucked it into her purse and walked back to Tom's flat.

She still thought of it as Tom's flat, the place where she was staying; it had not yet become the place where she lived. That continued to be her cottage in Wiltshire, which she was beginning to miss. Winters were messy and unpleasant in the centre of London, and the house in which Tom's flat took up the ground floor was an ancient and draughty one. The constant traffic roar was something she did not remember being affected by, when she had lived in London before.

Tom had not returned from his appointment when she came in, so she made herself a glass of hot lemon tea and curled up on his sofa to read the pamphlet.

For an official hand-out it was written in an unusually

idealistic manner, with high-sounding sentiments about the wisdom of the world being contained in its literature, and sprinkled with quotes about the state of the art from writers like Victor Hugo, Charles Dickens, Thomas Mann, John Steinbeck and Fyodor Dostoevsky (the multinational motif was present from the outset).

The official name of the scheme was the European Repository of Knowledge, and it had two main stated functions.

The first was to create what amounted to the world's largest reference library of contemporary thought, freely accessible to all, a fount of wisdom and a source of intelligence for posterity. (And so on.)

The second was to provide a subsidy for creative writers, one that would be adequately funded, free of political influence, non-judgmental and distributed without regard for what the leaflet called 'discriminatory or specialist literary criticism'. The subsidy would be calculated according to a simple formula and paid in ECUs, optionally convertible into national currencies at the standard (non-floating) rates of exchange. These rates were listed in the leaflet. As Gordon had said, the amount of the subsidy was arrived at by a simple formula, using a table in which the relevant numbers were inserted and then calculated.

Alice read all this, thinking ruefully that for everything she had disliked about Gordon Sinclair, and for all the good reasons she had for distrusting and even fearing him, he had at least put her on to this. There appeared to be no catch, no snags . . . at least, not in her present predicament.

The main condition of the subsidy, at which she would normally have baulked, was that to receive the money the writer had to sign away all copyright in the work. A new class of copyright had been created, called World Discretionary Copyright. Under this, the original creator of a piece of work accepted that the needs of society were greater than his or her own, and consented to assign copyright to the common weal, formerly known as the public domain.

Under normal circumstances Alice would not even have considered releasing her copyright – it being just about the only thing in the world a writer unarguably owned – but it was obvious to her now that *Six Women* was never going to be published. It had been taken from her as surely as if a thief had managed somehow to steal her copyright. She couldn't get it published, she couldn't let anyone read it . . . and she certainly had no hope of ever making any more money from it.

When she had read the form through from beginning to end, she put on her coat again and set off to find her car. This was parked in a side street in Acton, several miles away, requiring a journey on the Tube whenever she wanted to get to it. (There was no hope of parking anywhere near Tom's flat, at least not without paying a fortune in either fines or garage fees.) She hadn't driven the car since her abortive visit to Manchester the week before, and when she reached it she found it already covered in leaves, bird droppings and traffic grime. the engine started at the first attempt, so she drove to the large filling station on Western Avenue, bought two gallons of petrol, then took the car through the automatic wash. Afterwards, she returned to her side street and found another place to park.

Before she left she reached under the passenger seat, groped about under the loose carpet, and found her computer disks exactly as she had placed them.

Back at the flat, she switched on her computer and loaded the document containing the first part of *Six Women*. She read through enough of it to be sure that the long sojourn in the car had not somehow distorted the text, then began printing it out.

An hour later, Tom came home.

The printer was still screeching slowly through the long job while they were eating supper, and at last Tom asked her what she was doing.

'I can't do anything else with it, so I'm going to submit *Six Women* to the intervention fund.'

'The slush mountain?'

'Why do you call it that?'

'It's an open joke, isn't it?' Tom said. 'The biggest slush pile in the world.'

'I thought it was a bit more serious than that.'

'It was a lousy idea in the first place, it was set up by dimwitted bureaucrats, it's run by bickering politicians, and it's financed by arms deals to the Third World. Apart from that it's a great institution.'

'Oh,' said Alice.

'Were you serious about sending in your book?'

'I was until you said all that.'

'Sorry . . . I just don't think serious writers should have anything to do with it. That's all.'

'Tom, I need some money.'

'There is that,' he said. 'By the way, you owe me for rent.'

Alice found a cold green pea on her plate, and flicked it at him. It bounced off his shoulder.

'I thought it was a good thing,' she said.

'The writers' organizations are against it. The Society of Authors warns members not to take it too seriously, and the Writers' Guild actively campaigns to have it boycotted.'

She had now been with Tom long enough to know when

he was about to launch into one of his lectures.

'Surely anything that puts money in writers' pockets can't be such a bad thing?' she said.

'But which writers? And who's a writer? Any damn fool who can put together a few sheets of typewritten paper qualifies for a grant. Didn't you see that article in *Private Eye*? Someone typed out the first thirty pages of the London telephone directory, and was sent a cheque for seven thousand pounds.'

Alice said nothing, listening to her printer working away in the next room.

'You know what happens to intervention butter?' Tom went on. 'They store it for a couple of years, then sell it off cheap in the Third World. That's exactly what's happening to the manuscript mountain. Publishers in the Far East are churning out books based on intervention literature. They pick them up cheap from Luxembourg, there's no writer to pay, no messing around with permission or royalties or anything like that. The books are typeset by optical scanner, they're printed on junk paper, and then they're shipped in bulk back to Europe where they're sold for about a quarter of the price of real books.'

'Well, I need the money,' Alice said diffidently.

She stood up and moved away from the table, ostensibly picking up some of the dirty plates to take into the kitchen, but in reality looking for an excuse to get out of the room for a few moments. She was already learning that when Tom started one of his lectures she invariably ended up feeling inadequate, wimpish and on the defensive.

'And what do you think publishers do with the books they change their minds about?' Tom said. 'There's always Luxembourg. I can't think of a publisher who hasn't off-loaded a dozen unwanted books this year. It's usually enough to cover all their costs and overheads, pay off the author, and show a useful little profit.'

Alice passed Tom on her way from the kitchen to the next room, where she had set up her desk and computer.

'It's convenient to governments too,' he said. 'Once a manuscript is in the warehouse, it's virtually impossible to find it again. There's no catalogue, and new stuff arrives in such immense quantities that there's no hope of there ever being one. All they can do is log the title and the author's name, and dump it on the pile with everything else. So anything that's politically embarrassing finds its way to Luxembourg sooner or later, and no one will ever locate it again. The perfect solution! Two years from now, there won't be any such thing as modern literature. There'll just be unpublished manuscripts written by rich non-writers.'

Sitting at her desk Alice could hear his voice through the open door. She watched the head of her computer printer moving to and fro with its busy noise, the words forming magically on the continuous paper. After a few minutes the printer reached the end of the current document, and paused. Alice loaded up the next document.

She removed the large pile of pages already printed, then squatted happily on the floor, tearing off the detachable sprocket-hole strips from the sides, and separating each page and laying it face down with all the others. Tom was still talking in the next room, explaining how intervention literature was funded. Alice remembered Eleanor talking about the fund, and laughing at the very thought of it. For herself, she was just content to take the clean pages from the printer and stack them up in a pile, getting a new manuscript ready.

31

*A*LICE HAZLEDINE
   After a great deal of detailed examination of the file, I decided to place some interventions in the Hazledine file before closing and deleting it.

Her degree as Alice Stockton became third class. The coroner's verdict on David Andrew McLennan became open, with cross-referenced implications to Alice's file in the Police National Computer for potential drug abuse. She was refused a visa for the USA. The building society joint mortgage with William Hazledine was recorded as having been foreclosed. Her credit card borrowing limits were halved, automatically placing both current balances into default. I marked her tax file for special attention by the Inland Revenue investigations branch. I removed her complaints about William Hazledine from the marriage counsellor's file. Her driving licence was cancelled following a conviction for dangerous driving. She became HIV positive.

I was still entering these interventions when my office received a request from Alice Hazledine for a personal interview.

Although this was unusual in normal cases, it did not actually surprise me when it came from her. Quite apart from the sexual attraction, she had always struck me as intelligent and practical, and the fact that we already knew each other lent intriguing extra possibilities to the prospect of meeting her. Unlike previous occasions, this would be on my terms.

I fixed the appointment for a day when I had no other engagements, and during a period when I knew Guy Lawley would be away. I finished my datanet researches, and made full notes on the official disposal of her manuscript. The fate of this was therefore decided in advance, whatever might be said at the interview. For her, there was no conceivable advantage in coming to see me, although I would not say the same for myself.

When she arrived on the appointed day I made her wait in the outer office for twenty minutes, then had her shown in. She looked calm and determined, and I noticed she was carrying a small leather attaché case. When she sat down she placed this on the floor beside her. She was dressed in a dark-maroon skirt, a grey blouse and a black jacket. She was wearing light make-up and earrings, and her hair was tied back with a ribbon. The effect was altogether more pleasing than the one created by the pullovers and jeans she had usually worn when I saw her before.

'Did you have an enjoyable drive up here, Mrs Hazledine?' I said.

'I came by train. Why don't you call me Alice?'

'Because we are no longer in Wiltshire. I am acting in my official capacity, and you are here to see me in that capacity. Would you care for a drink? Coffee . . . or tea?'

'No thanks.'

'It was you who applied for this interview. I must point out that personal interviews are granted exceptionally, and I agreed to see you only because we have happened to meet socially and, if I may say so, under very pleasant circumstances. This is very much to your advantage.'

'That's what I thought,' Alice said. 'You presumably know why I'm here?'

'It's up to you to state your business.'

She glanced over her shoulder at the door.

'Is anyone likely to cone in?' she said.

'No, but if you would prefer it, I can lock the door. You may also ask for a third-party witness to be present.'

'I don't think that's necessary.' She picked up the case, and opened it.

There was nothing inside. She placed it on my desk. 'I've come to collect my manuscript, Gordon.'

'While we are in this office, you have to call me Mr Sinclair. To which manuscript do you refer?'

'The manuscript of my book.'

'I don't know which one you mean. You will have to describe it.'

'It's called *Six Women*.' I gave no response she could interpret. She went on, 'It's a manuscript of about three hundred pages, double-spaced, and printed by a personal computer. The first page has the title and my name on it. I write as Alice Hazledine, but my real name and address are printed at the bottom of the first page. I also want back the computer disks on which it was written.'

'And why do you think I might have this manuscript?' I said.

'Because it was impounded by the Home Office.'

'Then you should take your search to the Home Office.'

'Are you denying you have it?' she said.

'I want to know why you think it's here.'

She said, 'Because your firm has taken over internal intelligence work from the security services. You have a privatized contract with the Government to act as censors.

You monitor television, radio, films, newspapers, magazines and books, and have wide powers to suppress the freedom of speech. You have statutory authority to collect fees from the media you censor, your firm makes large profits, and you, Mr Sinclair, are an extremely powerful man.'

She had always struck me as one of those women who find power sexually irresistible, but I said, 'We are not censors. Our work here is editorial.'

'That's a specious distinction. An editor clarifies meaning, but a censor distorts it.'

'We ensure that no misunderstandings can arise about government policy. That's an editorial function.'

'Then it's the same thing. What I want is my manuscript back, and I want to know what I have to do to get it.'

'That all rather depends on whether or not I actually have it.'

She was looking flushed, and I realized that her apparent calmness on arrival had been appearance only.

She leaned towards me, and said more quietly, 'Since we are alone, and you say no one will interrupt us, and because we already know each other, could we please drop this pretence?'

'Very well,' I said. 'Your manuscript has been judged by three independent assessors. They say it is subversive and in breach of Crown copyright. I too have read it, and I agree with their opinion.'

'So you do have it!'

'In a manner of speaking.'

She gestured impatiently at me. 'What does *that* mean?'

'I don't have it in my personal possession.'

'But you know where it is.'

'Yes.'

'Then may I please have it back?'

'No. That's not possible.'

'Why?'

'Because you are a professional writer, Mrs Hazledine. If I were to give it to you, you would undoubtedly try to have it published. Even if that were technically feasible, I wouldn't allow it. Any attempt to have it published would cause it to be seized again.'

'What if I were to give an undertaking that I wouldn't?'

'Then why should you want it back?'

'Because I *wrote* it! I spent more than a year working on it. I'm not even allowed to keep a copy of it for myself!'

'That's correct. The book is subversive and in breach of copyright.'

'But it's completely innocent! How can biographies be subversive? And the book is original . . . are you implying that I plagiarized it?'

'You don't know your copyright law, Mrs Hazledine. The latest Act, taken with the Official Secrets Act, establishes that Crown copyright will be breached by any work which is declared by a minister of the government to infringe security.'

'But you're not a government minister!'

'I'm an appointed agent of the Home Secretary. I take these decisions on his behalf, and in this case my decision is final. The interview is concluded.'

I stood up.

Without moving from her seat, Alice said, 'I'll go to any lengths to get it back.'

'There's no appeal procedure.'

'I didn't mean that.' I had started to walk around the office, and she was turning in her seat to follow me. 'I came to see you personally, because I felt certain I could change your

opened wide with fear. When I tightened the knot she tried to get to her feet, but I kicked her down. I forced her legs open and pushed my way in, but she was dry and tight, and she struggled too much. Her face was now red, and her eyes were bulging.

I proceeded to beat her, using my fists against the side of her head; she slumped, and collapsed across the carpet. She was gasping for breath.

I rolled her over on her back, then released her hands. I arranged her legs wide apart, and her arms loose by her side. I knelt over her, and, gripping her pantyhose in both hands, I tightened the knot around her throat. She struggled desperately, beating weakly at me with her hands, her back arching away from the floor. Gradually her resistance failed, but after she became still I held the knot tight for a long time. I stared at the whites of her eyes, saw the wet pinkness of her extruded tongue.

I went to the interactive computer terminal, and quickly deleted her file, an action that simultaneously removed all trace not only of her but also of my mother.

She was certainly dead. I stood over her with my cock rigid in my hand. My ejaculate sprayed over her stomach, then dribbled down to collect in a small pool on the floor by her side.

32

ALICE WAS SITTING cross-legged on the floor of Tom's bedroom, with her possessions piled up in boxes and suitcases around her, and waiting for Tom to return with the rental van. Jimmy was already in his plastic carrying case, pre-emptively trapped half an hour before, and now curled up awkwardly in a sulking mound of angular fur, resigned to the indignity of being moved somewhere else. She wished she could somehow communicate to him that his loss of freedom was only temporary, and that anyway it was in the cause of going home.

The doorbell rang loudly, so she walked slowly through to answer it, thinking it was Tom. Rather to her surprise it was a postman.

'Alice Hazledine?' he said. 'Special delivery. Sign this.'

He handed her a thick square package, wrapped in bright-orange padded paper. She took it without realizing what it was, and only as she closed the door did she notice the return address printed in small letters on the label. She saw the words *'Entrepôt Littéraire'*, and *'rue de'* something in Luxembourg, and the weight of the package told her the rest.

She returned to the room where her possessions and her cat were waiting, and tore the wrapping apart.

Her manuscript was inside. No one appeared to have read

it, or even looked at it, because it was still held together with the elastic bands she had used when she sent it off: a big thick band in one direction, two smaller ones in the other, carefully placed so that the title and her name could be clearly seen. (This had been one of the instructions in the leaflet.)

A slip of good-quality paper had been tucked under the elastic bands, and she took this out. It was folded concertina-style, with each page laid out identically to all the others, but written in a different language: each language of the Community was represented, French, German, Greek, Italian, Portuguese, and so on. The English version was found in the third fold.

It said:

Your manuscript has been found unsuitable for inclusion in the European Repository of Knowledge, and is being returned free of charge to the address from which it was sent.

You are assured that no person has read your work, and no opinion, negative or otherwise, has been passed on it. No literary, political, national, ethnic, linguistic, moral, racial, religious or other criticism is implied or intended by or should be construed from this refusal.

No record of this refusal has been kept, and further submissions will not be jeopardized or prejudiced by this refusal.

For your future guidance, this work was refused acceptance for the following reason or reasons (where reason or reasons may be given without risk of offence):

Underneath, someone had written in ballpoint: 'Manuscript called (title) SIX WOMEN by (author) Alice Hazledine

283

already lodged.' An hour later, as Tom drove the rented van westwards along the M4, Alice told him what had happened.

'I suppose it's my own book that's already there,' she said. 'It would be too great a coincidence otherwise. What I can't decide is who placed it there. My bet is Gordon Sinclair.'

Tom was silent for a while, then said, 'I think it was probably your publisher. I told you . . . publishers do this regularly. I suspect that as soon as they got wind of trouble from the Home Office, they sent a photocopy across to Luxembourg by courier before anyone came round to take it away from them. They paid you the rest of the advance, didn't they? It came through almost at once, without any delay? You see, once the manuscript is accepted by the people in Luxembourg . . .'

Alice turned away to stare at the fields of winter wheat slipping past. The sky was grey, the low clouds heavy with rain. She saw the rise of Salisbury Plain, just visible in the gloom. The cat was asleep in his transport case, or at any rate lying still, waiting the journey out.

As they drove through Ramsford, on the way to Alice's house, they passed the newsagent's in the High Street. A placard for the local paper was outside, with the headline: 'MILTON MURDER - SUSPECT HELD.'

Alice asked Tom to stop, so he pulled the van over to the side of the road, and waited while she ran into the shop to buy a copy. She handed over the cash to the counter assistant, then ran back to the van without looking at the front page. She could feel certainty boiling inside her. When she was back in the van, she spread the paper so Tom could see it too.

The headline said: *Eleanor Hamilton's Son Charged With Murder.*

Alice shouted, 'I knew it was him! They got him! I told you

Gordon had done it!'

Tom was reading the account in the newspaper, leaning over with a very serious expression.

'He's only been charged, Alice,' he said. 'There will have to be a trial. That won't take place for several months, and until then - '

'Yes, but he did it! And you know what . . . it was me who put the police on to him!'

Alice was grinning happily, feeling more cheerful about the world than she had done in several weeks.

'I hope you produced some evidence,' Tom said.

'No. I didn't even try!'

'Then what did you do?'

'I sent an anonymous letter, and told them Gordon had done it.'

Tom frowned. 'What did it say?'

'That Gordon killed his mother, and that they should ask him where he was on the night she was murdered.'

'Where was he?'

'I've no idea. I just thought they ought to ask him. Whatever he told them, it obviously wasn't good enough.'

Alice wanted to leap out of the van and dance around in glee. She felt entirely vindicated. Of course she had no proof against Gordon, and was likely never to have anything concrete . . . but anyway that sort of investigation was up to the police. Alice knew that the police wouldn't charge someone just because they received a letter from a crank . . . but what she did know was that if they were *already* suspicious, a letter might persuade them to pull the suspect in and give him a grilling. Whatever evidence they had turned up on their own, they seemed to have had enough to charge him.

As they drove towards her cottage, Tom was lecturing her on the amorality of sending anonymous letters, and how nothing could justify sending them, no matter what the results might be. Alice was watching the winter hedgerows, the brown fields, the lowering sky, and she thought: I'm home!

She tapped the hard plastic lid of Jimmy's carrying case to rouse him, and to try to make him look at the scenery. The sullen misshapen heap of fur would not deign even to raise his head.

An hour or so later, with her possessions unloaded into the house, and with Jimmy freed to explore the garden and lane, Alice went back with Tom in the van to London. She collected her car from the side street in Acton, gave Tom a big and affectionate kiss, then drove back alone and at high speed to Wiltshire.

The cat was waiting for her on the lawn, and he yowled at her until she fed him. She warmed up some tinned soup for herself, then sat contentedly listening to the radio until it was time for bed.

The cat was already there, waiting for her to join him.

Twelve days later an envelope arrived from Luxembourg.

Inside was an announcement that the manuscript (title) *Five Women* by (author) Alice Stockton had been accepted for deposit in the European Repository of Knowledge. A bank draft for the sum of £13,872.73 was enclosed.

Alice rang Tom and told him.

'You're learning,' he said.

'Yes,' she said. 'Come and see me this weekend.'

THE GLAMOUR
Christopher Priest

All Richard Grey wanted was to recover, to return to normal. For four long, painful months he had been convalescing after the horrifying injuries that he sustained when a car bomb exploded near him.

He could remember the years he spent as a cameraman, covering stories all over the world, and he could remember taking a break from his career, but there was a profound blankness where his memory of the weeks before the explosion should have been. It was as if his life had been re-edited and part of it erased.

But then Susan Kewley came to visit him and she spoke of those weeks. And what Richard wanted most was a glimpse of what that time had held for the two of them. But the glimpses he is afforded take him into a strange and terrible twilight world – a world of apparent madness, the world of 'the glamour'.

Christopher Priest's rich and subtle narrative is mesmerising and profoundly moving, as compelling and as deceptive as a Hitchcock film.

0 349 12810 3
ABACUS FICTION

Abacus now offers an exciting range of quality fiction and non–fiction by both established and new authors. All of the books in this series are available from good bookshops, or can be ordered from the following address:

Sphere Books
Cash Sales Department
P.O. Box 11
Falmouth
Cornwall TR10 9EN.

Please send cheque or postal order (no currency), and allow 60p for postage and packing for the first book plus 25p for the second book and 15p for each additional book ordered up to a maximum charge of £1.90 in U.K.

B.F.P.O. customers please allow 60p for the first book, 25p for the second book plus 15p per copy for the next 7 books, thereafter 9p per book.

Overseas customers, including Eire, please allow £1.25 for postage and packing for the first book, 75p for the second book and 28p for each subsequent title ordered.